Half Crocked

Freaky Florida Investigations, Volume 8

Margaret Lashley

Published by Zazzy Ideas, Inc., 2022.

Copyright

For more information, write to: Zazzy Ideas, Inc. P.O. Box 1113, St. Petersburg, FL 33731

What Readers are Saying about Freaky Florida Investigations ...

"Hilarious, weird, and entertaining!"

"I am a mystery reader, but these books made me not care who done it. This Margaret Lashley is a game changer."

"Funny, unpredictable, pure Florida weirdness served up on a hard-to-put-down platter."

"Not too scary or over-the-top paranormal. A truly fun read!"

"The story lines are crazy, and all you want is more!"

"A funny cozy, science fiction, thriller, mystery all rolled into one great story!"

"I read a lot, and Kindle suggested your book. This is laugh out loud funny. Is everyone in Florida crazy?"

"Margaret Lashley has a knack for creating funny, small town strange, off the wall, but so endearing type of characters."

"If you enjoy laugh-out-loud comedy, this book is for you!"

Prologue

I took a sip of strawberry margarita and lay back on the squeaky, rusted-out lounge chair beside the not-so-sparkling pool of the Budget Motor Court.

I was in Treasure Island, Florida. It was the middle of August, and the heat was unbearable. But not as unbearable as the alternative—a life sentence for homicide.

So there was *that* ....

THREE MONTHS HAD PASSED since that fateful night when Grayson and I'd boldly gone where that nerd had never gone before.

That is, where we'd *almost* gone—until Earl had burst into the bedroom of the RV with some stupendous news that, to his addled brain, simply couldn't have waited one single, solitary second longer to spill.

As I lay there with my back roasting in the sun, the memory made my jaw clench. Despite ninety days of nonstop tequila and sunbaked solitude, I still couldn't erase the image of my cousin's idiotic face as he'd flung open the bedroom door and caught me atop Grayson, half naked.

"Bobbie!" he'd hollered. "Fantastic news! Your dad's auto shop is finally paid off!"

"What?" I'd screeched, frantically clutching at the edges of my unbuttoned shirt, trying to cover myself.

Grinning like a gorilla in a banana factory, Earl had waved a piece of paper at me. "See? It says right here in this letter from the bank. The loan on the property's been 'For Closed.'"

"What?" I'd yelled, then scrambled off Grayson. I'd snatched the bank notice from Earl's hillbilly paws, squinted at it, then glanced around wildly.

"You looking for these?" Grayson had asked. He'd leaned across the bed and handed me a pair of cheater glasses, then stuck a pillow over his lap.

One bespectacled look at the paper in my hand and my eyes had nearly bugged out of my head. "The bank says we haven't made a payment in *six months*!" I'd glared with disbelief at my giant bear of a cousin. "Earl, why on *Earth* didn't you make the mortgage payments?"

Lines had creased my cousin's Neanderthal brow ridge. "I *did*. I guess the checks must a bounced."

My jaw had dropped open. "But we gave you a *whole bagful* of money for the Mothman scat! What did you do with it?"

He'd winced. "I had me some unexpected expenses."

I'd shaken the foreclosure notice in his face. "Are you telling me you ate *twenty thousand dollars' worth of Fritos*?"

"'Course not, Bobbie. I spent it on my girls."

"Your *girls*?"

"Strip clubs can get pretty pricey," Grayson had said.

I'd turned and shot him some side eye. "How do *you* know?"

"Not *strip club* girls," Earl said. "*My* girls."

I'd whipped back around and narrowed my lethal gaze again on my shaggy-haired cousin. "Are you talking about Beth-Ann?"

Earl's giant, doofus head had cocked to one side. "Nope. I mean Sally and Bessie. Them fancy turtle ponds and custom chrome peerin' scopes don't come cheap, you know."

Arrgh!

I squeezed my eyes shut, trying to blot out the horrid memory. It didn't work. Restless, I turned over in my sun lounger. Then I sat up and took another huge slurp of the melted red slush in my margarita glass. The sucking sound as I reached the bottom reminded me of my life back in Point Paradise. It, too, was now officially down the drain.

I blew out a sigh, then reached over and set the empty glass atop the wobbly table beside my lounge chair. Absently, I twisted the sapphire ring on my finger. It used to belong to my Grandma Selma. She'd given it to me right before she passed. It was the only tangible anchor to the past that I had left.

As for my future? That remained to be seen.

My cellphone rang, startling me. I glanced at the display. My heart lurched. It was Grayson, my boss and private-eye instructor. I'd spent the last year training under him. Thanks to Earl, that was the *only* thing I'd managed to do with Grayson in that position.

I chewed my lip, debating whether to answer the phone. It was a call I'd been both anticipating *and* dreading for months—ever since the evening Earl had sabotaged Grayson's and my skyrockets in flight.

That night, I'd gone totally ballistic. I'd grabbed my Glock and run my cousin out of the RV. Then I'd chased him all the way across the Walmart parking lot, threatening to shoot him if I ever saw his stupid face again.

As I'd waved my pistol in the air like Annie Oakley on a bender, a cab had pulled up beside me. The driver, a woman whose face said she'd no-doubt seen it all before, rolled down the window and told me that I might want to put away the gun—*and* button my blouse.

In an instant, my anger had evaporated. It had been replaced by a tsunami of humiliation. Half naked and crazy in a Walmart parking lot? That had marked a new low for me—even by *my* sorry life's shabby standards.

Embarrassed beyond words, I wasn't able to face going back to Grayson in the RV. So I'd hopped into the old woman's cab and said,

"Take me somewhere I can drink myself into forgetting this night ever happened."

She'd laughed and said, "I know just the place. And cheer up, kiddo. I've lived long enough to know that time and alcohol can cure anything."

Hoping for all I was worth that the old lady was right, I'd texted Grayson from the backseat of the cab. I gave him *carte blanche* to retrofit the old RV we'd just bought—with two conditions.

First, Earl Schankles, utter bane of my existence, was not to be involved in the project in any way. Grayson was to do the modifications with the help of a conspiracy-theorist motor-head geek we called Operative Garth. And second, Grayson was to not contact me again until work on the RV had been totally completed. (At the time, my hope had been that this would allow the burning humiliation I felt to fade into a distant, eye-twitching memory.)

After typing these terms out on my phone, I'd sent the text to Grayson. Then the taxi lady had deposited me at the Budget Motor Court. Now, three months later, Grayson was finally calling.

Was I ready to face him?

With two margaritas working their magic in my gut, I felt pretty sure I was. But believe me, I'd needed every minute of the past ninety days to come to terms with my feelings about my future with Grayson.

I knew I wanted to be a P.I. And I was certain I wanted Grayson in my life. But did he want me?

Regarding my feelings about my cousin Earl, they were also crystal clear. Due to his negligence and stupidity, my jerk of a cousin had managed to destroy my past—and quite possibly my future—in one fell swoop.

As for the anger that still boiled inside me over the nuclear meltdown he'd made of my world? It hadn't even begun to reach its half-life.

Chapter One

I stared at my buzzing cellphone like it was a hissing rattlesnake about to strike. Uncertainty and anticipation kick-boxed inside my gut as I watched the phone vibrate, then shimmy across the cracked tabletop beside my lounge chair.

As it teetered halfway off the edge, I whispered to myself, "Come on, Bobbie. You're ready for this."

Before I could lose my nerve, I snatched up the phone, knocking my empty margarita glass onto the pool deck. My thumb hovered over the *answer* button. I took a deep breath.

You can do this, Roberta Drex. Just. Stay. Calm.

I clicked *answer*, then tried to sound breezy.

"Oh. Hi, Grayson."

"Drex! How are you?"

Tipsy. Tanned. Ten pounds heavier...

"I'm good. You?"

"Good."

I desperately wanted to say something charming and clever, but a sudden bout of awkwardness blocked my brain and tied my tongue. "Well, uh ... that's good."

"You sound good," Grayson said.

"Uh ... you sound good, too."

"Good."

We listened to each other breathe for a moment. After what seemed like an eternity, mercifully Grayson broke the silence. "Are you ready to see our new company vehicle?"

I blanched. "Oh. Uh ... yes. Sure! So you're done with the retrofit?"

"Of course. Otherwise, I wouldn't be calling. That *was* our agreement, wasn't it?"

Grayson's matter-of-fact tone made my heart sink.

So that's it. We're back to strictly business partners.

"Right." I hid my disappointment under a thin veneer of cheerfulness. "That was our agreement, all right."

"I'd like to give you a test drive." Grayson cleared his throat. "Uh ... I mean in the *vehicle*, of course."

I winced. Apparently, I wasn't the only one feeling completely weirded out by this. "Okay. Sure. When—"

"Excellent. I'll be by in five minutes."

"What?" I yelped. "You don't even know where I am!"

I waited for a reply, then realized Grayson had already hung up.

What the?

"You ready for another one?" a man asked, interrupting my panic attack.

I glanced up from my phone to see a young guy in shorts and an unbuttoned Hawaiian shirt. The blonde cutie's name was Ariel. He ran the slip-shod motel's shabby little poolside tiki bar.

"Uh, no thanks." I scrambled to my feet. Frantically, I grabbed up my towel and sunscreen.

"Okay. No problem," he said. "You don't have to leave."

Ariel picked up my empty margarita glass and glanced around, no doubt searching for the five-dollar tip I usually handed him whenever he served me a drink. I peeled a fiver out of my sweaty bathing-suit bra and handed it to him.

"See you this afternoon?" he asked, smiling hopefully.

"Uh ... I'm not sure." I hastily inched into my flip flops. "I think I may be checking out today."

The smile on Ariel's boyish face disappeared. "What? You can't leave, Miss Bobbie!"

"Why? Don't tell me you're actually going to *miss* me."

"I sure will." Ariel hung his head and stared at me with puppy-dog eyes. "How am I ever gonna pay for college *now*?"

FIVE LOUSY MINUTES.

My mind raced like a squirrel trapped in a room full of chocolate-covered acorns. After three months apart, Grayson had given me just five lousy minutes to prepare for seeing him again.

Typical man!

Sweaty, tipsy, and bloated like a pufferfish, I raced from the shabby pool area, my towel dragging on the ground behind me. Halfway to my motel room, I stubbed my toe on a crack in the sidewalk and blew out my left flip-flop.

"Seriously, Universe?" I growled as I hobbled up to my door.

After fiddling the lock open, I tumbled inside. I kicked off my other flip-flop, peeled off my sticky bathing suit, and made a beeline for the plastic shower stall for a quick rinse.

Sixty seconds later, sweat washed down the drain, I dried off with a threadbare towel. Then I rifled like a madwoman through the pile of semi-dirty clothes heaped atop a rickety bamboo chair wedged in the corner of the room.

After fishing through the crumpled pile for a shirt and shorts bearing the least noticeable strawberry margarita stains, I'd barely managed to button my blouse when a knock sounded at the door.

Crap!

A quick glance through the peephole confirmed it was Grayson. And he was looking as fit and professional as ever in his black shirt and jeans.

Double crap! No makeup. Not even time to brush my teeth! I bet my tongue is as red as a midlife-crisis Corvette!

Thankfully, my hair was passable. Three months apart had given it time to grow out—albeit only to the length of a man's cut. But as I ran my hand through my short, damp locks, I wondered why I even cared. Through the peephole, I'd seen that Grayson had regrown that horrible bushy moustache I hated. And his business-like tone on the phone had said what his words hadn't.

Face it, Bobbie. Your budding romance with Grayson is over. Nada. Zilch. Dumpster fodder.

Grayson knocked again. I straightened my shoulders and reached for the doorknob.

Here goes nothing.

I slapped on a smile and flung open the door. "Grayson! How did you know where to find me?"

His handsome head cocked to one side. "Good to see you, too."

I winced. "Sorry. It's just ... well, you caught me by surprise."

"Understandable." His green eyes glanced around the room. "Nice place you have here."

I put a hand to my heart—mainly to hide the strawberry-red margarita stain covering half my left boob. "I was trying to be budget conscious."

"Hmm," he said, noting the dated decor. "If *I* had picked this place, you'd have never ceased complaining about it."

He was right. I wouldn't have.

Am I that big a hypocrite?

Grayson's eagle eyes turned to study me. His left eyebrow rose half an inch. "Are those blood stains on your blouse?"

My free hand rose to cover a blotch on my belly. "Uh ... no. Hey! You never answered my question. How did you know how to find me?"

"GPS," he said, walking past me into the room.

"GPS?" I whipped around to follow him, hoping against hope I'd picked up all my dirty underwear. "Is that one of the new gizmos you installed in the RV?"

"No. GPS is a common cellphone app, Drex."

"Oh. Yeah, of course."

Grayson shot a furtive glance at a pair of underpants on the floor, but whatever he was thinking, he kept it to himself. "So, are you ready to see what Garth and I have done to Gabbie?"

"Gabbie?" I asked, kicking the panties under the bed.

"The RV. I named it. I hope you don't mind."

"Oh. No. That's fine. But why Gabbie?"

"Pack your things and I'll explain on the way."

I snatched my purse from the nightstand and tossed my room key on the bed. "I'm ready. Let's go."

Grayson eyed the mound of dirty shorts and shirts lying in a heap in the corner. "What about your clothes and whatnot?"

"I'll get new ones," I said, shoving Grayson outside.

"Good. I'd like to get going as soon as possible." As the door closed behind me, he eyed my blouse again. "Are you sure you're okay?"

I nodded. "Yeah. I don't know what they put in the strawberry margaritas around here, but even Mr. Clean doesn't have the muscle to get the stains out."

Chapter Two

Even though I'd prepared for the worst, I still couldn't quite wrap my head around what I was staring at.

Parked under a sagging palm tree in front of the rundown Budget Motor Court was an RV with more wear and tear on it than the cheap mattress I'd been tossing and turning on for the past three months.

"Isn't she a beauty?" Grayson asked.

My nose crinkled.

Not even close.

The RV's resemblance to my ugly-ass motel room was uncanny. Its dingy beige exterior perfectly matched the sulfur-stained shower stall in the bathroom. The dull orange and green stripes running along its sides echoed the not-so-groovy hues of my room's worn-out shag carpet and cracked avocado sink.

I blinked hard, wondering if I'd accidently fallen through some time portal back to 1974.

"Grayson, what exactly have you and Garth been doing all this time? This rattrap looks exactly the same as the day we bought it off Danny Daniels."

"On the *outside*, sure. That's the whole point. So we can travel incognito."

"To where? A third-world disco party?"

Grayson's shoulders straightened. "No. To our next investigation. It's in the center of the state, north of Orlando."

I cringed. "Not Point Paradise!"

"No. A little south of there."

Relief softened my tone. "Good. Well, given that it's Central Florida, I think the whole 'third-world vibe' you've got going on here should prove to be the perfect cover."

Grayson smiled. "Good. I was hoping you'd say that. We need to fly under the radar."

I shot him a sideways glance. "Why?"

Grayson's moustache twitched. "Never mind for now. Come take a look at the interior. I think you'll approve of the modifications."

As Grayson unlocked the side door to the RV, I paused and shot him a smirk. "Don't tell me. There's a mirrored ball hanging from the ceiling, isn't there?"

Grayson cocked his head. "Don't be ridiculous. There isn't nearly enough headroom."

I laughed. He smiled.

Maybe there's hope for the two of us after all.

"Is Garth in here?" I asked as I climbed the steps to the RV.

"No. He had a MUFON convention to attend."

I turned and shot Grayson a look of incredulity. "You passed up a MUFON convention for me?"

"Yes."

"I feel honored." I curtseyed and stepped inside the motorhome. Yet again, I found myself flabbergasted. But this time, it was for all the *right* reasons.

"Holy smokes!" I exclaimed as I took in the transformed décor of the main cabin. The rusty old stove and burnt-orange countertops were gone. In their stead was a gleaming new kitchen sporting stainless steel appliances and granite countertops. "Whoa! Is that one of those microwaves that doubles as a toaster oven?"

"It's a convection oven," Grayson said. "No more waiting for Pop Tarts two at a time from the toaster."

I grinned. "Sweet!"

"And look. Two refrigerators." Grayson waved a hand like a gameshow host. "One for food, and one for biological samples. No more mix-ups."

I thought about the Mothman mystery meatballs incident, and about Danny Daniels' tattooed foot stuck inside an empty Ding Dong box. But I decided not to go there. "Uh ... that's great."

"Did you notice the built-in coffeemaker?" Grayson asked, pointing to a contraption above the stove. "At the touch of a button, you can have your choice of espresso, café Americano, or cappuccino."

I grinned. "I have to admit, that's pretty cool."

"That's not all. Take a look in the bathroom."

My right eyebrow arched. "Why?"

"You'll see."

I quickly padded down the hall in my mismatched flip-flops. "Whoa! A real tiled shower!"

"With shelves for your 'lady stuff.'"

I whistled. "And a full-sized toilet. Nice." I frowned and glanced up at the ceiling. "What about the exhaust fan?"

Grayson stuck his nose in the air like a snooty butler. "Super deluxe."

I grinned. "Sweet. But how'd you find the room for all of this?"

Grayson shrugged. "I borrowed a bit of space from the bedroom."

"Oh."

I stepped down the hall and snuck a peek into the bedroom. The walls had been padded. Heavy metal mesh covered the windows. No doubt, Grayson had converted it into an electromagnetic monster trap, just like the one in the old RV. The only difference was the room was now considerably smaller.

And it had been furnished with a set of stacked bunk beds.

I winced.

Well, if that isn't the final nail in the romance coffin, what is?

"This looks good," I said, forcing a smile.

"You haven't seen the best part yet."

What? Adoption papers making us brother and sister?

I took a deep breath. "Go on. Show me."

Grayson opened the cabinets lining the hallway. "Black shirts and pants for both of us. Just like the ones I have on now. They'll be our official investigation uniforms."

I stared at him. "You gonna microchip me, too?"

Grayson's head cocked. "What?"

"Nothing." I sighed and opened another door in the hallway. Inside, a bunch of electronic gizmos blinked wildly on the shelves. "What's all that stuff?"

"The latest in electromagnetic radiation detection, satellite imagery, and alien tracking radar."

"What? No alien parasite remover?"

"Of course." Grayson opened another door, revealing a hodgepodge collection of glass bottles and plastic spray containers. "Thankfully, I was able to recreate nearly all of my original formulas."

"Fortunate indeed," I said, feigning enthusiasm. "What's in the tall cabinet, there?"

"That's been reserved for old-school paraphernalia."

"Old school?" Curious, I opened the door. Inside were an assortment of ropes, nets on poles, grappling hooks, frog gigs, fishing gear, bungee cords, a shotgun, and, strangely, a broom.

"What's the broom for?" I asked.

Grayson eyed me oddly. "For sweeping. Perhaps you've heard of it?"

Chapter Three

"I have to admit, these new travel chairs are sweet," I said as Grayson and I cruised down the road in the newly kitted-out RV.

Grayson nodded. "And they also double as flotation devices."

"What for?" I asked, shooting him a wary glance.

"In case of—"

"No! Never mind. I don't want to know."

"Okay." Grayson shrugged. "In case you're wondering, the chairs offer a complete 360-degree turning radius, for maximum maneuverability."

"You mean they spin?" I twirled around in my passenger seat like a kid in a Tilt-a-Whirl. "Woohoo!"

Dizzy, I slowly turned the chair back to face the windshield. That's when I noticed the dashboard looked like something from the helm of the Star Ship Enterprise. "What are all those lights and switch thingies for?"

"I'll explain later, when we're not underway."

I frowned. "So, what can you show me while we're moving?"

Grayson shot me a glance. "Open the compartment on your chair's arm rest."

I wagged my eyebrows. "What's in here? Some kind of ray gun? A light saber?"

"Just some creature comforts."

I popped the compartment open. "Wow. An actual built-in cup holder. Talk about your latest in high-tech gizmos."

"It's heated," Grayson said. "To keep the coffee warm."

"Seriously? Well, now we're talking! Hey, what are these buttons for?"

"The pink one is a seat warmer. The blue one is lumbar massage."

"No way!" I mashed the blue button, then nearly drooled as something akin to iron fingers began moving under the vinyl upholstery. They made their way up and down my back like a robotic masseuse.

Grayson's cheek dimpled, an indication he was grinning under that stupid moustache of his. "I take it you approve?"

I let out a contented sigh. "More than approve. I could almost fall sleep in this thing."

"Glad to hear it. Because that's your new bed."

I sat up with a start. "What? I have to sleep in a *chair*?"

"Not exactly. Swivel around to face the back, then hit the yellow button."

Grumpily, I did as instructed. At the touch of the yellow button, a cushy footrest appeared from under the chair and rose until it was even with the seat. Then the back of the chair slowly lowered until it was level with the butt cushion.

To my utter surprise and delight, the chair was now a bona fide bed. A *single* bed, but a real bed, nonetheless.

"Wow. This sure beats that old sofa bed," I said, wriggling my torso around like a pig in mud. Having grown accustomed to the low standards of the Budget Motor Court, the new chair-bed thingy felt like a slice of heaven.

"So?" Grayson asked.

I glanced over at him. "Okay. I have to admit it. This is pretty awesome."

He smiled. "I'm glad you approve. Now, let's get to work."

"Aye-aye, Captain."

I hit the yellow button again. Slowly, the bed turned back into a chair. I swiveled around to face the front. Then I turned my attention back to the mind-boggling assortment of knobs and buttons and blinking lights covering the dashboard.

"Gee, Grayson. This must be what the command deck of Enterprise looked like."

"You *do* know that was just a TV show, right?"

I smirked. "As far as we know."

Grayson's cheek dimpled again. "And here I thought *I* was the conspiracy theorist."

I reached for a big red button in the center of the dashboard marked with the letters EE. "Hey. What does this button do?"

"That's for E-level emergencies."

"What do you mean, '*E*-level emergencies'?"

"*Earl* level emergencies," Grayson said. "A shiny red button would be the first thing he'd press. So I made a dummy button just for him. It doesn't actually do anything."

I grinned. "You really *have* thought of everything. But honestly, Grayson. I doubt my dumb cousin is ever gonna set foot inside here."

Grayson's green eyes shifted from the road to me. "You're still angry with him?"

"Li'l bit."

Actually, the mere mention of Earl's name caused twin flames of anger and humiliation to roil up inside me afresh. But at least my fingers hadn't automatically balled into fists this time. I was making progress ... I hoped.

Grayson steered the RV into the left lane, then onto I-275 northbound. "You know you're going to have to face your cousin one of these days."

"Maybe. But not today." I glanced around at the fancy RV, itching to change the subject. "So tell me. Why did you name this thing Gabbie?"

"Ah. Well, GABBIE is an acronym. In the tradition of Operative Garth's BIMBO mobile."

"That giant cockroach tank?" I laughed. "Wow. What an honor."

Grayson totally missed my attempt at sarcasm. "I thought so, too. GABBIE stands for Grayson and Bobbie's Badass Investigative Explorer."

I snorted. "*Badass?* Whose idea was—?" I stopped midsentence and glared at Grayson. "Wait a minute! Why is *your* name first?"

Grayson turned and smirked at me. "Mainly because BAGBIE didn't have quite the same ring to it."

"You're right." I conceded and folded my arms across my chest. "BAGBIE sounds like the name of a Scottish butler."

"Exactly."

"Well, I totally get the badass part." I glanced around at the incomprehensible array of lights blinking on the dashboard. "So, how much did all this stuff cost, anyway?"

Grayson's eyes quickly shifted back to the road. "Don't concern yourself with that. After all the equipment is paid for, you'll still have a pretty penny left in your bank account."

I studied Grayson with suspicion.

I sincerely hope you don't mean that literally.

Chapter Four

After poking around the RV's new kitchen and bathroom, I returned to the driver's cab to discover Grayson had already driven completely through Tampa. He was now merging the motorhome onto I-75 northbound, in the direction of Ocala.

I wasn't sure what to say or do. The three months we'd spent apart had me feeling sort of estranged from Grayson. What had he been up to all that time? Surely he and Garth hadn't spent every waking minute under the hood of this RV, had they.

"So, what have you been up to since I saw you last?" I asked, casually flopping into the passenger seat beside him.

"Isn't it obvious?" Grayson shot an icy stare into the side-view mirror. "Upgrading the RV."

"Uh ... sure. But what else? Any new hobbies?"

Seriously, Bobbie? New hobbies?

Grayson shifted his serious stare to the road ahead. "I was going to save this conversation for later, but things are a bit complicated right now."

A lump clotted my throat. "You met someone, didn't you?"

"Yes. Did you?"

I thought about Ariel the pool boy, and the pizza delivery guy who'd come to know me on a first-name basis. They were people, right? "Yeah. Me, too."

Grayson's brow furrowed. "Look, I need to explain something about the last time we were together. I—"

"Don't sweat it," I said, cutting him off before he could pour salt into my wounded heart. "I'm cool with everything if you are. Agreed?"

Grayson eyed me carefully. "You sure?"

I gave him my best smile. "Of course I'm sure."

And now I will officially hate myself for the rest of eternity.

"YOU UP FOR SOME TACOS?" Grayson asked as I sat in my new, super-deluxe travel chair-bed thingy. Staring out the window as the world passed by, I felt listless and hopeless.

I wonder if this armrest has a suicide option ...

"Drex?"

"Oh. Tacos? Sure," I said. "I haven't had one since the last time we ate them together."

Grayson nearly steered the RV into a ditch. "Are you serious?"

"Not everyone has a one-track gut like you."

"I see. Let's stop at the Zephyrhills exit. Chatter on the ham radio indicates there's an excellent taco stand just off the interstate ramp in Westley Chapel."

"Sounds delicious," I said, even though my appetite had completely dried up.

Grayson glanced over at me. "We'll need to fortify ourselves for the journey ahead. It will take two hours and thirty-eight minutes to get to our destination."

"Where's that? Self-loathing?" I muttered under my breath. "I thought I was already there."

"What?" Grayson asked.

I shook my head. "Nothing." I studied my no-nonsense partner out of the corner of my eye. He appeared as calm and put together and handsome as he always did. In other words, he hadn't changed a whit. He was as irritatingly perfect and infuriating as ever.

"Grayson, I'm curious. How can you know down to the exact minute how long it'll take to get to wherever it is we're going?'"

"Easy. GABBIE told me." Grayson turned a knob on the dashboard. A sexy, female voice announced in a posh, British accent, "You will arrive in Astor in two hours and thirty-seven minutes, in light traffic."

I rolled my eyes. "Let me guess who chose *that* voice. Garth?"

Grayson nodded. "Correct. But our destination was *my* choice. And I must say, for an investigative intern, you show a surprising lack of curiosity about our new case."

I sat up in my chair. "Sorry. I had a few other things on my mind. Okay, so, fill me in. I'm all ears."

Grayson squinted at the rearview mirror. "We're headed to an unincorporated fishing village called Astor."

"Why? What's in Astor?"

Grayson shot me a knowing look. "Perhaps the real question is, what *isn't* in Astor."

I stifled a sigh. "Grayson, I'm not in the mood for games right now."

He shrugged. "Okay. Have it your way."

I waited a beat, then decided to pull up my big-girl panties and let our dead romance rest in peace. After all, it wasn't Grayson's fault. It was Earl's. I swiveled my chair to face Grayson. "Okay. I'll bite. So what *isn't* in Astor?"

Grayson's green eyes sparkled. "Three to nine of its residents, depending on whose headcount you believe."

"Huh?" I grunted. "Is that the size of the town? Geez. That's smaller than Point Paradise."

"Actually, it's larger. Astor's inhabitants numbered 1,595 according to the 2019 census."

My brow crinkled. "Sorry, but I'm not following you."

"Let me explain." Grayson glanced into the rearview mirror, then, at the last minute, he swerved onto the exit ramp for SR 56 like we were shooting a chase scene from *Fast & Furious*.

"Geez," I squealed, holding onto the arm rests for dear life. "I can see you didn't spend our time apart taking driving lessons!"

Grayson shot me a look. "Why *would* I?"

"Never mind." I adjusted myself back in my seat after being jerked akimbo. "What were you saying about Astor?"

"Oh. Right. While I was working with Garth on the retrofit, reports kept coming in over his ham radio about people disappearing from the area around Astor."

"Disappearing?"

"Yes. Garth explained the phenomenon has been going on for a few years now."

"*Years*? So what's the big hurry to get there *now*?"

Grayson glanced over at me. "Because three people went missing last week alone."

"Oh." My nose crinkled. "Any idea why?"

"I've got my theories."

I sighed.

I bet you do.

Chapter Five

"You've got to be kidding me!" I said, spewing a mouthful of greasy taco.

"Not at all," Grayson said.

I couldn't believe my ears. Grayson's theory about what was causing people to disappear from the tiny town of Astor, Florida had left me dumbstruck.

But, for the first time since we'd begun working together, I wasn't aghast because his idea was *implausible*. Just the opposite. It was *too* plausible—at least for the conspiracy nut I knew Nick Grayson to be.

"Alligators?" I asked, wiping grease from my chin.

"Yes. Alligator hunting season officially opened last week on August fifteenth," he said, as if that explained everything I needed to know about Astor's missing residents.

Grayson reached for another taco from the family platter he'd ordered. I shook my head in wonder. How could the guy eat enough food for a family of four and still have washboard abs? It was inhuman! And totally unfair!

I burped back early-onset heartburn. As usual, the taco place Grayson had picked was a dive. But I had to admit the tacos were incredibly tasty.

"So alligator hunting season started on the fifteenth," I repeated. "I don't see the connection."

Grayson's green eyes focused on me like lasers. "I told you. *Three people* have gone missing since then. Do you still not see the connection?"

I shrugged. "It could've been anything. Maybe they left on summer vacation. You ever think about that?"

But Grayson wasn't listening. His attention was focused on some guy who'd just walked into the restaurant. I admit the man looked suspicious. He had on a three-piece suit.

In Florida.

In the middle of August.

Grayson's emerald-green eyes grew dark. He locked them on me. "You ready to go?"

I glanced down at his plate and nearly gasped. "What? You still have two tacos left!"

He grabbed one and handed it to me. Then he took the other. "Come on. Follow me." Then he got up and made a beeline for the door.

"ALL RIGHT, WHAT THE hell is going on?" I asked as Grayson peeled out of the parking lot of the Mexican restaurant like we'd just committed a dine-and-dash.

"I didn't want to say anything. But I think we're being followed."

A tingle ran down my spine despite the heat. "By who? Don't tell me your new girlfriend's a psycho!"

"My new *what*?" Grayson gunned the RV like a NASCAR hotrod. It puttered for all it was worth up the entrance ramp to I-75 northbound.

"Girlfriend," I said. "You told me you met someone while we were apart."

"Yes. I met several people." Grayson checked the rearview mirror again. "None of them were women."

"Oh." I sat back in my passenger seat, uncertain whether to feel better now or worse. Then I realized if it really *was* over between the two of us, it couldn't get any worse. I chewed my lip. "So if you didn't meet women, who were they?"

Grayson cocked his head at me. "Men, of course."

"Ugh! I know that!" I swiveled to face him. "What *kind* of men? What did they want from you?"

"I'm not sure. Do you remember our last night together?"

How could I forget? My ears caught fire as I envisioned being in bed with Grayson, our lips pressed together, my bare chest against his. Then Earl burst through the door like that giant Kool-Aid pitcher in those commercials, splashing his idiot juice all over our budding flames of desire.

"Vaguely," I said.

"Then let me refresh your memory."

Sweat broke out on my upper lip. Was he really going to go there? "Uh ... okay."

"Danny Daniels was walking out of Walmart when a mysterious, hovering craft caught him up in a beam of light. He disappeared into the sky, leaving only his foot and two boxes of Ding Dongs behind in the parking lot as evidence."

"Yeah," I said, both relieved and slightly annoyed. "That's something I don't think I could forget if I wanted to."

"Right," Grayson said. "Well, during our time apart, I've been working with Garth and his spy network to analyze Daniels' foot. And to scour the internet for similar events."

My upper lip snarled in disgust. "Did you find any?"

"Unfortunately, no."

"Oh." I toyed with the controls on my chair. "Well, *I* did some research, too. In case you were wondering."

"You did? On what?"

"I watched two seasons of *Monster Hunters.* And almost every documentary Seth Breedlove ever made."

"So you studied fellow researchers' works," Grayson said without a hint of sarcasm. "Good use of your time."

"Uh ... thanks."

"And did you draw any correlations with what you watched and the events involving Danny Daniels?"

I swallowed hard. "Well, yeah. I think they could be related."

"How?"

"You know," I said. "Whoever's behind Danny's abduction has to involve aliens, the FBI, or a conspiracy between them both."

"Exactly!" Grayson said. "It's always aliens, the FBI, or a conspiracy between them both. Excellent, Drex!"

I shot him a sheepish smile. "Thanks."

Grayson studied me as he furthered his inquiry. "In addition to digital media, did you use any *underground* resources to aid in your background research?"

I chewed my lip.

If you count the underground tree roots turned into pulp to make newsprint for the National Enquirer, then yeah.

"Sort of," I said. "How about you?"

Grayson nodded, then checked the side-view mirror again. "Yes. I called Warren Engles."

I nearly blanched. Engles was this mysterious guy who had saved our butts a few times. But we'd yet to actually meet him in person. Given that Engles' aid always came with a price, we had yet to fully determine whether he was on our side or not.

"You told me you weren't sure whether Engles was really with the FBI," I said. "I thought you were worried he was only using you as bait to catch alien life forms."

"Correct," Grayson said. "I'm still not sure. You may be right about your theory Engles is only using us to track cryptids, then steal whatever evidence we gather."

"So you actually got in touch with him," I asked. "What did he say?"

Grayson frowned. "Nothing. I tried to call him, but his line had been disconnected."

My nose crinkled. "Oh. Why would that be?"

"Unknown." Grayson pursed his lips. "But after careful consideration, Garth and I concluded that it could only mean one of two things."

"Those being?"

Grayson locked eyes with me. "Either Engles is dead, or he already has what he wants from me."

I shook my head. "But Grayson, if either of those scenarios are true, why do you think you're being followed now?"

"I don't know. Whoever it is could be Engles' replacement. Or some other entity we're not even aware of."

A creepy feeling washed over me, giving me the willies.

Grayson glanced in the side-view mirror for the millionth time. "Then again, Drex, it could just be my imagination."

"I sure hope so."

"Me, too." He turned to me. "Do me a favor?"

"Sure. What?"

"If you spot a dark-blue sedan behind us, let me know."

Chapter Six

For the past half an hour, I'd kept my eyes glued to the side-view mirror, searching for the mysterious blue sedan that was either following us or was a figment of Grayson's warped imagination.

My bet was on the latter.

Working alongside Grayson, I'd come to learn that his version of "reality" was more fluid than most. Even so, more often than not, he'd proven to be right, despite the odds. So I kept vigilant.

"See anything?" he asked as we buzzed northbound along I-75.

"No. Still no sign of anyone tailing us."

"Good. Hold on." Grayson jerked the steering wheel hard to the right. The old motorhome groaned as we veered across two lanes, then took the Wildwood exit on two wheels.

"Geez, Grayson!" I yelled, sitting up and rubbing the spot on my head that had banged against the window. "Was that really necessary?"

"Given the uncertainty of our situation, I believe it prudent to take evasive measures. We need to lay low for a while, Drex. And I don't think we can lay much lower than Astor. It should serve perfectly as both a hideaway and a point to launch our new investigation."

I crossed my arms and stared blankly out the window. The old RV chugged east along on SR 44, past the obligatory string of grubby gas stations and generic fast-food restaurants that seemed to sprout up along interstate exits like toadstools after a rain.

"Gee," I said. "If this area is any indication, you're right. I don't think we *can* get any lower." I stared into the side-view mirror. "Well, at least no blue sedan pulled off the interstate behind us. I guess no one was following us after all."

"Or they lost our trail," Grayson said. "Either way, I think we're in the clear. For now."

I swiveled in my chair to face Grayson. As I studied my weird, intense, and oddly attractive partner, I wondered if I should be worried. And if so, who should I be more worried about? The blue sedan folks, or him?

"Grayson, say there *is* someone after us. If they're replacing Engles, they'd be doing what *he* did, right? Tracking us in hopes we lead them to alien life forms or cryptid creatures."

"Correct." Grays kept his eyes fixed on the road ahead. "Their mission would be to steal whatever evidence we gather. I suspect as part of their mutual alien-FBI cover-up operation."

I stifled a laugh. "But you said you think *alligators* are to blame for the disappearances in Astor."

"Yes. I don't see your point."

"And I don't see yours!" I shook my head. "Grayson, there's nothing *weird* about alligators. They're not monsters or aliens or even cryptids. So why would *they*—actually, why would *you*—care that a couple of rednecks ended up as gator bait?"

Grayson turned and focused his green eyes on me like twin laser beams. "Because I have reason to believe we might not be dealing with an *ordinary* alligator."

I gulped. Then I had a flashback of a movie I'd watched back at the motel. "Wait a minute. Don't tell me we're off to chase a mutant alligator some kid flushed down the toilet!"

Grayson scoffed. "Don't be ridiculous. That's not possible."

"Why? Because giant gators can't actually fit down sewers?"

"No. Well, yes. That and the fact that legends of giant alligators *predate* indoor plumbing."

My brow furrowed. "Huh?"

Grayson swerved to miss a roadkill possum, then launched into one of his academic dictums. As annoying as they could be, I suddenly realized I'd actually missed them.

Geez. I need to get a life!

"You see, Drex, ever since Europeans began settling Florida in the 1800s, there have been reports of huge alligators along the St. Johns River. That's the same river that runs through Astor."

I eyed him dubiously. "Okay, I'll bite. How huge we talking about?"

"Much too large to fall within the normal range of *Alligator mississippiensis*. Which, for adult males, can be up to fifteen feet in length."

I chewed my lip. "So you think there might be some kind of supermutant alligator running amok? Like Hogzilla, only Gatorzilla?"

Grayson shrugged. "That's *one* explanation."

I shot him a smirk. "But you have another one, I'm guessing?"

"*Deinosuchas*."

"Gesundheit. You need a tissue, or is there some robotic nose-wiping contraption built into that fancy spaceship dashboard of yours?"

Grayson eyed the dash. "Hmm. That's not a bad idea. But no." He turned and studied me. "I didn't sneeze, Drex. I said, 'Deinosuchas.'"

"Huh?"

Grayson rubbed his chin. "Yes, I do believe we could be witnessing the return of Deinosuchas, the terrible crocodile."

"Terrible crocodile?" I laughed. "What'd the poor thing ever do to *you*?"

Grayson's brow furrowed. "It's Greek."

I smiled. "With you, it usually is."

Grayson frowned. "I meant, Deinosuchas comes from the Greek words *deinos*, meaning terrible, and *soukhos*, meaning crocodile."

"I figured," I said, twiddling with the buttons on the armrest. "But Grayson, your hypothesis doesn't make any sense. With the exception of a handful of saltwater crocs in the Keys, Florida doesn't *have* crocodiles. We've got *alligators*. Not exactly the same thing."

Grayson smiled. "I totally concur with your excellent scientific reasoning, Drex."

I nearly fell out of my super-cushy chair. "You *do*?"

"Yes. You see, Deinosuchas is a misnomer."

"A misnomer?"

Grayson nodded. "Studies of the creature's braincase suggest Deinosuchas was more closely related to alligators than crocodiles."

"Really?" I snorted. "I wonder what studies of *Earl's* braincase would suggest *he's* most closely related to."

"What?"

I smirked. "Nothing. So, tell me more about this dyno-mitus thing."

Grayson's shoulders stiffened. "*Deinosuchas*. Fossils of the species have been unearthed all along the East Coast."

"Fossils? Grayson, just how long ago did this thing roam the Earth?"

"Deinosuchas lived during the Cretaceous Period. Around 82-73 million years ago, give or take a million."

I sighed. "Kind of like the cash in my bank account."

"Excuse me?"

"Nothing." I glanced out the window at a tumbledown trailer on the side of the road. It was the most interesting thing we'd passed in miles. "So tell me. How big did this dinosaur-gator thing get?"

"Deinosuchas could reach lengths of up to twelve meters."

I frowned and looked over at Grayson. "What's that in American?"

"Thirty-nine feet."

"Geez! That thing was a *monster*!"

"*Is* a monster," Grayson corrected.

I laughed. "Come on. You don't really think it could've survived all those millions of years, do you?"

Grayson glanced over at me. "Of course not. But both dinosaurs and alligators descended from a common ancestor over 200 million years ago. So, I'm deducing we're witnessing another example of iterative evolution."

"Wait a minute," I said. "I remember you talking about this before. Something about some abracadabra bird that came back from the dead?"

"The Aldabra rail."

"Yeah. That's the one."

Grayson rubbed a spidery forefinger across his bushy moustache, then launched into his signature brand of scientific spiel.

"As you may recall, Drex, the flightless Aldabra rail was driven to extinction by predator species introduced to its isolated island home. But once those predators vanished, the once-extinct, flightless bird re-evolved itself into existence using dormant genetic markers still present in its flighted kin."

My face puckered with skepticism. "Hold on. Gimme a second to catch up with your crazy train of thought. You're saying that environmental conditions in *Florida* have changed, and are now favorable again for an extinct species of alligator to return and reclaim its place in the ecosystem?"

Grayson beamed. "That's *precisely* what I'm postulating. The Aldabra rail proves that it's possible. So it's not beyond reason to speculate that the time of Deinosuchas has also returned."

That depends on whose "reason" we're talking about going beyond, isn't it?

I shook my head. "I still think it's a nutso idea. But let's say for the sake of argument that you're right. Why would this thing come back *now*?"

Grayson's cheek dimpled. "Excellent question, Cadet. During the last century, man nearly succeeded in driving alligators to extinction in

North America. By 1973, they were actually on the endangered species list."

"So?"

"Perhaps this near-extinction event triggered the forces of natural selection to favor a return of the species to its original, massive size."

I frowned. "What for?"

"Natural selection favors adaptation. If the Alligator as a species is to survive the rise of Homo sapiens, perhaps size *does* matter in determining who will ultimately win the struggle to become the next apex predator."

I grimaced. "That's a pretty scary thought."

"Why? Because the return of Deinosuchas could mean that humans would no longer be on top of the food chain?"

I chewed my lip. "Well, yeah, that too. But the scariest part is that your theory actually makes sense."

Grayson blanched. "I beg your pardon?"

"Nothing." I turned and stared out the window at the endless marshland bordering either side of the road. It dawned on me how easy it would be for a monster-sized alligator to hide amid the thousands of unexplored acres of dark-water swamps choked with cypress stumps, cattails, and water hyacinths.

A creepy feeling ran up my spine. I turned to Grayson. "What did those dino-sookie things look like, anyway?"

Grayson shrugged. "Actually Deinosuchas' overall appearance was quite similar to modern-day alligators."

I frowned. "So if we spotted a huge gator out there, how could we tell if it was a normal one, or one of your monster-saurs come back from the dead?"

Grayson turned and locked eyes with me. "Easy. If it was a full-grown Deinosuchas, it would be as big as a school bus."

Chapter Seven

After leaving the interstate, Grayson and I spent the next hour and a half traversing one stretch of nondescript back-country road after another. As we roamed further and further from polite society—and then from civilization as I'd come to know it—we formed a zigzag pattern above Orlando through the heart of a mostly forgotten stretch of the Sunshine State.

If you asked me, it had been forgotten for good reason.

The boggy swamplands, mosquito-infested pine woods, and occasional abandoned buildings we'd passed along the way almost had me homesick for lowly little old Point Paradise. I was about to send out a rescue flare when I spotted a light at the end of the tunnel.

It was a restaurant out in the middle of nowhere called Over Yonder Pizza. I opened my mouth to make a snide comment, but spotted another sign even more ridiculous-sounding. It read, *the Royal Order of the Moose Lodge.*

Seriously?

Grayson eased off the gas. As we came to the intersection of Highway 40 and Alternate 445, he stopped the RV.

"What's wrong?" I asked, uncertain which prospect I feared more—a blue sedan full of goons, an alligator the size of a bus, or that this godforsaken spot we were at was Astor.

"*You have arrived at your destination*," announced the sexy, female voice of the RV's navigation system, sealing my fate.

I groaned. "You've gotta be *kidding* me."

Astor was too far north of Disney to offer any of its comforts or attractions, yet was still far enough south to offer all of Florida's oppressive heat, humidity, and, to my surprise, *traffic*. In other words, Astor offered the worst of all possible worlds.

"What's your issue?" Grayson asked. "I told you we needed to lay low."

I shook my head. "Yeah, but I wasn't expecting *this* low. What's the plan? Dunk ourselves under the swamp water and breathe through straws?"

"Astor *must* have its charms," Grayson said as a steady procession of cars and trucks whizzed by the rural intersection. "As you can see, it appears quite popular."

"With who? Possum hunters?"

Grayson gunned the engine and squeezed the RV into a break in the traffic. "Keep an eye out for the Rangler RV Resort. It should be coming up soon along the main drag."

My brow furrowed in wonder. "I don't get it. What are all these people doing out here in the middle of nowhere? There's nothing out here but palmettoes, run-down thrift stores, and mosquitos."

"It's the draw of the river," Grayson said. "The St. Johns is just off to the right."

I squinted out the dirty passenger window as we cruised past a smattering of run-down buildings. I couldn't spot anything resembling a waterway. "Are you sure?"

"Positive."

We drove past a brick post office the size of a box of Saltine crackers. "If this is the main drag, I'd hate to see the warmup act," I quipped.

Grayson glanced my way. "If you're implying that Astor's not much to look at, I concur. However, the town's current name suits it better than its original one."

I snorted. "What was this dump called before? Dis-Astor? Astor-Roid?"

"No. *Manhattan*."

I nearly choked on my own spit. "Come on, Grayson! You made that up!"

Grayson's chin rose an inch. "I did not. It's an historical fact. Actually, this whole area was founded nearly 150 years ago by William B. Astor, Jr. He was a descendant of John Jacob Astor, America's first multi-millionaire."

My nose crinkled. "Why on Earth would a millionaire want to live *here*?"

Grayson shrugged. "Perhaps William Astor wanted to create his own thriving metropolis. That could explain why he originally gave the town the rather ambitious moniker of Manhattan."

I glanced around at the rundown storefronts loitering along the edges of the streets like abandoned orphans, tossed out to fend for themselves amid the open stretches of untamed palmettos and pine woods. "Looks like this guy Astor's ambition fizzled out pretty quickly, if you ask me."

"*Au contraire*," Grayson said. "To his credit, William Astor was a true visionary. He built this town from the ground up."

I laughed. "What *else* did he have to build it from? Back then there was nothing *but* dirt. Can't say there's much more than that here *now*."

"The town was quite something back in the day," Grayson said, ignoring me. "William Astor constructed a botanical garden and a hotel here. A century and a half ago, he transformed this area into a sought-after destination for steamboats navigating the St. Johns."

My nose crinkled. "Nice for rich travelers, I guess. But I'd have hated to be dragged out here in the middle of nowhere, just to tend plants and make beds for a bunch of hoity-toity snobs. The working-class folks must've hated it."

Grayson shook his head. "I don't think so. I think the townspeople actually liked William Astor. Otherwise, when he died, why would they have renamed the town in his honor?"

"A great honor, indeed," I quipped.

We passed a singlewide trailer by the side of the road. A crude steeple and cross had been nailed onto the trailer's sagging metal roof, turning it into a makeshift church. "Face it, Grayson. Either way you look at it, Astor's glory days are well behind it."

Grayson sighed. "You may be right. The last major construction project in the town was nearly a hundred years ago, when they built the bridge across the St. Johns River."

"Geez. So tell me. What the heck are all these people doing driving around here?"

Grayson glanced over at me. "According to my sources, this area still offers one of the best places to fish and hunt in Florida."

"Holy crap!" I gasped.

"What? You must've realized by now that tracking down Deinosuchas would involve *hunting*."

"Uh ... that's not the problem."

"Then what *is*?"

I nodded toward the side of the road. "Take a look at our fabulous accommodations."

Grayson turned and spotted the Rangler RV Resort. He tried to hide it, but I'm pretty sure I saw him flinch.

I mean, how could he not?

Sitting thirty feet off the highway on the left was a massive wall constructed entirely of used tractor tires. Stacked eight feet tall and filled with cement, they were a monument to redneck ingenuity. An opening in the wall was guarded by a heavy, wrought-iron entry gate.

A sign on the gate read, *Rangler RV Resort. No Loitering.*

"Gotta dig that prison ambiance," I said as monster trucks, ATVs, and campers with out-of-state tags whizzed by on Highway 40 like sheet metal bats out of hell.

Grayson's chin rose an inch. "Some people would call the construction a resourceful reclamation of recyclable materials."

I smirked. "Yeah. And some people used to call this place Manhattan."

"Well, there's no turning back now," Grayson said. "I procured the only campsite available for fifty miles."

I sighed. "Well, on the bright side, we've already solved one mystery."

Grayson cocked his head. "What's that?"

"I figured out why there's so much traffic speeding by."

"Oh. Why?"

"Because nobody can wait to get the hell out of here."

Chapter Eight

Grayson pulled the motorhome up to the prison-like iron gate of the Rangler RV Resort. As we sat anticipating the delights surely awaiting us behind the massive, tractor-tire walls, I heard the blare of a not-so-distant gunshot. Even then, no one came out to greet us. Not even an escaping prisoner.

"I'm going to honk the horn," Grayson said.

I grabbed his arm. "Wait! It's not too late. We can go hideout somewhere else. Like Fukoshima, maybe."

But it *was* too late. Suddenly, the gate swung open with a painful *creak* that set my teeth on edge. A thin, wiry old man wearing Wrangler jeans, a flannel shirt, and a dirty cowboy hat limped up to the driver's side window.

"Y'all got a reservation?" he asked, then let loose a stream of nasty brown tobacco juice from the side of his mouth.

"Yes. Drex, party of two," Grayson said.

I did a double-take. "Where do you think we are? The Redneck Ritz Carlton?"

The man squinted a wary eye at the battered clipboard in his hand. As he pondered what was written on it, I pondered whether the *Gunsmoke* Festus lookalike could even read.

"Well, there you are," he said finally. His skeptical scowl morphed into a brown-toothed grin. "Y'all got our deluxe spot number 33." He looked up from the clipboard at us and winked. "Howdy. I'm the head honcho around here."

"Don't you mean the head *warden*?" I said under my breath.

"Huh?" the guy grunted.

Grayson shot me a look, then turned back to the clipboard cowboy. "Nice to meet you, sir."

"Name's Tommy Tarminger," he said. "Here, put this parking pass on your windshield."

He handed Grayson a slip of green paper. I was startled to see that Tommy's fingers clutching the pass were made of silvery metal.

Apparently, Tommy noticed that I noticed.

"Lost my arm up to the elbow a few years back," he said.

"Chain saw?" I asked.

Tommy grinned. "Nope."

"Wood chipper?" I guessed again.

"Nada." Tommy's shoulders straightening with pride. "Ol' Chomp hisself got ahold a me couple years back. Took him a taste and didn't like it, I guess."

"Chomp?" Grayson asked.

Tommy's withered, unshaven face blanched with surprise. "Y'all ain't never heard a *Chomp*?"

"No," Grayson said.

"Huh." Tommy scratched behind his left ear with his metal claw. "When y'all asked for a huntin' guide, I figured you was here for the contest."

"What contest?" I asked. Then I whacked Grayson on the shoulder. "*What* hunting guide?"

"The Chomp Chase," Tommy said. "Astor's annual gator huntin' competition. Happens this time every year, you know. Durin' the duration a legal alligator huntin' season around here."

"Oh. *That* Chomp," I said, shooting Grayson some side eye.

"Y'all sure was lucky to get the last campin' spot we got," Tommy said. "Tell the truth, y'all only got it on account of a cancellation. Buddy Barlowe was supposed to be there. He went missing two days ago. Found his boat floatin' out in the middle of the river. Wife called up lookin' for his deposit back yesterday, right before you called."

"What happened to Buddy?" I asked.

"Don't rightly know." Tommy leaned forward until his head was halfway in the driver's window. He clicked his metal pincer fingers like a pair of castanets. "Best I can figure, Ol' Chomp liked the taste of Buddy a whole lot better'n' he did me."

"AHH. NOTHING LIKE THE great outdoors," I quipped as Grayson maneuvered the RV into "deluxe" camping spot number 33.

Far from the rural camping idyll I'd envisioned, our premium campsite bore a strong resemblance to a convenience store parking lot in a low-rent neighborhood. Though our little slice of heaven was only twenty feet from the riverbank, it was also only fifteen feet away from the resort's derelict-looking camp store.

"Beggars can't be choosers," Grayson said. "We were lucky to get this spot."

I glanced around. "Nope. I'd say luck forsook this place a long time ago."

The so-called store wasn't much more than a rusty, metal shed the size of a two-car garage. It leaned precariously beside the river's edge on a concrete slab riddled with cracks big enough to blow out an industrial-strength flip-flop. (I'd recently become somewhat of an expert in this field of study.)

As I took in the ambiance of the neon lights advertising beer, bait, and beef jerky, I was surprised to see the shop also had two gas pumps located on the river side. They were anchored into the crumbling concrete pad.

Oddly, the store's main entry door also faced the river, rather than the campsite. Confused, I glanced around. Then it hit me. Most of the establishment's intended clientele arrived here by boat.

To either side of the store, rickety docks of weathered pine boards lined the riverbank. They jutted out into the water like the tines of a giant, gray comb. A haphazard flotilla of boats crammed every nook and cranny like a hoard of hungry wood lice.

Jon boats. One-man canoes. Fancy airboats. Flats skiffs. Each floated side-by-side, occupying every square inch of available dock space. As the ragtag armada bobbed up and down in the gentle wake, their hulls rubbed together, creating an orchestra of squeaks and groans akin to the musings of a drunken violinist.

Hands on my hips, I stared at the scene and muttered, "Welcome to the Redneck Riviera."

"Beautiful, ain't it?" a voice sounded behind me.

I turned to see Tommy Tarminger hobbling my way. "I see y'all done found your spot without me."

"Yes, sir. Seeing as it was the only one left, it wasn't too difficult."

I glanced around at the other campsites occupied by RVs, tents, and pickup trucks—both with and without camper tops. But strangely, besides me, Tommy, and Grayson, there wasn't another soul in sight.

"Where is everybody?" I asked.

"Gettin' some shut-eye," Tommy said. "Them folks at the Florida Wildlife Commission done declared gator huntin' a night sport. Only allowed from 5 p.m. to 10 a.m."

"Oh."

Tommy turned to Grayson, who was studying the river through a pair of binoculars. "Y'all gonna be ready when my cousin Denny comes by at eight to take you out?"

Grayson lowered his binoculars. "Yes. Thank you, Mr. Tarminger. We'll be ready."

Tommy tipped his grimy cowboy hat. "All-righty, then. I was just makin' sure. I figured y'all might be tired after all that fishin'."

"Fishing?" I asked.

Tommy's beady eyes gave me the once over, then stopped on my left boob. "It ain't easy keepin' the blood and guts off when you're cleanin' fish. That's why we got them sinks over yonder at the docks."

Tommy's metal hand pointed toward the docks, then shifted direction like a weather vane. "We also got us a special shower stall for washin' all the guts off'n ya. It's right over there, behind the store."

"Thanks." Awkwardly, I raised my hand to cover the strawberry margarita stain on my shirt. "I'll keep that in mind."

"You're welcome," Tommy said. "So, you got a name?"

"Oh. Sure. I'm Bobbie."

"Ha!" Tommy laughed, as if he'd just won a bet with himself. "So you *are* a feller."

I grimaced and ran a hand through my short, red hair. I thought about setting the record straight, but couldn't see the point. Besides, if I was going to be trapped in a camp full of roughneck fishermen, being one of the guys might have its advantages.

"Yep, I'm a guy all right," I said, lowering my voice an octave.

Grayson's Spock eyebrow went up.

Tommy nodded. "Thought so. Well, good luck huntin' tonight."

"Thanks."

He turned to leave.

"Hey, Tommy!" I called after him.

He turned back around. "What?"

I hooked a thumb toward the bait store. "Any chance they carry Jose Cuervo?"

Chapter Nine

After a three-month hiatus from Grayson, sharing sleeping quarters with him again was going to take some getting used to.

I figured tequila would help.

So, while Grayson was in the bathroom, I snuck over to the bait shop. The crusty, cigarette-smoking old lady running the register told me she was fresh out of Jose Cuervo. So instead, she sold me a bottle of what she swore was, "The next best thing."

I scurried back to the RV like a hobo with a fresh pocket rocket, still wearing my dirty shirt and carrying my bottle in a brown paper bag. Grayson was still in the shower, so I plucked a gleaming glass from the posh new kitchen cupboards and scooted into the plush, leather bench of the cozy banquette.

Suddenly, I felt as if this RV may be too fancy for the likes of me. Feeling anxious, I twisted the metal cap from the quart container of tequila and started to pour a glass. "Screw it." I tipped the bottle up and took a couple of slugs straight from the rim.

"Ah!" I wagged my eyebrows devilishly.

No dirty glass equals no dirty evidence.

Feeling smug about my covert operation to get a buzz on, I went for a third swig. As I flinched against the sting of the alcohol, something caught in my windpipe. Suddenly, I couldn't breathe!

"Aack!" I tried to cough, but I couldn't catch any air. I was suffocating to death! Panicked, I jumped up and tried to Heimlich myself with a swift punch in the gut.

It hurt, but it didn't work.

"Aack," I gasped. Pressure was building in my lungs like a helium balloon hooked to an aircraft engine.

Gulping for oxygen, I scrambled out of the kitchen booth and made a beeline for the bathroom. I was about to kick in the door when Grayson stepped out, a towel wrapped around his otherwise naked body.

"What's going on?" he asked.

One look at my blue face must've answered his question. He twirled me around, gave me a bear hug, and squeezed the living daylights out of me.

"Fwoomp!"

That was the sound I heard as the lump in my throat cleared my tonsils and flew past my lips. Limp in Grayson's arms, I sucked in a life-giving breath.

"Stay calm and breathe," Grayson said, carrying me to the banquette. He set me in the booth, then went over and picked something up off the floor and tossed it onto the table in front of me.

I stared, aghast at the object that had been clogging my windpipe. It was a fat, white worm the size of my pinkie.

Accordion-shaped like a crinkle-cut French fry, the grotesque insect had nasty-looking dark spots on both ends.

"Dear mother of god!" I gasped. "How old was that tequila?"

Grayson picked up the bottle I'd been chugging before being rudely interrupted by the oversized maggot.

"That isn't a worm, Drex. It's the larva of gusano de maguey."

"I don't care *whose* larva it is," I hissed, trying not to retch. "Get it out of here!"

"I don't understand why you're so upset. The label clearly reads, *Monte Alban Mescal Con Gusano*. In other words, mescal with moth larvae."

My mouth fell open. "Wait a minute. The worm in the tequila bottle! I've heard about this. They say if the worm dies right after it hits the booze in the bottle, the tequila is good."

"Just another urban legend, I'm afraid," Grayson said, adjusting his towel.

"What do you mean?"

"Well, first off, this isn't tequila. It's mescal. To be tequila, it has to be made from at least 51 percent Blue Agave cactus. Mescal can be made from any variety of maguey succulents."

"How do you know all this stuff?" I asked, trying not to stare at his killer abs.

He smirked. "A thirst for knowledge, coupled with an eidetic memory."

"Oh, yeah. I forgot about the memory thing."

"And I, of course, did not."

I smiled wanly. "Because of your memory. Ha ha. Very funny. Uh ... thanks for saving my life and stuff."

"You're welcome."

I took the bottle from Grayson. "So this isn't tequila? But there's still a worm inside. How do you account for *that*?"

"As I've already explained, that isn't a worm, Drex. It's a moth larva."

I glanced at the squishy-looking blob on the table. "To borrow a phrase, Grayson, 'A grub by any other name would still be as disgusting.'"

"They're not disgusting." Grayson reached over and picked up the larva. "Quite the contrary. These little protein-rich gems are eaten regularly in Mexico—without tequila or any other form of liquid courage."

He lightly squeezed the grub between his fingers, causing the ends to bulb out.

My stomach heaved. "Yuck and double-yuck, Grayson." My face puckered with disgust. "Tell me, if those things are such a delicacy in

Mexico, how'd this one end up in a tequila bottle? Excuse me—*mescal* bottle?"

"Not by accident, that's for sure. Its inclusion was absolutely intentional. Though the reasoning behind it might not be quite so forthright."

"What do you mean?" I asked, praying the pulsing worm between his fingers wouldn't burst and send a spray of grub guts all over me.

Grayson smiled down at this wormy little friend. "Popular belief is that adding the larvae changes the flavor of the liquor. But it's more likely the truth that the tradition began as a marketing ploy to lure the naïve American market away from tequila and back to mescal."

I stared in morbid fascination at the bulbous larva being squeezed between Grayson's long, thin fingers. "I don't get it. How could putting a bug in this booze make it *more* appealing?"

Grayson smirked. "To borrow a phrase from *Spaceballs*, 'Merchandizing.'"

"Huh?"

"Clever ad campaigning," Grayson said. "They used to run advertisements claiming that the presence of the larvae in mescal brought purity, virility, and good fortune."

I sneered. "Did they mention choking to death?"

Grayson ignored me. "It didn't seem to matter that Mexicans themselves never drank mescal con gusano. In fact, the Mexican Standards authority prohibits adding insects to a tequila bottle."

I shook the bottle at him. "Then how did that nasty thing get in here?"

"As I said, that's not tequila, Drex. It's *mescal.*" He tossed the larva back onto the table. It landed with a sickening plop. "Mescal is different. I thought I just explained all that."

"Ugh! Fine." The thought of that yucky white maggot being lodged in my throat mere minutes ago made me want to heave. "Grayson, are we done here?"

"Yes, I suppose so. Why?"

"Because I need to go throw up."

I WAS AWAKENED BY THE distinct feeling of a hand gripping my thigh. I'd fallen asleep in my new chair-bed thingy. The room was dark. The hand squeezed my thigh again.

"Are you up for it?" Grayson whispered.

A hot wave of fear, excitement, and lust shot through me like meat gravy that had been left out on the counter overnight.

"Up for it?" I asked, my mouth suddenly as dry as sand.

Grayson released his grip on my thigh. "Yes. Denny Tarminger should be here soon. I can go gator hunting alone if you're not up for it. You were sick earlier."

"Oh." I sat up in my chair. "No. It's okay. I feel better. We got any coffee?"

"I'll fix you a cup while you change your clothes."

I glanced down at my margarita-splattered shirt. "For a gator hunt? I don't see the point."

"Those red stains all over your clothes make you look like the victim or the perpetrator of a deadly assault."

I snorted. "We're at a fishing camp, Grayson. Who here *doesn't*?"

Grayson stiffened. "Point taken. But still, I'd appreciate it if you'd change into the official investigative uniform I got for you."

I sighed and stood up. "Fine. I'll hop in the shower. You get that coffee going, and hang the clothes you want me to wear on the bathroom door. Deal?"

"Deal."

FOR THE SECOND TIME that day, I found myself on the verge of asphyxiation.

"Grayson!" I yelled through the bathroom door. "This shirt doesn't fit!"

While I appreciated the sentiment that my partner thought I wore a size extra-small, my recent bout with the moth larva had left me with a new found appreciation for being able to suck air into my lungs. And right now, I couldn't.

The tiny T-shirt Grayson had bought for me was hopelessly entangled around my neck and left elbow, and was about to strangle me alive!

I rifled around in the medicine cabinet and found a pair of cuticle scissors. As I used the tiny blades to hack myself free from the black polyester death trap, the bathroom door cracked open.

"Are you okay in here?" Grayson's voice wafted through the opening in the door. "I heard you grunting."

"Yes." I made a final snip to free myself from the suffocating grip of the T-shirt serial killer. "Just need a slightly bigger shirt."

"Got it." A moment later, Grayson's hand appeared through the crack, holding a crisp, black shirt on a hanger. "Here. Wear one of mine for the time being."

I snatched the shirt from Grayson's hand. "Thanks." I slipped Grayson's shirt on over my head. It wasn't as loose as I thought it would be, but it did the trick. My boobs were no longer squashed like pancakes. And I was no longer on the verge of blacking out due to lack of oxygen.

"Thanks for the loaner," I said as I emerged from the bathroom.

"You're welcome." Grayson was standing at the ready with the promised cup of coffee. "I made you an Americano. Given your recent near-death experience with a Mexican larva, it seemed apropos."

"Very funny." I grabbed the cup, then flopped into the booth and took a sip. "Hey. This is actually good!"

Grayson's cheek dimpled. "So you approve of the upgrades we made to the RV?"

"Well, this one, at least. But I can't believe you set up this whole case investigation without even consulting me."

Grayson cocked his head. "I thought that was what you wanted. For me to take charge of things."

"Of the RV renovations, yeah. But not *everything*. How am I supposed to learn how to be a PI if you keep doing all the stuff yourself?"

Grayson frowned. "Are you unhappy with the internship? Is that why you had me stay away?"

Heat seared my earlobes. "No! It's just that ... Well, to be brutally honest, I needed time for the embarrassment to die down."

Grayson appeared confused. "What was there to be embarrassed about?"

A loud knock sounded at the side door.

"That must be Denny." Grayson walked over and opened the door.

"Sorry I'm late," a raspy voice said.

"Not at all," Grayson said. "Come in."

An old woman dressed in camo from head to toe stumbled through the door. She straightened herself up and said, "I had to wait for the darned booze shipment to get here."

"*You're* Denny Tarminger?" I asked.

"You're darned tootin'," she said. "Hey! How'd you like that mescal I sold you?"

Chapter Ten

"We're going to hunt alligators in *this*?" My bulging eyes fixated on a battered, square-bowed old skiff harboring more patches than a pirates' convention.

"Well, she ain't purty, but she's got championship bones," Denny said.

I glanced around for some alternative—*any* alternative to this floating death trap. Two near-death experiences were my limit for the day.

But as I looked around, I saw there wasn't any other choice. Denny's dilapidated boat was the last one remaining of the armada that had, a few hours ago, been lined up bow-to-stern along the rickety dock in front of the bait store.

In the fading light of dusk, the worn-out boat floundered gracelessly in the water, like the upturned carapace of a drowned cockroach. Even Grayson, who was usually cavalier about such things, appeared skeptical.

"Excuse me, Ms. Tarminger," he said. "Could you please explain exactly what you mean by 'championship bones'?"

Denny rubbed the white hairs poking from her chin. "Sure thing. You see, 'bout ten years back, me and my huntin' partner gigged Ol' Chomp in the eye in this very same boat."

My nose crinkled. "Well, the boat certainly makes for an eyesore, I'll give you that."

Denny glanced around furtively at the empty dock. "Huh. Looks like everybody else done got a head start on us."

I raised an eyebrow. "You think?"

"We'll just have to use that to our advantage," the old woman said. "All them fellers went upstream. We'll head downstream instead."

"Sounds good to me," Grayson said. "Let's get going."

Denny took a step toward the boat, then froze. She patted the pockets on her camo vest and said, "Oh. Just missing one thing before we set off."

"What's that?" Grayson asked.

She held out a gnarled hand. "You got my three hunnert dollars?"

"DENNY'S SNORING AGAIN," I whispered in the dark, then nudged Grayson.

We were sitting side-by-side on the hard, molded bench seat bisecting the middle of the worn-out skiff. A pillowcase-sized bag of Cheetos was wedged between us.

Denny Tarminger was hunched over on the bench at the back of the boat. She'd motored us up to a stand of cattails along the bank, tied the boat to some reeds, and instructed us to, "Sit, watch, and wait."

Then she'd promptly nodded off.

We'd been "sitting, watching and waiting" for over an hour, with nothing to show for it but a gut full of Cheetos and an impressive assortment of bug bites.

"You'd think for three hundred bucks she'd have ponied up for some seat cushions," I grumbled. "My butt is killing me."

"No life preservers, either," Grayson said. "Hmm. I wonder if this Cheetos bag could serve as a makeshift flotation device."

"Get real, Grayson. That old woman has no idea what she's doing out here. Can we go now? *Please*?"

"No." Grayson glanced up and down the river. "Deinosuchas is out here somewhere. I know it."

"Ugh. Even if you're right, we'll never find it with that old woman as our guide. Her snoring's enough to drive a bear away. Why'd you pick her, anyway?"

Grayson's shoulders straightened. "She was the only one available on short notice. Plus, I liked the name Tarminger."

I swatted at a moth flitting around the dim glow of our kerosene lantern. It was our only light source besides the stars and sliver of moon overhead.

"Seriously? You chose that old bat because you *liked her name*? I thought you were a *scientist*. That's hardly a rational reason."

Grayson shrugged. "Rationality isn't the only force that compels our actions, Drex. As Emily Dickenson once penned, 'The heart wants what it wants, or else it does not care.'"

My right eyebrow arched with surprise. "That's pretty poetic of you."

He sighed. "I've been reading the classics lately."

I thought about the last thing *I'd* read. It was a tabloid article entitled, *I had Bigfoot's Baby*.

"What's so interesting about Tarminger?" I asked. "What is it, anyway?"

"Tarminger isn't an actual *thing*. It's the corruption of the word *harbinger* by an author named Dodsley. He first used it in a poem he wrote in 1594 called, *A Knacke to Knowe a Knave*."

I shook my head—half in admiration, half in stupefied astonishment. "It amazes me how much weird stuff you know. You're like a Cheeto-munching encyclopedia."

"The taking of poetic license has a long and varied history," Grayson said, dusting Cheeto residue off the thigh of his black jeans. "It's vital to the evolution of language."

"What do you mean?"

"Well, for instance, Edgar Allen Poe made up the word *tintinnabulation* simply to add alliterative flair to his poem, *The Bells*. It's now an official word. It means a tinkling or ringing sound."

I smiled. "Huh. That's kind of cool."

"Yes. But tarminger, I'm afraid, didn't stand the test of time. It remains a mere jot in the history books. An unappreciated misspelling of the word harbinger—which, of course, means something that signals the approach of another."

"Like flowers are harbingers of spring," I said.

Grayson's green eyes glowed. "Precisely!"

Suddenly, a piggish snort erupted from Denny Tarminger. Her head dropped. Then she let out a long, squeaky fart. "Pfffvvrrtt!"

Grayson's eyebrow rose an inch. "I hope that's not a harbinger of more flatulence to come."

"Geez." I waved a hand in front of my face. "Did she eat that or did it die inside her?"

"Undeterminable. And I don't care to repeat the experience in order to gather corroborating evidence." Grayson reached over and nudged the old woman on the shoulder.

"Huh?" Denny grunted, snorting herself awake. She sat up and blurted, "Y'all see a gator?"

"No," I said. "It's so dark out here we can barely see our hands in front of our faces. But we certainly *smelled* some ghastly creature. Right, Grayson?"

"That so?" Denny's beady eyes shifted left to right. "Here, let me turn my headlamp on. Sorry I didn't have no extra ones for you two."

"Understandable," I said sourly. "What should we have expected for a mere $300?"

A *click* sounded in the dark. Denny's headlamp blinked on, casting an eerie, yellowish glow over the inky water. I nearly gasped with delight. The lamplight revealed a veritable constellation of glowing red dots floating on the surface of the river.

"Look at all those lightning bugs," I said. "It must be mating season."

"Them ain't bugs," Denny said. "Them's eyes. *Gator* eyes."

My smile took a nosedive. "What! How is that possible?"

"*Tapetum lucidum*," Grayson said.

"Huh?" Denny and I grunted.

Grayson set down the bag of Cheetos and cleared his throat. "You see, cats and alligators both possess a structure in the backs of their eyes called the tapetum lucidum. It reflects light back to photoreceptor cells, allowing them to make the most of low-light environments."

"Huh," Denny grunted. "That tapin' lucifer thing's what makes their eyes glow wicked red at night?"

"Yes. It allows them to see in the dark without the aid of infrared headlamps, such as yours."

Denny cackled like an old crone. "Well, I'll be. Learn somethin' new every day."

I chewed my lip, my eyes glued on the sea of red dots bobbing in the water all around us like devil rubies. "How can there be so many alligators in one spot?"

"I got the answer to that," Denny said. "This here St. Johns River is ideal habitat for the slitherin' creatures."

"No shit," I said. "How many you think are in this river?"

Denny shrugged. "Don't know for sure. But a few years back, some fancy biologists come up in here and tried to count up the gators. Best they could figure, river's got over fifty per square mile. But if you ask me, I think it's more'n that. 'Specially during mating season."

My nose crinkled. "Mating season? When's that?"

"It was over last month." Denny chuckled. "Should a heard all the bellerin'! All these here gator eyes we're lookin' at now are pro'lly males. The females are busy guarding their nests. Their young'uns ought to be hatching out any day now."

"Intriguing," Grayson said. "Denny, you seem to know a good deal about alligators. What more can you tell us about the one called Ol' Chomp? You said you saw it yourself. How big would you estimate the creature to be?"

Denny grinned crazily, like Jack Nicholson in *The Shining*. "Ol' Chomp? He was big enough to snap Tommy's arm off at the elbow like it was macaroni. That big enough for you?"

Grayson frowned. "I'm sorry for his loss. But can you give me an idea of how large Ol' Chomp appeared, compared to other alligators you've seen?"

Denny's lips twisted. "Bigger. A *whole lot* bigger. Poor ol' Tommy's arm didn't look no bigger'n a boiled turkey neck hung up inside Chomp's humongous ol' jaws."

"Fascinating." Grayson glanced down the skiff's rickety bow. "Chomp must've been at least as big as this boat."

Denny smiled and shook her head. "*Twice* as big. Anyways, y'all ready for some marshmallows?"

"Uh ... not me," I said. "I'm not hungry." Given the sea of predatory eyes glaring at us like we were appetizers on a floating charcuterie tray, having a nibble was the last thing on my mind.

"Not for eatin'. For chum." Denny tore open the plastic bag. "Nothin' gets a gator goin' at night like the white glint of a marshmallow floatin' on the surface. Pro'lly reminds 'em of a bloated fish belly."

My nose crinkled. "Not picky eaters, are they?"

"Nope. Not at all." Denny laughed and tossed a handful of marshmallows into the water. "You know what? I like you two. So I'll tell you a little secret."

"What's that?" Grayson asked.

Denny winked. "I don't think it matters a whit what you use to chum for gators. Been my experience they'll eat plum near anything, given half a chance."

My lip snarled. "You don't say."

"I *do*," Denny said. "You'll see for yourself when the hunters come back and start guttin' their catch. Seen everything from turtle shells to license plates tumble outta them gators' split innards."

"Intriguing," Grayson said. "What's the oddest thing you've seen ingested?"

"You mean ate by a gator?" Denny shrugged. "Let's see. Spark plugs. Huntin' hounds—well, what was left of their dog tags anyways. Bullet casings. Bobcat claws. Even a whole deer carcass once."

Grayson's eyebrow shot up like Spock's. He grinned at me. "Now *that's* taking the word 'omnivorous' to the extreme, wouldn't you say?"

I shook my head. "Grayson, we're out here in the middle of nowhere, in a leaky old boat, surrounded by hordes of hungry gators that can swallow a deer in one gulp, and you're making jokes about their eating habits?"

"Don't you worry yourself none," Denny said, leaning over to pat my knee. "This here boat is unsinkable."

I frowned. "I sure hope you're—Unk!"

My body suddenly catapulted sideways.

Something had just slammed into the side of the boat.

Something huge.

The force of impact sent all three of us skittering to the left side of the skiff. The sudden shift in weight had the old boat tilting wildly in the gator-infested river.

"Dear lord!" I screeched as black water poured in over the side. "We're gonna capsize!"

Chapter Eleven

"Everybody hold on!" Denny Tarminger hollered as the shabby old skiff listed ever closer to capsizing and dumping us into the mouths of a thousand waiting alligators.

"We ain't goin' down! Not on my watch!" the old woman bellowed, then leapt into action like Bruce Willis trapped on a doomed hillbilly jungle cruise.

Denny sprang headfirst toward the upturning hull. Her gnarled fingers grabbed ahold of the rising side of the boat. For half a second, she hung there by both hands like a scrawny, albino bat. Then, with a grunt worthy of a rutting boar, she hoisted herself up into a full-body curl.

Before I could even scream, "We're all gonna die!" Denny's bodyweight acted as counterbalancing ballast. The upturning hull slammed back down onto the water. In a flash, we were back to languidly floating in the river as if nothing had happened. Our brief interlude with certain death was over.

"See?" Denny said, grinning and patting the side of the boat. "What'd I tell you? This baby's *unsinkable*."

"Well done." Grayson reached over to shake her hand. "You're remarkably spry for a woman your age."

"Thanky." Denny slapped a bucket into Grayson's outstretched palm. "Now, get busy bailing."

"Wait a minute," I said, confused and sopping wet from the experience. "Am I the only idiot who wants to know *what the hell just rammed us?*"

"Oh, *that*," Denny said. "It was pro'lly a log. Or it could a been Ol' Chomp hisself. I think he remembers this boat."

I gulped and locked eyes with Grayson. "Is that possible? That the gator would remember this boat?"

Grayson shook his head. "Unlike humans, reptiles don't have the capacity for episodic memory. They can't remember specific events with clarity." He rubbed his chin. "However, they *can* build associations."

I didn't like the sound of that. "Associations?"

"Yes. For instance, if they're fed by the same human every day, they will probably begin to think of food whenever they see not just *that* human, but any human in general. The same goes if a gator is attacked by a human. It could develop a negative association, and begin to act defensively around all humans."

I glanced around at the dark water surrounding us. "So you're saying that Chomp couldn't actually be holding a grudge against Denny, or this boat?"

"Not this boat specifically," Grayson said. "But with boats and humans *in general*, yes. And the more events the gator experiences, the stronger those associative instincts will become."

I chewed my thumbnail. "So, if Ol' Chomp is one of these Deinosuchas things, he's probably had a lot of time to build his associative instincts."

Grayson nodded. "That stands to reason. But unless we can get the gator to return so we can get a better look at it, there's no way to tell for sure."

Denny rubbed her chin. "You know, there may be *one* way to get Chomp hisself to come back."

Grayson's eyebrow went angular. "Really? How?"

"By dangling Ol' Chomp's favorite bait." The old woman shot us a lascivious wink. "Either of you wanna give me a hand?"

I grimaced. "What?"

"Gimme a *hand*," Denny repeated. She waved her gnarled hand in the air, pinching her thumb and fingers together like a crab claw. "You know. A *hand*? Like Tommy did?"

Grayson and I stared at her blankly.

Denny frowned. "It was a joke." She sighed and let her pincer-hand drop. "Ah, well. I guess you had to be there."

DESPITE MY THREAT TO throttle Grayson to death in his sleep, he refused to order Denny to motor us back to the safety of the dock. From what I could tell, he wouldn't be satisfied until he'd picked the old woman's addled brain clean of every tidbit it contained about Ol' Chomp and the people who'd allegedly gone missing at the hands—or should I say *jaws*—of the legendary beast.

Held captive, I became an unwilling witness to the pair's odd ramblings. Among other things, I learned vicariously that alligators could run faster than humans, climb trees, and consume a quarter of their body weight in one meal. As far as I was concerned, what the hell else did anyone need to know about the hideous reptiles?

"So, what can you tell us about the three men who went missing last week?" Grayson asked Denny.

The old woman popped a marshmallow into her gap-toothed maw and cackled. "Well, for one thing, they wasn't all men."

I gulped. "They weren't?"

"Nope. One was Shirleene Parker, the town floozy."

My nose crinkled. "What happened to her?"

"Don't rightly know. Last people seen a her, she was floatin' down the river in a flamingo inner tube."

I shook my head. "Why?"

Denny shrugged. "Shirleene always was partial to pink. Anyways, nobody's seen hide nor hair of her since."

"And the others?" Grayson asked.

"You mean Buddy Barlowe and Fatback Taylor?"

I nudged Grayson. "Isn't Barlowe the name of the guy who had our campsite?"

"Yes." Grayson turned to Denny. "What can you tell us about them?"

"Buddy and Fatback?" Denny shrugged. "They was good old local boys. Wouldn't hurt a fly. Mainly because they was always too busy feuding amongst themselves."

"What were they fighting about?" I asked.

"Just something that happened way back when they was kids."

"Could you elaborate?" Grayson asked.

"Only when I consume milk products," Denny said.

Grayson cleared his throat. "I meant, could you provide more information on the source of Buddy and Fatback's discord?"

I rolled my eyes. "What started their feud, Denny?"

"Oh." The old woman frowned. "They was out fishing in the river one day. Fatback was using an old cane pole. Anyhoo, he went to cast it and hooked Buddy in the eye on the backswing. On the cast, he pulled Buddy's eyeball clean outta the socket."

"How tragic!" I said.

Not to mention totally gross!

Denny nodded. "At least it wasn't no total loss. Fatback caught hisself a five-pound bass with it."

Grayson stifled a snort.

I grimaced. "That's not funny."

Denny laughed. "Buddy didn't think so, neither. It's been fifteen years. Him and Fatback still fight about it every time they get together. Or, at least, they *did*."

My nose crinkled. "Why'd they hang around together if they annoyed the hell out of each other?"

Denny shrugged. "Better the devil you know, I guess."

Grayson shot me a smirk, then glanced over at Denny. "Were they together when they disappeared?"

"Yep. Out fishin' on the river, like usual. River Patrol Officer named McVitty found their boat. It was drifting along the riverbank, empty. That was two or three days ago. Not a word from either of 'em since."

"Do you think they might've killed each other?" I asked.

"Doubtful," Denny said. "Unless one of 'em growed teeth big enough to bite the boat in half."

I gasped. "What?"

"They found the boat barely floating," Denny said. "Side hull was missing a chunk out of it. Nothing left of Buddy and Fatback to be found. Not even Buddy's bobber eyeball."

My upper lip twitched. "Bobber eyeball?"

"Yep. Buddy couldn't afford no glass eye, so he used a fishin' bobber instead."

I grimaced at the thought. "That must've looked weird."

Denny shrugged. "Eh, it bugged out a little bit, but other than that, it looked purty natural to me. Buddy drawed an eye spot on it and everything."

"You said they were out fishing when they disappeared," Grayson said. "Were they looking for bass?"

"Nope. They was after gators. Same as you two."

"How do you know?" I asked.

The old lady plucked another marshmallow from the bag. "They found one a Buddy's gator buoys floating in the wrecked boat."

"Gator buoys?" I asked. "How does that work?"

Denny popped the marshmallow into her mouth. "Some folks around here hunt gators with harpoons. You know, like in that movie *Jaws*. You tie a buoy to a harpoon, then shoot it into the gator's back and wait for the buoy to tire the critter out."

"Is that legal?" Grayson asked.

"Yep. Them boys—"

A huge splash sounded nearby. Denny stopped mid-sentence and turned toward the noise. As she did, her infrared headlamp illuminated the center of the black river. The light glinted off a white, head-sized object moving slowly through the water about ten feet from the boat.

I squealed. "What the hell *is* that?"

Denny grabbed a flashlight from her camo vest and aimed it at the object. What I thought was a decapitated skull turned out to be a gallon milk jug. Somehow, it was moving slowly up river, against the current.

"Well, I'll be," Denny said. "That's one a Buddy's gator buoys."

"How can you tell it's his?" Grayson asked.

Denny adjusting the aim of the flashlight. "See that eyeball drawed on it?"

"Yes," Grayson said.

"That's Buddy's signature."

"Oh," Grayson said. "Did he use an eyeball icon because he had a fake one?"

Denny shook her head. "Nope. He done it because Buddy couldn't spell worth a hoot."

Chapter Twelve

"Keep your arms and hands pressed to your sides," the young boy said.

Sweat trickled down my forehead as I waded up to my armpits in the murky river. The boy was two steps ahead of me. The dark water swirled around his mullet-covered neck.

All around us, the monstrous, scaly heads of alligators bobbed on the surface, encircling us like a school of hungry piranhas.

"They can't turn their heads sideways," the boy said. "So stay straight as a board. Don't let anything stick out that they can latch onto."

"Easy for you to say," I said. "You don't have boobs."

Suddenly, a terrible scraping sensation scratched down my back, followed by the unmistakable snap *of a gator's jaws.*

"One of them just tried to take a bite out of me!" I whimpered.

"Don't panic," the boy said. "Like I told you, they can't latch onto a vertical target."

I took another hesitant step.

Maybe the boy was right. But even if he was, what were we supposed to do when we got to shore? Waiting on the other side of the riverbank was an alligator as big as a Grand Safari stationwagon!

It opened its jaws and bellowed.

"Whoooaaaannk!"

"What the?" I gasped, jerked awake by the horrendous noise.

It sounded again. "Whoooaaaannk!"

This time, I recognized it as the obnoxious blare of an air horn. I sat up in my chair-bed and checked the clock on the dashboard. It was 5:30 a.m.

"What the hell is going on?" I grumbled to myself.

I pulled aside the privacy curtain covering the front cabin's windshield and windows, and pressed my nose against the glass of the passenger window. Either a military coup was taking place at the Rangler RV Resort, or the motley hordes of gator chasers were arriving back from the hunt.

I rolled down the window and hollered at a guy passing by. "Hey, what's happening?"

"Breakfast bell." He pointed toward a food truck parked beside the bait store. The vehicle, an old white panel van, was surrounded by hungry rednecks—just as I'd been surrounded by hungry gators in my dream.

I scowled. "At 5:30 in the morning?"

"Yeah. We're all just getting back."

"Oh." Suddenly self-conscious, I lied. "Sure. Us, too."

He nodded. "Y'all have any luck?"

We're still alive. Does that count?

I shook my head. "No. You?"

"Nope. Hey, I'm Willie, by the way." He pulling his wallet from his camo vest.

"Bobbie. Nice to meet you."

"Likewise." Willie glanced back toward the food truck. "Look, man, I gotta go. I gotta get in line before Cheech sells out."

"Cheech?" I asked, but Willie was already gone. He was making a beeline for the food truck.

"Who the hell gets up for breakfast at the crack of dawn?" I grumbled. But as I rolled up the window, I caught a whiff of baking bread, mingled with cinnamon and sugar. My gut growled.

I mashed the yellow button on my armrest. My bed turned back into a chair. I spun around and yelled, "Grayson! Get up! It's time for breakfast!"

"I'LL TRY THE GATOR-tail breakfast burrito, my good man," Grayson said when we finally made it to the head of the line at Cheech's food truck.

"Sorry. Just sold out," the thin, sweaty guy doling out gravy said.

"What about the cinnamon buns?" I asked.

He dragged a hand through his shaggy, black bangs. "Guy ahead of you got the last one."

I stomped my foot. "Crap. What've you got left?"

"Biscuits and gator gravy," he said. "Can fry you an egg, too, if you want."

I nodded. "That'll work. We'll take two, please."

As Cheech filled our Styrofoam plates, Grayson forked over the money. We grabbed our breakfasts and searched for a place to sit. But again, we'd come too late in the game. All the picnic tables were overrun with bleary-eyed men in various stages of beard growth and personal hygiene abandonment. But to be fair, it *was* August. Even at 6 a.m., the air was already as hot and muggy as a bowl of pea soup.

"Over here!" someone yelled.

I turned to see Willie waving. He was perched on a log by the fish-gut showers. I ambled over to him, Grayson in tow. As we got close, I noticed with envy that Willie was munching on half a cinnamon bun.

"They were out of those by the time we got there," I said. "They any good?"

Willie took a bite of the bun and nodded. "Yep. Just about anything that comes out of Cheech's food truck is. Y'all have a seat."

Willie scooted down the log. Grayson and I sidled up to him.

"So you guys didn't have no luck last night?" Willie asked.

I shook my head. "Only the bad kind."

"I disagree," Grayson said. "I thought it was a productive experience, given that it was our first time gator hunting. Though I'll admit I'm not totally convinced of our guide's proficiency."

"Huh?" Willie grunted.

I smirked. "He means our guide was a bit sketchy."

"Oh." Willie licked his lips. "Who was it?"

"Denny Tarminger," I said.

Willie laughed. "That old lady? She don't know nothin' about catchin' gators."

I glared at Grayson. "I knew it! And you paid her $300!"

Grayson shrugged. "I could've saved $50 with the gator/hog combo. But porcine pursuit seemed irrelevant to our investigation into Deinosuchas."

Willie's brow furrowed like a bulldog pup's. "What'd he say?"

I sighed. "Never mind. Willie, why do you think Denny's not a good gator hunter?"

"Cause as far as I know, she ain't never done it afore." Willie set his plate down and grinned. "I bet she and Tommy pro'lly told you all about how them two gigged Chomp in the eye. Am I right?"

I frowned. "Yeah."

"Well, don't believe nothin' them two says. Truth is, back in the day, they was kissin' cousins. That is, they was until Denny's daddy caught 'em playin' second base and shot Tommy's arm off."

I grimaced. "Geez!"

Grayson's brow furrowed with skepticism. "I suppose alligators don't like marshmallows, either."

"No," Willie said. "Now *that there's* the god's honest truth. But you can't catch a gator with 'em. They ain't got no grip to 'em. For that, you need the old B&B combo."

"The old *what*?" Grayson asked.

"Broom plugs and a bang stick," Willie said. "Every gator hunter worth his hindquarters knows that."

I shot Grayson a smug smile. "Oh well. Lesson learned. Denny's no good. And there aren't any more hunting guides available. I say we just pack up our stuff and—"

"Hold on," Willie grunted. "Seeing as how y'all are hard up, and seem like nice folks, I got a guy I might could hook you up with."

"You do?" Grayson smiled. "We'd be grateful for the information, wouldn't we, Drex?"

I shot Grayson some side eye. "Sure."

"All right, then." Willie grinned. "Now the feller's fairly new to the sport, mind you. But he's got a real passion for it. And from what I seen a him, he's a might more trustworthy than that there Tarminger clan ever was."

"Excellent," Grayson said. "Do you have his number? Maybe he'd be free to take us hunting tonight."

"I can do you one better'n that." Willie tipped his head to the left. "Here he comes now."

I glanced in the direction pointed out by Willie's unshaven chin. Lumbering toward us was a big, bear of a man. I instantly recognized his monkey-in-a-banana-factory grin.

"Earl Schankles!" I hissed. "What are *you* doing here?"

Chapter Thirteen

The sight of my cousin Earl tromping toward me made me jump up from the log, forgetting the plate of biscuits and gator-gravy in my lap. It spilled onto the ground.

I turned and glared at Grayson. "If you think I'm entrusting what's left of my crappy life to *that* jerk, you're crazy!"

Willie shriveled like a spider caught in a hairdryer blast. "Y'all know each other?"

"Unfortunately, *yes*," I hissed.

"Come on, Bobbie," Earl said, his face as earnest as a rescue-shelter mutt. "Gimme a chance."

"No way!"

"I can do it, I swear." Earl held his Redman cap in his hand. "Since I seen you last, I been studyin' up to be a real-life gator hunter."

I laughed bitterly. "Oh yeah? *Prove* it."

Earl's brow furrowed. "How?"

I folded my arms across my chest. "You can start by telling me what the hell *you* know about alligators."

Earl puffed out his barrel chest. "Well, I know there's only two kinds of 'em in the whole wide world."

"Really?" I sneered.

"Yeah." He stuck out a meaty index finger and began to count. "One, you got you the American kind. What we got here. It's called Alligator *mississippiensis*." Another fat finger popped up. "And two, you got that there Chinese kind in China. They call it Alligator *sinensis*."

I glanced over at Grayson. "Is that true?"

Grayson appeared as surprised as I was. "Yes."

Earl beamed with pride. "And I know how to tell 'em apart, too."

I eyed him skeptically. "How?"

Earl grinned. "The Chinese ones has got on little pointy hats."

My face dropped an inch.

Mother of god, we're doomed.

DESPITE THROWING A hissy fit that would've made Tanya Harding proud, Grayson wouldn't budge. Earl was to be our new gator hunting guide, and that was that. Against my will, I followed Grayson and Earl back to the motorhome, dragging my feet the entire way.

Overruled by Grayson, who was my boss and, more importantly, in possession of the only set of keys to the RV, I fumbled along behind the chummy pair in a state of shock and disbelief. Less than a day ago, I'd been sipping margaritas poolside at the beach without a care in the world. Now, I was back in cahoots with a pair of off-kilter jerks who seemed intent on playing craps with my life.

"Woooeee!" Earl hollered as he stepped through the side door of the RV. "This place is a regular Taj Ma-what'cha-call-it!" He reached in the fridge and pulled out a beer. "Bet all this fancy stuff put a big-ol' dent in your bank account, Bobbie!"

"No more than *you* did," I grumbled.

He winced. "Sorry again about losin' your dad's shop."

"Yeah." I ground my teeth. "Get real, Earl. What do you know about gator hunting?"

"More'n you think. An' I say the first order of business is to get yourself a waterproof cellphone case like this 'un." Earl pulled an orange plastic case from his pocket and swung it by the lanyard it was attached to. "But let's save all that stuff for later. Right now, we need to get us some shuteye so we're all geared up for the hunt this evening."

Grayson's gaze shifted my way. "Sounds like professional advice to me."

I frowned. "Well, that makes *one* of us."

Earl took his cue to leave and headed for the door. Maybe he was smarter than I gave him credit for. "I'll be back at three o'clock to give you all your first lesson."

"Where are you going to sleep?" Grayson asked.

"Oh, don't you worry about me, Mr. G. Me and Bessie got it all worked out."

I WAS IN MY CHAIR-BED sleeping off the carb-and-grease overload of Cheech's biscuits and gator gravy when a familiar sound began grating on my subconscious nerves. I awoke to hear Earl's annoying voice. He was yucking it up with Grayson in the kitchen. I got up to join them, fully prepared to share my sour mood with the world.

"There she blows," Earl said. "You want some coffee, Cuz?"

I unclenched my jaw. If Earl could make nice, I guess I could, too. "Sure. That'd be good."

Earl sprung up and grabbed a mug from the cupboard. "So I hear y'all went out gator huntin' last night with Tommy Tarminger?"

"No." I snatched the empty mug from Earl's hand. "You're wrong. It was his cousin, *Denny* Tarminger. So what?"

Earl shrugged. "Nothin'."

"Thought so." I set the mug in the automatic coffee dispenser and pressed the button marked *cappuccino*.

"Only thing is," Earl said, "iIf my recollector's right, Tommy Tarminger's the name of that feller from the bank. The one what took over your dad's place."

I gasped and whirled around. "What?"

"See for yourself." Earl fished inside the breast pocket of his camo vest and pulled out an envelope. "This here letter come for you last week."

I snatched the envelope from his hand, then read the hand-scrawled note inside it.

"That polecat!" I screeched.

"What's in the letter?" Grayson asked.

I scowled. "Earl's right. Tommy Tarminger bought my dad's auto garage in a foreclosure deal. Now he's making me an offer to buy the place back—for $42,000 *on top of* the remaining mortgage!"

"You gonna do it?" Earl asked.

"Are you crazy?" I hissed. A vein throbbed at my right temple. "I'd sooner shove $42,000 down the butthole of a hippopotamus than give it to that pincer-handed pirate!"

Grayson rubbed his chin. "Hmm. Art imitates life."

I glared at him. "What are you babbling about?"

"Apparently, Tarminger actually *is* a bastardization of the word harbinger. In this case, I'd say it's a warning for us to keep an eye out for deceit."

"The seat of what?" Earl asked.

I shook my head and glared at the letter in my hand. "I don't know about all that harbinger business, Grayson. But I'm totally on board about the bastardization part."

Chapter Fourteen

I slurped down my last swig of cappuccino and stared at my cousin. The big lug was sitting across from me at the banquette, his face a wordless plea for forgiveness. He'd cost me my love life and my family business. Other than that, he was an okay guy ...

I blew out a sigh. If I was being honest with myself, I'd have to admit I'd given up on my dad's auto garage when I'd left with Grayson a year ago. Earl defaulting on the mortgage had just made it official. But his ruining my chance at romance with Grayson? That was harder to let go of.

I groaned inside. Earl flouncing in and inserting himself into our investigation wasn't making it any easier to forgive him. Once again, I was being forced to put my life in Earl's big, bumbling hands. To say I was happy about it would've been a lie. But given the way my blood was pulsing in my temples, I figured I'd better try to come to terms with it before I blew a blood vessel.

I pursed my lips into a sour grin. "So, what're you gonna teach us about gator hunting, Professor Pinhead?"

Earl tapped a finger to the side of his noggin. "Ever' thing I know, in due time. But the first order a business is we gotta go get somethin' to eat. I'm hungrier'n a bear comin' out a hypernation."

My eyes narrowed. "Is this just another stall tactic?"

Earl blanched. "Stall? What would I be stalling about?"

"I could go for some lunch, myself," Grayson said, glancing down at his cellphone. "The Blackwater Inn is supposed to have the best food in town. According to this, it's right on the St. Johns. That means it offers scenic views of the river, as well."

"Sounds good to me," Earl said.

Grayson looked up and smiled. "I'll grab my binoculars. We may be able to spot Chomp while we dine!"

"Oh, goody," I said. "And maybe Deinosuchas will serve us dessert."

"Come on, Cuz," Earl said, climbing out of the booth. "You'll like the Blackwater Inn. They got anything fried in the world you could want. Includin' green beans and dill pickles."

My nose crinkled. "How do you know that?"

Earl shrugged. "I might a been there a time or two. Come on, let's get goin'. I got a hankerin' for some a their fried gator tail and big ol' Pepsi Cola."

I frowned. "They got anything stronger than Pepsi?"

"Yes." Grayson studied his phone. "It says here, 'We proudly serve Pepsi products and a full bar for your ultimate thirst-quenching desires.'"

"Full bar?" I sighed. "Well, all righty then. I'm in."

THE BLACKWATER INN didn't look nearly as fancy as I'd pictured it in my mind. But then again, compared to the other dilapidated-looking establishments we'd passed along the way, Astor didn't exactly set a very high bar.

Even so, I was surprised when Earl pulled his black monster truck up to a bland, institutional-looking, red-brick building. The second story, made of wood paneling, was painted the cheery color of battleship gray.

"How quaint," I quipped. "Looks like this place used to be an elementary school. Or maybe a public health clinic. Or possibly the DMV."

"It tastes better'n it looks," Earl said, shifting into park.

I sighed. "I would certainly hope so."

I undid my seatbelt and climbed out of the truck. The first thing I spotted were the humongous red letters running across the second story of the restaurant. They spelled out *Blackwater Inn*. To the left of them hung a medieval shield or coat-of-arms thingy.

The shield was divided into four brightly-colored panels. One quarter sported the image of a fish. Another, a hunk of meat shaped like a turkey leg or a ham. A third section showed two wine glasses clinking together. The fourth one, well, I couldn't quite make it out.

"What is that?" I asked, squinting at the sign. "A pair of scissors?"

"A crossed knife and fork," Grayson said. "After all, this is—"

"Y'all quit jabberin' and come on," Earl hollered, sprinting for the entry door. "Let's get inside and order afore the crowd gets here."

"What crowd?" I asked, noticing the parking lot was empty.

Earl tried the door. "Dang it! It's locked!"

Grayson motioned toward a sign by the door. "It would appear they don't open until 4:30. It's only 3:37."

"I'll never make it," Earl groaned. "I'm parishin' to death!"

I rolled my eyes. "Quit whining. There's got to be some place around here that's open."

Earl pouted. "Dang it. But my belly was set on some gator tail."

"Let's get back in the truck and head down Highway 40," Grayson said. "I saw another restaurant that's also on the river. According to the app, it just over the bridge. A place called McGatorTail's."

"Huh," Earl said. "Think they got any gator tail there?"

WHEN EARL SPOTTED THE sign for McGatorTail's, he stomped the gas so hard we rocketed over the small, hump-backed bridge in the road. All four of Bessie's tractor tires went airborne, sending my stomach into a cartwheel.

As we hit the asphalt again, Earl shifted gears like a NASCAR pro. He hooked a hairpin left onto the road leading to the restaurant, then floored it again until we reached the parking lot. Once there, he mashed the brakes so hard we spun a 360, then slid perfectly into the parking spot closest to the front door.

"Woohoo!" Earl hollered. "Like a glove!"

"Geez, Earl!" I yelled, elbowing him in the gut. "You're gonna get us killed before we have a chance to get killed!"

Earl shot me a funny look. He flung open the door, jumped down out of the driver's seat, and hit the ground running straight for McGatorTail's front door.

"Think he's hungry?" Grayson asked, unbuckling his seatbelt.

I smirked. "What was your first clue?"

"Aww crap on a Sears catalogue!" Earl hollered.

"What?" I called out from the cab of the truck.

"There's a dang board nailed across the front door. Says they're closed for good."

I elbowed Grayson. "You think they meant 'good' as in *permanently*, or "good" as in for the welfare of all mankind?"

Grayson's cheek dimpled. "Debatable." He pulled out his cellphone. "Let me see what else is out here."

As Grayson perused our other options, Earl paced the parking lot in front of the monster truck, wringing his hands and bellowing, "What are we gonna do now?"

"Quit your bellyaching," I said. "We'll find something. Come on and get back in."

As I watched Earl stomp back toward the truck, I suddenly got the feeling we were being watched. A shiver ran up my spine. McGatorTail's was tucked along the St. John's River just adjacent to the bridge. Bordered by water and woods, it should've been picturesque. Instead, the whole place had a creepy, derelict vibe about it.

Besides us, there was only one other car in the crumbling, trash-strewn lot. An old, rusty white Buick. From the looks of it, the car must've either broken down and been abandoned there, or somebody's murdered corpse was stuffed inside the trunk ...

Grayson said he thought we were being followed.

I broke out in a case of the heebie-jeebies.

What if the guys in blue sedan decided to change vehicles?

"Hurry up, Earl!" I yelled as he reached for the door handle. He pulled himself up and inside the monster truck. "Come on! Let's get out of here."

"Fine with me, Cuz."

"So crank the engine, already!" I ordered.

"Geez! Hold your horses."

I glanced around again, half expecting to see Freddy Kruger coming at us with a chainsaw. I was about to tell Grayson about the Buick when I noticed a sign in front of the parking space where it sat. Bright red lettering on the white sign spelled out a warning; *Bridge Tender Only. All Others Towed.*

Bridge tender?

I looked up at the bridge and spotted a small, one-man watchtower attached to side of the bridge span. I nearly laughed with relief. Then I felt foolish. I was sure Grayson had already figured all that out, and hadn't even considered it worth mentioning.

"I found another restaurant online," Grayson said, looking up from his cellphone. "According to this, it's open, now, too."

"What's the name?" I asked.

"Who cares?" Earl said. "I'm hungry enough to eat a dad-burn tomahawk!" He turned the ignition, shifted into reverse, and floored it.

As my head jerked back from centrifugal force, I spied something in the rearview mirror. It was tucked away in the corner of the lot, hidden by a pair of beat-up dumpsters.

"Hold on!" I yelled, grabbing Earl's arm. "Isn't that Cheech's food truck?"

"Lawd a-mighty," Earl hollered. "We're saved!"

Chapter Fifteen

"Cheech!" Earl bellowed out the driver's side window of his monster truck. "What're you doing out here in McGatorTail's parking lot?"

"Shhh!" Cheech's eyes darted left and right as he came out from behind the dumpsters. "Keep your voice down. I'm trying to keep a low profile."

"Why?" I asked, scooting across the bench seat and jumping out of the truck behind Earl.

Cheech stared at the asphalt. "Because I don't have permission to park my food truck here."

I glanced over at the dumpsters. Not only was Cheech's food truck there. Right next to it was a one-man tent and a pull-behind trailer the size of a pickup bed.

"Are you *living* here?" I asked.

Cheech swiped at his shaggy, black bangs. "Just temporarily. Until I get back on my feet."

"How'd you fall off of 'em?" Earl asked.

"The way most people do around here." Cheech frowned. "I missed a couple of house payments and pinch-a-penny Tarminger pulled the rug out from under me."

"You mean Tommy Tarminger?" I asked.

"Yeah. The dirt-bag offered to let me stay in my house—for twice the rent as my old mortgage payment."

My face pinched with anger. "I know the feeling. He got my dad's mechanic garage the same way."

Cheech shook his head. "Sorry to hear that. You know, the worst thing is, the jerk marks his territory. Like it's some kind of pissing match."

"What do you mean?" Grayson asked.

"Tarminger paints everything he owns this ugly-ass blue. Like the color of dirty Ty D Bol."

My eyes shifted over to Earl. "Did he ...?"

Earl nodded sheepishly. "Right over your daddy's hand-painted sign, too."

My jaw clenched. "What a turd!"

"We're not his only victims," Cheech said. "Look around. Half of this town's turned Tarminger blue."

"What's in the trailer back there?" Grayson asked.

"Everything I have left in the world, thanks to Tarminger. Besides the food truck, I do lawn work and odd jobs on the side. Around here, most work is seasonal, so money can get pretty tight. Especially in the summer. We all do what we can to get by."

"If the local economy's so bad, where did Tommy Tarminger get *his* money?" Grayson asked.

"The old fashioned way," Cheech said sourly. "He inherited it."

AFTER A DELICIOUS LUNCH of fried gator tail from Cheech's food truck, we returned to the Rangler RV Resort and napped until five o'clock. Then Earl came and woke us up for our first lesson on how to hunt down gators, Florida-style.

The only problem was, I wasn't ready for a lesson. Or for Earl. But I *especially* wasn't ready for a *lesson from Earl.* Sleepy and grumpy as a teenager in first-period homeroom, I stumbled out of my chair-bed, grabbed a cup of coffee, and slid into the booth, intent on giving the substitute teacher a hard time.

"Earl, just how'd you end up choosing gator hunting for a new profession anyway?" I asked.

Earl shrugged. "I couldn't think of nothin' better to do."

"So it was a process of elimination," Grayson said.

"Yeah," I snorted. "As in nobody else would hire him."

Earl shook his head. "Naw. It wasn't like that. I did it on account a I figured, why not do what I like to do best? And that's huntin' and fishin'." He smiled, then his face suddenly went limp. "Oh! I mean, besides chasin' monsters with you two, a course!"

Yeah, right.

"Doing what one loves turns work into play," Grayson waxed poetic.

I smirked. "Grayson, you're turning into a regular Shakespeare."

"Oh, no," Earl said. "You can't shake no spears at no gators. Least, not here in Florida, anyways. The FWC don't allow it."

I thought about trying to explain things to Earl, then decided there was really no point, spear or otherwise. "Okay, Earl," I said. "You're doing it because you love hunting and fishing. I get that. But why *Astor*, of all places?"

Earl grinned. "It might surprise you, Cuz, but the alligator is Florida's official state reptile. And this here area is gator-hunting heaven. The whole town's all run-through with man-made canals, just for the intense purposes a allowin' a man his God-given right to go out fishin' and huntin' right outta his own backyard."

My nose crinkled. "Seriously?"

"He's correct," Grayson said. "Astor's located entirely within the Ocala National Forest. It's an unspoiled paradise for alligators and all sorts of wildlife to thrive."

"See, Bobbie?" Earl proudly tapped a finger on his fat temple. "I done my homework. The St. Johns is 310 miles a natural-born gator habitat. And it flows northbound, hookin' up with a pile of freshwater springs and lakes on its way to the Atlantic. That includes ol' Lake

George. It's the biggest lake in Florida, 'cept for Lake Okeechobee, a course."

Grayson locked eyes with me. "As you can plainly see, that equates to ample space for Deinosuchas to live and breed."

"Dino *whut*?" Earl asked.

I shrugged. "Some dumb prehistoric alligator Grayson thinks is eating people around here."

"That so?" Earl's eyebrows rose an inch. "Like the ones in the movies? Ha! I *knew* they was real!"

"It's called Deinosuchas," Grayson said. "And there's every reason to believe it could exist."

"Every reason?" I scoffed. "Come on, Grayson!"

Grayson's shoulders stiffened. "Alligators have remained virtually unchanged over the past 65 million years. They were already basking in rivers like the St. Johns when other dinosaurs were becoming extinct."

I shook my head. "Okay. For the sake of argument, let's say you're right. How could an alligator the size of a bus ever get enough to eat around here?"

"Oh! I know!" Earl said, raising his hand. "Them critters'll eat anything they can get their jaws around, from grapefruits to wild hogs."

"But why haven't we *seen* them?" I asked. "Why aren't these humongous gators just walking down the streets and snatching people off their lawn chairs?"

"Who says they ain't?" Earl asked.

"Alligators are ambush predators," Grayson said. "But if they spot an opportunity, they can run up to thirty miles an hour in short bursts."

Earl nodded. "That's plenty quick enough to snatch grampa right outta his undershorts."

Grayson agreed. "Like I told Drex, up to nine people have been reported missing along the St. Johns over the last three years."

I chewed my lip. "But if Deinosuchas is to blame, wouldn't somebody have seen one by now and reported it?"

Grayson locked eyes with me. "Not if they didn't survive the encounter."

A shiver went down my spine. "Oh."

"So," Earl said, slapping his palm on the table. "Y'all ready for your first lesson in how to catch one a these monster gators?"

I grimaced. "Do we have a choice?"

Grayson shot me some side eye. "We're ready."

"Good." Earl scratched behind his ear and glanced around the RV. "So, y'all got a broom around here anywheres?"

Chapter Sixteen

I nearly spewed a mouthful of coffee all over the banquette table. "A *broom*?"

"Yep," Earl said.

"What do you need a broom for?"

"Sweeping," Grayson said, studying me from his spot opposite me in the booth. "Perhaps you've heard of it?"

I shot him some side eye. "Tell that joke again and you may discover some brand new uses for a broom handle."

Earl smiled. "Well, that's kinda what I wanna show you all."

"Really?" I said. "Knock yourself out. The broom's in the hall closet. The one where Grayson keeps his pile of 'old school' contraptions."

Earl padded to the hallway and opened a cabinet door. "Got it!" he called out, then ambled back to the booth with the broom.

"Okay, Einstein," I said. "How are we gonna catch gators with a broom? Beat them over the head until they're unconscious?"

"I *wish*," Earl said. "But that'd be illegal. You see, Bobbie, in Florida, when it comes to gettin' gators they's all kind a laws you gotta follow."

"What kind of laws?" Grayson asked.

Earl held the broom like a rifle and looked down the "barrel" handle at us. "Well, for one, you can fish for gators with a line, but you can't use no hooks."

"No *hooks*?" I frowned. "Why not?"

Earl shrugged. "Who knows? I don't make the rules. I just figure out a way around 'em."

"So what's the work-around?" Grayson asked.

"Huh?" Earl grunted.

"What do you use instead of hooks," I said.

"Oh." Earl grinned. "I use what they call the 'wooden peg method.' Lemme show ya."

Earl laid the broom across the kitchen counter. Then he pulled a small hacksaw from his back pocket and began sawing a chunk off the end of the handle.

"What the?" I said.

"See this?" Earl held up a two-inch section of broom handle.

"Yeah." I laughed. "What are we supposed to do with that? Tie a string around it and paint it white like a marshmallow?"

Ponder puckered Earl's face. "Huh. I might have to try that one a these days. But no. What we're gonna do is wrap this here peg in bait. Then, when a gator swallers it, it gets stuck in its craw and you can reel 'em in."

"Interesting," Grayson said, examining the broom plug. "Once the prey item has been ensnared, what happens next?"

"You shoot 'em," Earl said.

I grinned. "Cool. I'll finally get to use my Glock."

"Oh, no," Earl said, shaking his head. "Them folks at the FWC don't look kindly on us using what they call 'conventional firearms' on a gator."

I frowned. "What? Why not?"

Earl shrugged. "Like I said, I don't make the laws. I just work around 'em."

"So what's the work-around?" I blurted, beating Grayson to it.

Earl grinned. "A bang stick."

Grayson's eyebrow triangulated. "A bang stick?"

"Yep. I got us one right here. Hold up a second."

Earl walked over to the RV's side door, opened it, then leaned out and grabbed something.

"Here she is," he said, pulling in a length of metal pipe about eight feet long. Attached to one end of it was some kind of odd, piston-looking thing. A six-inch strand of bare-metal wire ran from the piston thing to the main pipe, making a small, noose-like loop.

"How does the apparatus function?" Grayson asked.

Earl pointed at the piston thing. "This here is what they call the powerhead. You load it with a round of live ammo. Me, myself? I prefer a .44 caliber bullet. Anyways, once you reel the gator to the side of the boat, you jab the powerhead end of the bang stick into the back of the critter's head. It goes off and shoots a single round right through the gator's brain."

I stared at the contraption. "Does that thing really work?"

Earl grinned. "If you don't believe me, Bobbie, you can always reach over and stab the gator with a knife. That's legal, too. Or you can shoot 'em with a huntin' bow."

My upper lip hooked skyward. "Or, here's a thought. I could skip all this fun and not go hunting at all."

"ARE YOU SURE YOU KNOW what you're doing?" I asked Earl as we headed for his boat, our arms laden with spears, gigs, snares, fishing poles, and a cooler full of Dr Peppers and Little Debbie snack cakes. The night air was as dark and thick as a Sasquatch beard.

"Yep. And afore you ask, I got me a legal alligator trappin' license and two tags authorizin' me to bag two gators here in Lake County. Set me back nearly three hunnert and fifty dollars."

"Of *my* money, I bet," I muttered under my breath.

Grayson froze in his tracks in front of me. I nearly ran right into him. "What about *us*?" he asked Earl. "Don't *we* need licenses, too?"

Earl shook his head. "Nope. I can bring along one non-huntin' passenger free a charge."

"Uh, Earl?" I said. "I know it's dark and all. But in case you haven't noticed, there are *two* of us."

Earl winked and started walking again. "Don't you worry about that none, Bobbie. If'n we get stopped by anybody, I got a work-around for that, too."

I scrambled to keep up, my arms full of fishing nets and oatmeal snack cakes. "What kind of work-around?"

"We'll cross that snag when we get hooked up on it," Earl said, stopping in front of a skiff tied to the dock.

"*This* is your boat?" Grayson asked.

"Yep."

I looked up from balancing the snack cakes in my hands. Earl flicked on his headlamp, casing a green pall on the skiff floundering in the water in the fading light of dusk.

My mouth dropped open. "You're kidding."

"Nope." Earl beamed. "Got me one heck of a deal on it from the old lady what runs the bait store."

"TWO HUNDRED DOLLARS?" I muttered, climbing into Denny's battered, square-nosed scow. "I can't believe that woman had the nerve to charge you that much to buy this junky old boat."

"Don't be ridiculous, Bobbie," Earl said. "I didn't buy it. I just rented it for the night."

I nearly swallowed my tonsils. "For two-hundred—"

Grayson put a hand on my shoulder. "Just let it go. At least we all have headlamps this time."

I closed my eyes and took a deep breath. "Fine."

As we pulled away from the security of the dock, our infrared headlamps shone a greenish-yellowish haze, illuminating the cattails and lily pads lining the shore of the murky, black river.

Earl's initial gator-hunting training session had lasted until after six o'clock. So, for the second evening in a row, we were the last group to set off for the night's gator hunt.

Not that I minded. Once again, I'd been saved the embarrassment of being seen by the other hunters in Denny's ludicrously rundown boat. Plus, every minute of delay had given me a few more precious moments before I had to endure sitting on a hard, plastic seat in the middle of a bug-infested river, listening to the droning on of bullfrogs, cicadas, and my cousin's mindless jabber.

The asthmatic old outboard coughed and putted as we slowly motored away from the rustic comforts of the Rangler Resort. Once again, I found myself sandwiched between two men as opposite as bookends—and I was the meatball stuck in-between.

As we motored out, the hot, soggy air began to condense on my skin. I closed my eyes and said a prayer.

Hey, Universe? If I'm doomed to die inside a giant alligator's maw, could you please do me a favor and make it happen sooner rather than later?

Chapter Seventeen

"Then you got your gator-tail lasagna, your gator tail and grits, your gator-tail sausage—"

"We get it, Bubba Chump," I said, kicking Earl in the shin hard enough to send the shabby old boat wobbling in the wake of my annoyance.

We'd been anchored off the riverbank behind McGatorTail's for over an hour. I'd yet to see a single set of red gator eyeballs glaring back at me. And, to be honest, I couldn't have been happier about it.

I was pretty sure it was Earl's constant jabbering that was keeping the creatures at bay. Even so, there was only so much a girl could stand—even if it was in her own best interests. Earl's imaginative ways to prepare gator meat had me completely fed up. If I heard him utter one more way to eat gator I was going to skewer him and feed him to the blasted creatures myself.

"Could we *please* change the subject?" I begged.

"Well, what you wanna talk about, then?" Earl asked, rubbing his shin.

"Shouldn't we remain silent?" Grayson asked. "To avoid disturbing our prey?"

"Far as I can figure, gators don't care a mite what we say about 'em," Earl said. "And you know why?"

I frowned. "Why?"

Earl snorted. "'Cause they got *thick skin*. Get it?"

"Ha ha," I said.

"That skin's what makes 'em such good eatin'," Earl said. "Keeps the meat tender. Did you know you can fricassee a—"

"What about your monster gator?" I blurted at Grayson. It was official. I'd reached the point of desperation where even *learning something* seemed more appealing than the current situation.

"What do you mean?" Grayson asked.

"You know," I said. "What else can you tell us about Dino sookie?"

"Deinosuchas," Grayson said. He turned his gaze toward Earl. "As I told Drex, I believe the 'terrible crocodile' actually has an alligator's braincase. My theory is that it's resurrected itself iteratively after nearly being driven to extinction by man."

"Huh," Earl grunted. "I wonder what kind a trucks them men used to drive 'em there in."

I shot an *I-told-you-so* smirk at Grayson. "What can I say? Earl's got the braincase of a lemur. Yet we're out here entrusting him with our lives. Oh happy day."

"Braincase?" Earl asked. "I heard a belts and boots made outta gator hide, but I ain't never heard of nobody making a suitcase out of a gator's brain afore."

"She's referring to the braincase of Deinosuchas' skull," Grayson said. "Fossil evidence shows it was more closely related to alligators than crocodiles."

Earl laughed. "So you're sayin' this critter's half-crocked?"

My eyebrow shot up. For perhaps the second or third time in my life, something Earl said actually kind of made sense.

Earl jiggled the line tied to our broom-handle bait. "Hey Mr. G. What'd your ol' dino-gator look like, anyways?"

"Pretty much like today's modern alligator," Grayson said. "Except for its size. At maturity, Deinosuchas could've reached up to forty feet long."

"Lawdy!" Earl let go of the line like it was electrified. "That's purty sizeable all right. I bet one a its choppers was as big as a slice of Aunt Vera's pecan pie."

"You'd be right about that," Grayson said. "And its hemispherical osteoderms would be as big as turtle shells."

"Its hemi-engine Oscar Mayer *whut*?" Earl asked.

"Hemispherical osteoderms. The scaly patches along its back."

"Oh." Earl nodded. "So *that's* what them things is called. Bet this critter's hide was tough as steel."

"Deinosuchas was indeed a formidable creature," Grayson said. "In its heyday, it was the apex predator up and down the eastern coastal regions of North America."

"Huh," Earl grunted. "I don't get it, Mr. G. If this Dino-dookey thing was king of the jungle, what in tarnation killed it off?"

"Environmental changes, most likely. Changes that led to a reduction in abundant food sources. Actually that's why I think Deinosuchas may be on the comeback."

"What do you mean?" I asked, reaching for the carton of Little Debbie oatmeal pies.

Grayson grabbed the carton and shook out one for himself. "In the past hundred years, the human population has expanded exponentially. We now number into the billions. But even as we expand our reach deeper and deeper into new habitats, we're actually less and less prepared to survive in them."

"I don't believe that." I turned the snack cake carton upside down and shook it. "Dang it! We're out of Little Debbie's!"

Grayson sighed. "My point exactly. Homo sapiens has grown soft as a species. I'm convinced we've reached a point where we're so ill-adapted to our natural environment that we're now just a virus mutation away from species annihilation."

"Geez." I stared longingly at Grayson's snack cake. "You gonna eat that?"

Grayson shook his head and glanced out into the open water. "We grow weaker. Meanwhile the alligators grow stronger. Their elegant, near-perfect design has remained virtually unevolved for millions of years, including their perfectly adapted reptilian brain."

Earl laughed. "Hey, Mr. G. If gators has got reptile brains, what've we got? Monkey brains?"

"Well, yes and no. Mammals possess both reptilian and mammalian brains."

Earl's eyes grew wide. "You mean we got *two* brains?"

I snorted. "What a goober!"

Grayson shot me a pained look, then turned to my cousin. "Actually, Earl, we have *three*."

The whites of Earl's eyes shone in the moonlight. "We got *three* brains?"

Grayson nodded. "In a way, yes."

I crossed my arms and smirked. "*This* I gotta hear."

"So I have your attention?" Grayson asked, then ripped into the Little Debbie. "You see, the basal ganglia in the human brain are referred to as the reptilian complex. This area controls our self-preservation behaviors to ensure survival of our species."

"Self-preservation behaviors?" I asked. "What do you mean?"

Grayson looked away. "You know. The four F's. Feeding, fighting, fleeing and fff ... uh ... fooling around. As in mating."

My nose crinkled. "Seriously? Is that some scientist's idea of a joke?"

"Not at all." Grayson studied me. "The contributions of the reptilian brain are not to be made light of, Drex. Like I said, they provide us with our basic survival instincts."

"Then what do we need our other two brains for? Wining and dining?"

Grayson groaned, then turned his attention to Earl. "You see, Earl, over millions of years of evolution, mammals developed two new brain sections."

"Cool!" Earl said.

"Yes. Cool, indeed. First came the limbic system. It allowed us to form and store memories, giving us the ability to learn. Then, around 200,000 years ago, our brains underwent something akin to a cosmic Big Bang. The neocortex was formed, opening us up for higher thinking."

"Big Bang?" I laughed. "Isn't that scientist-code for 'We don't know what the heck happened.'?"

"I prefer to think of it as scientific poetic license," Grayson said. "But in a way, you're correct, Drex. No one has yet been able to explain the sudden expansion of the human brain to allow for philosophy, self-reflection, and even psychic powers."

"Sounds to me like the hand a God reached down and made us smart," Earl said.

I laughed. "Yeah. Too bad you skipped Sunday school that day."

Grayson shrugged. "At this point in our understanding, Earl's explanation for the neocortex is as good as any other. At any rate, to make a long story short, the neocortex and limbic system now work together to regulate human thoughts and emotions, along with sexual arousal. Theirs is a divine dance of the human brain I've poetically coined, *limbic pentameter*."

"I don't get it," Earl said.

Grayson cocked his head and smiled. "You see, it's a rather clever corruption of the musical term, *iambic pentameter*."

"I still don't get it," Earl grunted.

Grayson cleared his throat. "Iambic—"

"He made it up, Earl," I said, cutting Grayson off. "What it boils down to is that we mammals—well, at least *most* of us—are smarter than your average reptile. Right, Grayson?"

Grayson shrugged. "Actually, that would depend on the situation and the action required."

My upper lip snarled. "Huh?"

"Take the Everglades, for instance," Grayson said. "The recent introduction of pythons has tipped the balance in favor of reptiles. Mammals like raccoons, possums, and even bobcats are dwindling. Despite their advanced mammalian brains, they're losing the battle to the so-called 'primitive-brained' reptiles."

I frowned. "But I don't see how that applies to us humans."

Grayson held up a spidery finger, as if to accentuate his point. "While we no longer live in the same world as primitive man, we still encounter potentially life-threatening situations on a regular basis. The same reptilian brain that kept early man alive still functions within us pretty much the same as it always has."

"You mean our 'fight or flight' response?" I asked.

"Precisely."

"So, what's your point?" I asked.

"It's this. Our reptilian brain is smart enough to save our skin, *unless* we allow our mammalian brain to override it."

My brow furrowed. "How do we do that?"

"By overthinking. Classic analysis paralysis." Grayson locked eyes with me. "Allowing thoughts and emotions to override our primitive gut instincts can prove deadly."

"How's this for gut instincts?" I said, and snatched the Little Debbie from Grayson's hand.

"Why do I bother?" Grayson muttered.

"Huh," Earl grunted. "You mean to tell me that if it weren't for our gator suitcase brain, we pro'lly wouldn't a made it this long?"

Grayson's green eyes brightened. "That's *precisely* what I'm saying. You see—"

Suddenly, a terrible howl pierced the night.

"Aaaughhooo!"

A second later, somewhere nearby, a man's blood-curdling scream echoed across the water. A splash sounded, followed by an eerie, whooshing noise.

"What the hell is that?" I asked, nearly jumping into Grayson's lap.

We aimed our headlamps in the direction of the sound. In the center of the river, something huge submerged into the tannic water, causing a wake so strong it made our boat wobble.

"L ... l ... let's g ... get the hell out of here!" I stammered.

But there was no need for my mammalian-brain ramblings.

Earl's primitive reptilian brain had already sprung into action. He was yanking the pull-chord on the outboard motor like a one-armed lumberjack in a log-sawing competition.

Chapter Eighteen

As soon as Denny's old boat touched the dock back at the Rangler RV Resort, I leapt off the battered skiff and ran for the motorhome like the ground was made of lava. I swore the whole way there that if I made it inside the motorhome without being eaten alive, I'd never go gator hunting again.

But I never made it to the RV.

Instead, I was ensnared by the heavenly aroma of my favorite kind of cuisine—food being cooked by somebody else. I stopped in my tracks and turned around. In the dim light of dawn, I spotted Cheech's food truck and made a beeline for it.

"Good morning, Cheech!" I said, running on the adrenaline high of making it back to shore alive. "What's cooking?"

"Not much, yet," he said, whipping something in a bowl. "I'm just setting up."

"But I smell something delicious. Cinnamon rolls?"

He laughed. "No. What you smell is my early-bird special."

"What's that?"

"I warm up the stove every morning by cooking yesterday's grease with the leftover coffee. People around here call it red-eye gravy. Comes served over day-old biscuits."

"Grease, coffee, and biscuits?" Earl said, coming up behind me. "Them's the three staples of life!"

"Sounds like the nectar of the gods to me," I said, reaching for my wallet. "We'll take three."

I WOKE UP FROM MY AFTER-breakfast nap to discover I had the RV to myself. Neither Grayson nor Earl were anywhere to be found.

Heaven!

I seized the opportunity to call my best friend, Beth-Ann. She was a Goth-dressing beautician from my hometown of Point Paradise.

"Bobbie!" she said. "How's my favorite beach bum?"

"Good. But listen. I'm calling about Earl. I thought you agreed to keep tabs on him for me."

"I am. I mean, I *was.* Until he took off for a job a few days ago."

"Uh-huh. Did he happen to mention what *kind* of job?"

"No. And I hated to ask him, Bobbie. It's the first spark of life I've seen in him lately. He's been mighty upset about losing your family's garage."

My brow furrowed with surprise. "He's actually been upset?"

"Devastated is more like it. He's been moping around my beauty shop, wringing his hands and moaning loud enough to scare my customers off. He even gave me his two-headed turtle to look after, saying he was an unfit parent for Sally."

I winced. "Geez. I didn't realize he was taking it so hard."

"Believe me, he *is*. I hope he hasn't done himself a harm."

"What *I* hope is that he doesn't do *me* a harm. Don't worry about Earl. He's here with me and Grayson in Astor."

"He is? Thank goodness!" Beth-Ann's voice lowered an octave. "Hey, wait. You're back with Grayson?"

"Yeah. He picked me up in the new RV the day before yesterday."

"And you didn't think to call me until *now*?"

"Uh ... I've been busy."

Beth-Ann cackled. "I *bet* you have. So, are you two hitting the sack together?"

"Hardly. In fact, I don't think Grayson missed me at all."

"Why do you say that?"

"I dunno. It's like he's been reset back to his original factory settings. He even regrew that horrible moustache!"

"Gee." Beth-Ann sighed. "The only thing more repellant than that moustache would be if he took up smoking cigars."

"I know, right?"

"Well, it was your idea to give him space, Bobbie. You told him not to call you."

I winced. "I know. But why did he have to choose *that* moment to finally start listening to what I say? I thought maybe we could pick up where we left off. But what chance do I have with Earl around? Honestly, Beth-Ann, I think my virginity is growing back."

"I hear you, sister. But hey, if you two aren't doing the deed, what *are* you doing?"

I chewed my lip. "Searching for a giant alligator."

I heard Beth-Ann gasp. "Like the ones in the movies?"

"Yeah. Except we've only got broom handles for bait, and Earl Schankles as our guide."

"My word."

"Exactly." I blew out a breath. "On that note, did you get my last will and testament I mailed you?"

"Yes. Earl gets everything if you bite the dust."

"Incentive for you to keep dating him. He needs somebody to look after him."

"He's not *that* big an imbecile."

"I know. It's just our thing. Earl and me insulting each other, I mean."

"Yeah, I know. But seriously, Bobbie. You're not dying or anything, are you?"

"No. But even if I was, with my luck I'd come back reincarnated as myself."

Beth-Ann's laugh was drowned out by the familiar roar of Bessie's hemi engine.

"Crap. Listen, I gotta go Beth-Ann. Just remember, if anything happens to me, take care of yourself—and my jerk of a cousin, too. Okay?"

"Sure, but—"

I clicked off the phone. The door to the RV burst open. Earl and Grayson came tumbling in.

"Where have you two been?" I asked.

"Re-provisioning." Grayson set two Walmart bags down on the banquette table.

"We needed us some better bait," Earl said. "So we found us a Walmart Supercenter in Deland, twenty miles from here."

Earl set a couple of sacks on the kitchen counter, then reached in one and pulled out a wadded up ball of pink plastic the size of a Thanksgiving turkey.

"What the heck is that?" I asked.

"A pink flamingo float," Grayson said.

"You know," Earl said. "Like the one Shirleene Parker, the town floozy, was last seen in."

My nose crinkled. "Uh, what am I missing here?"

"The floozy part," Earl said, and padded off down the hall.

I turned to Grayson. "Could you please explain what the heck's going on here?"

"I have a theory, Drex."

"What theory?"

"I believe the color pink could be an attractant for Deinosuchas. The roseate hue has proven to have a calming effect in institutional settings."

I stared at the lump of plastic. "It must be true. I'm already beginning to feel like I'm in an institution."

"Here she blows," Earl said, emerging from the hallway carrying an inflatable woman in his arms. The expression on her face was either one of surprise, or she was about to consume an Oscar Mayer wiener.

"What the?" I yelled. "*This* is what you spent my money on, Earl? A blow-up doll?"

"No ma'am," Earl said. "Grayson already had her."

I gulped, then glared at Grayson. Then I took another look at the doll and nearly swallowed my tonsils. "Wait a minute. Is that thing wearing my *Wilshire wig*?"

Grayson looked away, his cheeks burning. "You weren't using it. Why let it go to waste?"

My eyes bored holes into Grayson. "And my *bikini, too*?"

"You weren't using *it*, either," Grayson said. "And as I mentioned, if Shirleene Parker is a victim of Deinosuchas, the creature may be attracted to pink. Or women."

"Or floozies," I grumbled.

Earl laughed. "Them *are* the three staples of life."

I shot Grayson a death glare. "Seriously. Is that all you have to say for yourself?"

Grayson grimaced. "Did I mention we also bought a boat?"

Chapter Nineteen

I tumbled out of the RV and stomped across the campsite behind Grayson and Earl. Hooked to Bessie's trailer hitch was a sleek, steel-gray flats boat.

"Great," I grumbled. "You wouldn't let *me* buy a new RV, but you two went off and bought a brand new *boat*?"

"Not brand new," Grayson said. "Just new to us."

"We bought it off another gator hunter," Earl said, running his hand along the boat's smooth, fiberglass hull. "This here's a primo gator-huntin' vessel. The shallow draft is perfect for runnin' rivers and marsh. And see here? It's got T-Lock gunnels, two-foot side height, and a hull shape built for quick turnin'."

"Yeah, yeah," I said. "The real question is, does it have any patches or cracks in the hull?"

"Narry a one," Earl said, beaming with pride.

I unfolded my crossed arms. "Well, at least we won't have to bail while we hunt. But if this boat's so great, why was the guy selling it?"

"Don't know," Earl said. "But he throwed in his gator tags, too. Now we can take us *four* gators."

"Why would he do that?" I cast a suspicious eye over the shiny, too-good-to-be-true, V-shaped boat.

"Don't know that, either." Earl patted his new prize like it was a prize hound-dog pup. "All the feller said was he wasn't never gettin' on the river again."

"Why not?" I asked.

Earl shrugged. "As a 'matter of self-preservation,' whatever that means."

My eyebrow rose half an inch. I shot Grayson my best WTF look. "Why would the guy have said such a thing as that?"

"Indeterminable. All I can say in his defense is this; the reptilian brain doesn't lie."

AFTER AN HOUR OF LISTENING to Earl beg and plead, I finally agreed to give him another chance and go out in the new boat that evening. But I'd added two stipulations. One, we were to leave only under cover of darkness. And two, all the other hunters had to be launched and long gone.

Being seen in Denny's unseaworthy scow had been humiliating enough. That problem was solved. But a new one appeared in its stead, in the form of a new passenger. One I didn't approve of one little bit. The guys had named her Ms. Floozy. She was my inflatable, pornographic body double.

I glanced over at the couch where the inflatable woman sat in a most unladylike position. In addition to my Wilshire wig and bikini, the blow-up tramp now sported a pink flamingo float around her waist and an open-mouthed look of horror on her face.

I can relate, sister.

Dying in the jaws of a gator was one thing. But I wasn't about to be caught dead sitting next to Ms. Floozy in a fishing boat. I had to draw the line somewhere, didn't I?

So while we waited in the RV for the cover of darkness, Earl tried to get me and Grayson up to speed on the delicate art of gator hunting. It was enough to make me long for that bottle with the worm in it ...

"What's the duct tape for?" I asked Earl as he tossed it into a utility bag he was packing for the trip. "Don't tell me it's to patch Ms. Floozy over there in case she springs a leak."

"Nope. This here duck tape's to wrap around the snout a the gators we catch."

"Why? I thought we were gonna shoot them in the brain with that bang stick thing of yours."

"We are. But let me learn you somthin', Cuz."

"What?"

This ought to be rich.

"These here reptilian critters can fool ya. Even when you think you done shot 'em good and dead, they been known to come back to life and chomp a body's leg off. That's why we *professionals* tape their mouths closed fast as we can, whether they're dead or alive."

My nose crinkled. "Geez. If a bullet to the brain doesn't kill a gator, what can?"

"This here." Earl held up a Bowie knife. "Them FWC fellers recommend using a big ol' knife to sever the gator's spinacular column right below its head. Then you stab it in the brain, to make sure it's really dead."

I grimaced and turned to Grayson, who was sitting across from me, researching something on his laptop. "Is Earl right? Can a half-dead alligator really bite your leg off?"

"Theoretically, yes," Grayson said.

I winced. "Geez!"

Grayson closed his laptop. "Actually, alligators possess one of the most powerful bites in the animal kingdom. I just read about a recent study involving wild and captive alligators. Researchers found that large individuals can bite down with a force of 2,960 pounds. That's over 13,000 newtons."

"Dang it!" Earl said. "When we was at Walmarts, I done forgot to get the Fig Newtons!"

AS WE MOTORED DOWNRIVER toward the bridge in our shipshape new boat, up ahead I caught the familiar put-put sound of a wheezing outboard motor. It wasn't long before we overtook the other vessel. As we pulled alongside it, I was surprised to see Tommy and Denny Tarminger floundering away together in that battered old boat of hers.

"What are you two doing out here?" I asked.

"We decided to try our luck at hauling in Chomp for ourselves," Tommy said. "Somebody posted some serious prize money for the beast."

"How much we talkin' here?" Earl asked.

"Cash money? Five grand," Denny said.

Earl whistled. "Sweeeet!"

I stood up in the boat and glared down at Tommy in his two-bit cowboy hat. "Haven't you already taken enough money from other people?"

"I beg your pardon?" Tommy said.

I felt Grayson's hand tugging at my thigh. "Leave it," he whispered.

I sighed and sat down. "Fine. Let's get out of here and get this over with."

"You got it," Earl said. He revved the engine and we left the unsavory pair awash in our wake.

"Where are we heading?" I asked.

"Back by the bridge," Grayson said. "Where we encountered something big submerging last night."

"Something big enough to bite a leg off?" I asked. "Or swallow one of us whole?"

"Indeterminable."

"Great." I sighed, let my shoulders slump, and resigned myself to my fate.

Well, at least this time we're not bobbing around in Shitty Shitty Bang Bang.

Chapter Twenty

"There's the bridge," Grayson said as the ghostly white arch over the river came into range of our headlamps. "Drop the bait."

"You got it, Chief." Earl took his hand off the engine throttle. "Gimme a hand, Bobbie."

"I'm not touching that thing!"

"Suit yourself." Earl reached over and hoisted Ms. Floozy from her seat. He checked that the broom-chunk covered in bait was still dangling from the rope around her waist, and that the flamingo pool float hadn't sprung a leak. Then he unceremoniously flung the blow-up doll into the river.

As Ms. Floozy splashed down into the dark water, the impact nearly upended her. Her legs flew up obscenely. When her startled face reemerged from the river, my Wishire wig—the best wig I'd ever owned—had been lost at sea.

Dang it!

Scowling, I took a medicinal swig from the flask full of mescal I'd hidden in my camo vest. It was the only thing keeping me from grabbing the metal bang stick and whacking both guys over the head with it. Well, that and the idea of going to jail for homicide, no matter *how* justifiable it would've been.

I chose instead to sit in silence and give the alcohol time to do its work. As I waited for the mescal to kick in, I kept my eyes glued to Ms. Floozy. Her shiny, bald-headed visage trailed slowly behind us in her pink inner tube like a ghost in some mannequin-themed horror movie.

Where's Freddy Kruger when you need him?

"LOOKS LIKE WE'VE GOT company," Grayson said, his voice startling me from my mescal-induced haze.

In the distance, I heard another boat approaching. But it wasn't the coughing put-put of the Tarminger scow. In the pale moonlight, I made out the gleam of a white hull. A second later, I saw the glint of a windshield built into a small, square-shaped cabin.

"Watch out, they're coming up fast," Grayson said as the boat blew by Ms. Floozy. The wake sent her tumbling upside down. Her long, pink legs jutted out of the water like an overturned mallard.

"Geez," I said. "I hope whoever these jerks are, they don't *capsize* us."

Earl put a hand on his forehead. "If'n they do, remember. I wear an extra-large."

I reached for my flask to anesthetize myself further from Earl's stupidity. Suddenly, a flashing blue light blinked on above the approaching vessel. A voice over a loudspeaker said, "River patrol. Cut your engines."

"Aww, crap!" Earl said. "I was a-feared this would happen." Earl turned off the engine, then leaned over and snatched a bag from the boat console. "Listen up, you two. *Grayson*, you ain't fishing. You're just my passenger."

"Roger that," Grayson said.

Earl turned to me. "Bobbie, you got a huntin' license." He slapped a laminated card into my palm.

"What?" I held the card up to the moonlight. "Wait. This has Aunt Vera's name on it!"

"Yep. I went by to see her at the old folks' home. She give me her sweet potato pie recipe, and her blessin' to get a huntin' license in her name."

"I'm gonna give you a blessing of my own, Earl!" I shoved the card back at him. "This is the stupidest idea you've had yet! Nobody's going to believe I'm a 73-year-old woman!"

"In the dark they might. Hear me out."

"Why should I?" I growled.

"On account a Aunt Vera's artificial hip, she qualified for a Person with Disabilities huntin' license. It costed $22 instead a $270."

"So what?"

My cousin's basketball-sized head cocked like a confused puppy's. "I thought you'd be glad I was thinkin' economical."

I stared at him, stupefied by his unique brand of incomprehensible logic. "Huh?"

"Now, come on, Bobbie. Time's a wastin'." Earl glanced back at the patrol boat that was slowly trolling up beside us. He shoved something into my hands. "Here, put on this here white wig and chin-hair beard."

My face dropped two inches. "You've got to be kidding me. I'm not doing that!"

"Okay. Have it your way. But huntin' gators without a license is a third-degree felony in this here state. Punishable by up to five years in prison and $5,000 in fines."

A spotlight wavered over us. The voice over the loudspeaker said, "I'm going to need to see your licenses."

"I can't believe this," I grumbled. I turned away from the light and slapped the white wig over my skull. In my haste, I dropped the chin beard. It wafted into the black water like a cotton-candy spider.

Crap.

Wig secured, I turned to see Earl leaning across the side of the boat, handing the patrol officer his license. The guy in the boat was probably in his mid-fifties. Caucasian. With a set of crooked, misshapen teeth.

"Only me and my Aunt Vera is huntin'," my cousin said. "My friend here is just spectatorin'."

"Looks in order," the man said, handing Earl back his license. "And you, ma'am?"

Trying to appear older, I scrunched up my face and spoke in a wobbly voice. "Vera Mosely, sir." I handed Earl my license to give to the officer.

"I think something fishy's going on here," the officer said, looking up from studying my license. "Are you really a woman?"

My eyebrows went slack.

That's *your problem with this?*

I was about to give him a piece of my mind, when I thought about the consequences. I pasted on a smile. "I sure am, officer."

"I'm going to need you to prove it," the man in the patrol boat said.

"Prove it?" I gulped. "How?"

"Stand up and show him your breeder hips," Grayson said. "That ought to suffice."

Every molecule in my mescal-soaked brain wanted to kick all three of their rotten heads in. But unable to see any other way out, I slapped on a fake smile and stood up.

"Now wiggle your hips," the officer said.

Dumbfounded, I did as instructed.

The officer broke out in a laugh. "I was just joking!" He handed Earl back my aunt's license. "Anybody can see you had a few kids back in your heyday. Any chance you and Denny Tarminger are twins?"

I smiled as the veins in my temples throbbed like a pair of hammered thumbs.

Any chance you got those teeth out of a costume-shop joke bin?

"No, we're not related," I said, snatching Aunt Vera's license from Earl's hand.

"Well, you all be careful hunting out here." The officer handed Earl a business card. "And if you could, I'd appreciate you all keeping an eye out for the three folks that went missing on the river last week."

"We will," Grayson said. "Do you have any clue what happened to them?"

"Not a one," he said.

"Denny Tarminger said Buddy Barlowe's boat was nearly bit in two," Earl said.

"I seriously doubt that," the officer said. "I've heard about big gators tipping kayaks and canoes, but I've never heard of one large enough to bite a flats boat in half. Heed my advice. Don't believe everything a Tarminger tells you."

"I heard *that*," I said.

"Be safe." The officer tipped his cap, throttled up his engine, and disappeared back down the river.

"Whew!" Earl said, a hand over his heart. "That was a close one!"

"Are you serious?" I jerked the white wig from my head. "That guy's an idiot. And he must be blind as a bat, too."

"My thoughts exactly," Grayson said. "Why else would he have nearly run over Ms. Floozy twice without even noticing her?"

Chapter Twenty-One

When morning broke, we were still on the water. Nothing had molested Ms. Floozy during the night. Not even a lonely gator hunter. So, under Grayson's orders, Earl hauled her inflatable butt back into the boat.

"Should we pull anchor and head back to the RV park, Chief?" Earl asked.

Grayson nodded. "Make it so."

"You got it." Earl cranked the trolling motor.

"Gimme the binoculars." I grabbed them from Grayson. "And Earl, throw a tarp over that obscene lump of plastic."

"What do you need the binoculars for?" Grayson asked. "We haven't seen an alligator in hours."

"I wanna find my Wilshire wig. That thing cost me a fortune!"

"Oh." Grayson patted my shoulder. "Don't worry. Pretty soon you won't need it."

"Pretty soon!" I hissed. "I thought my hair looked okay *now*."

Earl laughed. "I thought you wanted to be a *P*.I., Bobbie. Not a *G*.I."

"Ha ha," I grumbled. "Just shut your pie hole and get us out of here."

"Yes, sir." Earl saluted me, then upped the throttle on the engine.

"Wait!" I yelled.

"What is it *now*?" Earl grumbled.

I focused the binoculars on a spot by some reeds. "I think I see something."

"What?" Grayson asked.

"I don't know." I pointed to my left. "It's over there by that stand of cattails."

"Is it your wig?" Earl asked, maneuvering the boat in the direction I pointed.

I shook my head. "No. It's white."

Earl edged the boat closer to the reeds. "Is *that* it?" He laughed. "Bobbie, that ain't nothin' but an old Styrofoam worm bucket."

"Crap." I frowned. "Wait a second. I think there's something inside it."

"Yeah. Worms," Earl said.

I shot him some side-eye. "Just get us a little closer, okay?"

"All right already, Major Payne." Earl maneuvered the boat to within a foot of the reeds.

"Is that what I think it is?" Grayson asked.

"Oh my lord!" I gasped and let the binoculars fall from my eyes.

"Let me use those," Grayson said, taking the binoculars from me.

Earl shook his head. "If that don't beat all."

Caught in the reeds was a worm bucket, all right. But it didn't contain any wriggling creatures. Instead, it was filled halfway to the top with some kind of pinkish-brown goo. And floating in the center of the goo was an eyeball. Or, to be exact, a bobber with an iris and cornea drawn on it with magic marker.

I grimaced. "That's gotta be Buddy Barlowe's eyeball. But what's that other stuff?"

Grayson's eyebrow did its Spock impression. "My guess would be it's also Buddy—but in the form of half-digested stew."

"Well I'll be," Earl said. "Now that there's what I'd call a bucket a dead-eye gravy."

Chapter Twenty-Two

"It appears Buddy Barlowe was one early bird who didn't *get* red-eye gravy, but was turned *into* it," Grayson said.

I watched in morbid fascination as he leaned over and plucked the Styrofoam container from the water. Then, using a long, thin finger, he poked the fake eyeball floating in the mystery goo.

I fought back a retch. "Gross, Grayson! What are we gonna do with him? I mean *it*. I mean *him*?"

"Deliver him or it to the local authorities," he said.

"Huh," Earl grunted. "Kind a like a Buddy Barlowe take-out order. Hey, Mr. G. That come with fries?"

I shook my head. "You guys are sick. Keep that up, and you're both going to hell for sure."

"Speak of the devil," Earl said, nodding toward a boat in the distance. "Here comes that patrol man again. Bobbie, get your wig back on, pronto!"

"Crap!" I grabbed the cheap white wig and tugged it back onto my skull. Then I sat down, hunched over, and chewed my lip. "It's daylight now. He'll know I'm not old enough to be Aunt Vera!"

"She's got a point," Grayson said. He turned back to me. "Quick. Drex, get under the tarp and start snoring, like you do when you're sleeping."

My eyes narrowed. "I don't snore in my sleep!"

Grayson sighed. "Very well, then. Just be sure to explain that to the officer when he slaps you with a $5,000 fine."

"Ugh! I'm going, already." I dove under the tarp.

So this is what my life has come to. Hiding out from the law in a cheap wig under a plastic tarp next to a silicone sex doll with fish guts tied to her waist.

Ain't life grand?

"WHAT'S UNDER THE TARP?" I heard the River Patrol officer ask. I recognized his voice. It was the same guy from last night.

"Aunt Vera," Earl said.

I let loose a snore.

"She all right?" the man asked.

"Yes," Grayson said. "She's just sleeping it off. The old gal likes her mescal."

My ears caught flame.

Old gal!

"I see," the officer said. "Let me have a look at her, just to make sure."

I cringed.

Aww, crap! If he gets a good look at me, I'm going to jail!

I rolled over to try and hide my face, and ended up with my head wedged between Ms. Floozy's fake boobs.

Seriously, Universe? This is how my life is going to end? Death by humiliation? Fine! To hell with it!

I raised up on one elbow, ready to throw open the tarp and take my lumps. But as I reached for the edge of the plastic sheet, the boat rocked. I slipped and fell back onto Ms. Floozy. The impact caused her right boob to burst with a loud, fart-like sound.

The patrol officer laughed. "You know what? On second thought, never mind. Let the old gal sleep. No use letting the stink out of her Dutch oven."

"Yeppers," Earl said. "The old gas bag never could hold in her intestinational flatulence."

"Just like my Great Aunt Sophie," the patrol officer said. "So, did you all catch any gators last night?"

"No, sir," Grayson said.

"I thought I saw you wave me down."

"No, but we were going to," Grayson said. "Your timing is quite fortuitous."

"What?" the officer asked.

"Here," Grayson said. "We wanted to report we found this."

As I lay under the tarp with a slowly deflating Ms. Floozy hissing at me with her boob, I was left to imagine the officer's face when Grayson handed him the container full of Buddy's disgusting remains.

"Well now," the officer said. "That's something you don't see every day."

"Sorry we don't have the lid," Earl said.

"I'm sure I've got one in the boat," the officer said. "I collect up enough trash on this river every week to fill a dumpster."

"So, you think that's Buddy Barlowe?" Grayson asked.

"Well, that's Buddy's eyeball, for sure. I appreciate you handing this over. It's the first clue we've had about what happened to him. Where'd you all find it?"

"Just over there," Grayson said. "By that stand of cattails."

"Hmm. I wonder what this gooey stuff is."

"I think it could be Buddy as well," Grayson said.

"I was afraid of that," the man said.

"I theorize that an alligator got Buddy," Grayson said. "Then, at some point after ingestion, the creature became agitated and disgorged Buddy's remains before they were completely digested."

"You don't say," the officer said. "You got any theory on how some of his undigested remains came to land inside this bait container?"

"Just luck," Grayson said.

"Bad luck," Earl said.

"Well, what you say *is* possible," the patrol officer said. "A gator's stomach acids are as strong as vinegar. They can digest soft tissues in two or three days. Buddy's been gone four. Any bones in this stuff?"

"We haven't had time to check," Grayson said. "We just found it ourselves."

"How long do bones take to digest?" Earl asked.

"Depending on size and thickness, a couple of weeks or up to three months," the officer said.

"Golly," Earl said. "So you all think that soupy stuff really could be Buddy gravy?"

"Unfortunately, yes," the officer said. "Well, I better get this over to the station so they can send it to forensics. I'll get a crew out today to check the area for any further remains."

"Yes, sir," Earl said.

I couldn't see from under the tarp, but I'd have bet money Earl saluted the guy.

"Tell your granny I'm sorry I missed her," the officer said.

"My *aunt*, you mean," Earl said.

"Oh. Right. She looks a lot older." The officer snickered. "Good thing she isn't awake to hear that. Women can be mighty sensitive when it comes to comments about their age and beauty."

"Don't you worry. She's used to it," Earl said, his toe kicking me in the side. "She's been ugly since birth."

As I lay there next to Ms. Floozy, biting my tongue in half, I listened to the sound of the officer's engine fading and plotted my revenge against my idiot cousin.

Finally, I heard Grayson say, "The coast is clear, Drex."

I whipped the tarp off my head and hissed, "Earl Schankles, I'm gonna make your life a living hell!"

He laughed. "Sorry, Cuz, but we're too close a relations to start datin'."

Earl and Grayson glanced at each other, then burst out laughing.

As I sat up and extricated myself from the limp arms of Ms. Floozy, I realized those two jerks were enjoying this too much. *Way* too much.

Suddenly, a thought hit me like a squirt of warm bird poop.

"Wait a minute," I growled. "You guys set me up!"

Chapter Twenty-Three

"Set you up?" Grayson asked, watching as I gracelessly floundered my way out of the tarp and up onto a boat seat. "Drex, I thought *I* was the one around here in charge of conspiracy theories."

"Gimme a break." I scrutinized his face. "Admit it, Grayson. This whole gator-hunting trip was a set-up between you and Earl, wasn't it?"

"What you talkin' about, Cuz?" Earl asked, trying to look innocent.

"Grayson, you're just pretending to be after some ancient alligator monster, aren't you?" I whipped around to face Earl. "And *you*! A professional gator guide? Get real! This was all a ruse just to get the three of us back together, wasn't it?"

Grayson's chin inched closer to his neck. "I wouldn't call it a *ruse*, per-se. It was more like an ... *opportunity*. And in all fairness, Earl really *did* train to become a gator hunter."

Earl beamed. "I almost finished the whole course, too!"

"*Almost*," I spat. "What a surprise. Earl, the only thing you ever finished in your life was becoming a complete nincompoop!"

"Tone it down," Grayson said.

"Nincompoop *is* toning it down," I said. "Excuse me, but who just got called a gassy old hag?"

Grayson rubbed his chin. "I don't recall anyone using the term, 'hag.'"

My molars pressed together with enough pressure to bite through a knife blade. "Look. If I wasn't stuck on this boat with you guys, I'd march right out of here and never look back."

Earl cutt the throttle. "Gee, Bobbie. Me and Mr. G. didn't mean no harm by it. Honest. What's the matter? Don't you *wanna* be a private investigator no more?"

My eyes narrowed. "If it means being humiliated by you two every chance you get, then *no*!"

Grayson studied me with an expression too hard to read. "Look, Drex. I compliment you on figuring out our plan. But your attitude hasn't exactly made things a cakewalk for *us*, either. As your mentor, I suggest we discuss this further in private, when we get back to the RV."

"Fine," I said. "Perfect."

But it wasn't perfect. Far from it. As I turned and stared silently out at the river, a hard, dry lump grew larger and larger at the base of my throat.

Something had to give. And from where I sat, I felt *I'd* already given enough.

Chapter Twenty-Four

When we finally arrived back at the docks in front of the Rangler RV Resort, I was wet, dirty, exhausted, and hungry. Not exactly the perfect ingredients for a stellar mood.

I needed coffee.

Pronto.

Before I blew a gasket.

But my stringer full of bad luck wasn't ready to let me off the hook just yet. Breakfast at Cheech's was also a no-go. By the time Earl found an open slip at the crowded dock, we were just in time to watch his food truck speed out of the lot, leaving the other straggling gator hunters in a cloud of orange dust.

"Awesome," I said sourly. "Well, if you guys think *I'm* cooking breakfast, you can kiss my grits."

"Still perturbed?" Grayson asked, walking up beside me.

"Sure looks that way to me," Earl said, wincing from the weaponized glare I'd launched his way. "Aww, come on, Bobbie. Cheer up. I'd cook us up a batch a gator stew, but all we got is a *croc* pot."

The vein in my right temple twitched. I was about to have a caffeine-deprivation meltdown. "For the love of God, would you *can it*, Earl?"

Grayson unlocked the RV. Before he could take the keys from the knob, I pushed past him and sprinted to the coffee machine. I flipped the switch on, then rifled around the kitchen cupboard for the largest mug I could find.

"So when did you two set all this up?" I asked as I waited for the black elixir of life to perk its way into my cup. "That night in the Walmart parking lot?"

"Nope," Earl said. "At least, not that I can recollect."

"Seriously?" I watched Earl grab a box of Pop Tarts from the cabinet. "You can't remember? *That's* your cop-out?"

"He's telling the truth," Grayson said, grabbing a coffee cup and joining me in line at the machine. "That night, after you took off in a taxi cab, the glowing light that zapped Danny Daniels returned."

I nearly dropped my full coffee mug. "It *did*?"

"Yes." Grayson stuck his coffee mug in the machine and pressed the button marked *Americano*. "It came back and shone its laser beam down on Earl, just as he was climbing into Bessie."

"I ... I didn't know." I scooted into the banquette booth and shot Earl a look of concern. If he noticed, I couldn't tell. He was too busy shoving half a Pop Tart into his mouth.

I glanced up at Grayson. "So ... what happened? Was Earl hurt?"

Grayson inched into the booth opposite me. "I can't say for sure."

"Why not?"

"Before I could do anything to intervene, Earl peeled out of the parking lot. He took off down the street with the unidentified aircraft in pursuit. I ran back to the RV and tried to follow him, but got hung up at a traffic light and lost sight of him."

I nearly spewed my sip of coffee. "You stopped at a red light in the middle of chasing a UFO?"

"It was a matter of public safety," Grayson said. "An old lady in a walker was crossing the street. By the time my lane was clear, Earl had disappeared from sight. I tried to reach him on his cellphone, but he didn't pick up. I didn't hear back from him until three hours later."

"*Three hours*?" I turned to Earl. "Why?"

"On account a that's when I woke up," he said, then took a giant slurp of coffee.

I turned back to Grayson. "Woke up?"

Grayson nodded. "I drove around St. Petersburg for a couple of hours looking for him. Then I decided to go to Plant City and get help from Garth. But halfway there, I spotted Bessie parked along I-4, just outside Thonotosassa."

I glanced over at Earl. "You pulled off to take a nap?"

Earl shrugged. "That's just it, Bobbie. I don't know. You see, I ain't got no recollection of how me and Bessie ended up there."

Chapter Twenty-Five

I gasped. "Wait a minute! Are you saying Earl was abducted by aliens on his way to Garth's place?"

Grayson's brow furrowed. "Indeterminate."

Earl shrugged. "But we *did* determinate that I was missin' about two hours a time I cain't account for."

"Two hours?" My gut flopped. "Are you sure you didn't just forget about pulling into a convenience store and downing a six pack?"

"No evidence to support such activities was found," Grayson said. "I've been working with Garth not only on the RV renovations, but on trying to ascertain what actually happened to Earl and Danny Daniels in that Walmart parking lot."

"Somebody beamed Danny up," I said, scarcely believing my own recollection of the event.

Grayson locked his eyes with mine. "Whoever or whatever these entities are, I believe they're also behind the theft of the jar containing our vestigial body parts."

I swallowed hard. "*Entities*?"

Grayson nodded. "Whether they're of terrestrial origin or not, I have good reason to believe they're still following us."

I grimaced. "In blue sedans?"

Grayson nodded again.

I set my coffee mug down. "But ... why?"

"On account a drivin' a sedan's a lot faster than walkin'," Earl said, then shoved the rest of a Pop Tart into his giant maw.

Grayson locked eyes with me. "Garth and I believe they may be collecting human DNA in search of individuals with advanced abilities, in order to create human-alien hybrids."

I nearly groaned. "Not that tired old conspiracy theory again."

"Nature calls!" Earl said. "If y'all need me, I'll be in the can. Don't wait up."

I frowned. "But then again, they *did* let Earl go."

"My point exactly," Grayson said. "That action adds a certain credibility to my theory, don't you think?"

"Well, yeah. But if *that's* true, why on Earth would they keep Danny Daniels?"

Grayson rubbed his chin. "I've been wondering that, too. It could be they were going to return Danny, but experienced a transporter anomaly. You saw him struggling in that beam of light. His foot was severed when he kicked through the beam. Perhaps once Danny was damaged, he couldn't be returned."

My nose crinkled. "Are you saying there's some kind of intergalactic return policy?"

"Why wouldn't there be? Danny was damaged, therefore, he needed to be destroyed."

"By spontaneous combustion? You can't be serious."

"Why not?" Grayson said. "You remember the film clip I showed you when we first met. The one of the armed troopers storming a craft, releasing human children from their glass capsules?"

I frowned. "Along with a bunch of other hideous images you used in order to teach me not freak out under pressure. Yeah, I remember. But you said you didn't know if that clip was real, or from an old sci-fi movie or something."

"*Or something* being the operative term here." Grayson pursed his lips. "That *something* could've been evidence of human sampling by alien beings."

My anxiety was building like a pressure cooker full of butterbeans. "Get real, Grayson. If aliens existed, there'd be proof by now!"

"There *is* proof, Drex. Plenty of it."

"What?"

Grayson's shoulders stiffened. "Numerous unexplained signals from outside our solar system have been captured and documented by reputable agencies."

I shook my head. "Not that blasted 'WOW' signal again. That was *one* time. And it happened a million years ago."

"It happened in 1977."

I shook my head. "Right. And not a peep since. Seriously, Gray—"

"Drex," Grayson said, interrupting me.

I frowned. "What?"

"There's been a new one."

Chapter Twenty-Six

"I can't believe it," I said, staring at the article on Grayson's laptop.

After his outrageous claim that aliens were in contact with Earth, I'd made him show me proof. Grayson had found the article online, then shown it to me. And, as the saying goes, once I'd seen it, I couldn't un-see it.

"Did I get that right?" I asked, feeling stunned and confused. "They found *actual radio waves* coming from another planet in another solar system?"

"Correct. Believe me now?" Grayson reached across the banquette table, took the laptop from me, then proceeded to read the article out loud, just to reiterate his point.

"A narrow beam of 980 MHz radio waves were detected in April and May of 2019 by the Parkes telescope in Australia. The signal appears to have come directly from the Proxima Centauri system, just 4.2 light-years from Earth."

"But ...," I stammered. "Couldn't it just have been one of those bouncing radio waves thingies? Like the one that caused the *War of the Worlds* to rebroadcast?"

Grayson shook his head. "Not likely. The 980 Mhz radio band is one that human craft and satellites don't normally use."

I slumped back in my seat. "Oh."

"There's more," Grayson said. "Like the WOW signal, this one also had characteristics of a techno-signature. And perhaps more interestingly, while it was being observed, the signal shifted slightly, in a way that resembled the movement of a planet."

I winced. "Does this proximate century system have any Earth-like planets?"

"Proxima Centauri," Grayson corrected. "As far as we know, the system revolves around a single rocky body, and one gas giant."

Down the hallway, Earl flushed the toilet.

I closed my eyes.

Boy, can I ever relate to that ...

I WANTED TO DROP THE subject of alien communication. It was giving me the willies. I'd even braved the bathroom after Earl got out in an attempt to trade one earth-shattering scenario for another.

But Grayson wouldn't let it go. When I returned from my shower, he was still tucked in the booth, studying something on his laptop. He glanced up at me.

"Drex, did you know that the Parkes Telescope that discovered the signal I told you about is part of a new, hundred-million dollar Breakthrough Listen project?"

I sighed and slipped into the booth opposite him. "No, I didn't. But I have a feeling you're going to tell me."

"Well, yes." Grayson appeared confused. "Why else would I bring it up?"

Why indeed ...

"The Parkes Telescope's main charter is to hunt for radio signals from technological sources beyond our solar system."

"And it found one. Yay. I get it." I drummed my nails on the table, becoming more and more uncomfortable with the world as I knew it.

Grayson smiled, a faraway look in his eyes. "Think of it, Drex. That's just *one* project we *know* about, thanks to *Scientific American* and *The Guardian*. There could be dozens more we're yet to be made privy to."

Dear lord. I hope not.

"Okay, fine, Grayson," I said, a twinge of paranoia crawling up my spine. "Say aliens *did* come down from Alpha Centauri and fry Danny Daniels foot off. Then they chased Earl out of the Walmart parking lot in his monster truck. What in the world would they want with a pickle jar full of our spare body parts?"

"Most likely for human genetic sampling, like I've already explained. They must be searching for something uncommon. Otherwise, given all the reported abductions, they should have already collected a scientifically valid sample base by now."

A shiver ran down my spine. I thought about the scar on Grayson's abdomen where his extraneous appendage used to be. His family had nicknamed it his "nubbin." Its removal during his childhood had left him with the appearance of having two navels. Now it was in the possession of whoever took that blasted pickle jar. They also had the vestigial twin removed from my brain. What a bunch of sickos!

I locked eyes with Grayson. "My brain tumor thingy and your nubbin. Those were just deformities, right? Why would any alien in their right mind want them?"

Grayson shrugged. "Perhaps for their sheer novelty."

"Novelty?"

"Yes. Perhaps they were targeted by an intergalactic P.T. Barnum out collecting oddities from around the universe."

My nose crinkled.

Seriously? I'm not just a freak here on Earth, but throughout the known universe?

"The samples themselves would be of little value to a serious researcher," Grayson said.

"Why not?"

"Our vestigial parts possesses no points of comparison."

I frowned. "What do you mean?"

"Just like Mothman scat or chupacabra hair, DNA testing of samples can capture a genetic profile. But unless a verified *base specimen* is available for comparison, the genetic profile can only be categorized as an 'unclassified sample.'"

I shrugged. "So what?"

"Drex, a serious collector would want to classify his or her findings with a verified base specimen. After all, without provenance, all they would possess is two hunks of mystery meat in a jar."

"Oh. How do they get a verified specimen?"

Grayson reached out and took my hand. "The only way they would be able to validate their research is to collect a DNA sample from each of us."

A sense of dread crept up my spine. I swallowed hard. "Thus, the blue sedans."

Grayson nodded. "Precisely."

Chapter Twenty-Seven

After my discussion with Grayson, I couldn't sleep. Stalkers in blue sedans? Killer crocs? Alien abductions? No sex for two years?

I couldn't decide which was harder to wrap my head around. Either way, this wasn't exactly shaping up to be the life I'd envisioned fifteen years ago, when I'd stood in my cap and gown holding my freshly minted Bachelor's Degree in Art Appreciation.

After tossing and turning for nearly an hour, I sat up in my chair-bed and sighed. Then I dragged myself to the kitchen to get a swig of mescal.

As I fished around in the drawer I'd hidden the bottle in, I spotted Grayson sitting at the banquette in the dark like a ghostly apparition. Needless to say, I nearly slammed the drawer on my fingers.

"Jeezy-petes!" I squealed.

"Good. You're up," he said. "It's time."

I hid the bottle behind my back. "Time for what? To beam me up, Scotty?"

"Time for your annual evaluation."

I choked on my own spit. "My *what*?"

"As your private investigator mentor, it's time I conducted an annual review of your progress."

"Oh." I tucked the bottle in my back pocket. "So, how am I doing so far, boss?"

Grayson flicked on an overhead light, then tapped a finger on the table. "I have to say, your attitude could use some improvement."

I winced. "Can I get you a cup of coffee, sir?"

"It's a little late for that."

"Crap. I've already failed?"

"What? No. I don't drink coffee after five. It's bad for the digestion."

"Oh. Okay. Pop Tart, perhaps?"

"No. Sit down."

"Okay." I plunked into the banquette booth opposite him.

"First off," Grayson said, "let me begin by saying that the fact that you don't know the difference between entomology and etymology bugs me beyond words."

"Huh?"

Grayson smiled like a praying mantis. "It was a little joke. To lighten the mood."

"Oh." Sitting on the bottle hurt my butt cheek. "Ha ha. Good one, sir."

Grayson's brow furrowed. "I read in the managerial handbook that it was best to establish a friendly rapport before introducing hard topics."

I cringed. "Hard topics?"

"I'll cut to the chase. I'm not sure your personality is right for the job. Your attitude—"

"Look, Grayson. About my attitude. I don't really mean it. I've kind of had a few hard knocks lately, you know?"

"So you're saying the constant sarcasm is a ruse?"

"Huh? No. I've never faked a sarcasm in my life."

Grayson cocked his head. "Then you're genuinely unhappy with both your job and your colleagues?"

"No. What I mean is ... I use sarcasm as a defense mechanism. A way of coping with the stress."

"The stress of encountering cryptids?"

"Well, that and stuff like having to hide from cops under a tarp with a plastic woman whom you find more attractive than me."

Grayson stiffened. "I told you. I was only using it as a decoy."

I stifled a scowl. "Right. Anyway, about my attitude. I'm not saying I feel unhappy. It's more like *awkward*."

"You feel awkward?"

I shrugged. "Yeah. Half the time, I feel like I don't know what I'm supposed to be doing. And then, when I actually *do* something, I end up embarrassing myself. Being wrong all the time can get on a girl's nerves, you know?"

Grayson's eyebrow did its Spock thing. "Intriguing. I thought *I* was the one always in the wrong."

I smirked. "Well, you're *wrong* about that."

We locked eyes, then shared a brief laugh.

"I've missed moments like this," Grayson said.

"Me, too."

"Feeling better?"

I smiled. "Yes."

"Good." Grayson glanced down at his laptop. "Then let's get started with the evaluation."

I blanched. "What?"

"First off, do you have any questions?"

"Well, yeah. There is something I've been wondering about."

"What?"

"Do you think Deinosuchas roared? I mean, who's to say it didn't moo like a cow?"

Grayson stared at me blankly. "I meant questions about the *P.I. job*."

"Oh." I frowned. "See? That's exactly what I meant earlier. I'm awkward. I'm a screw-up! A screw-up who can't keep a job *or* a boyfriend." I let out a sigh. "I feel so dumb compared to you!"

Grayson sat back in his seat. "Compared to *me*? A science nerd whose parents dress up like Batman and Cat Woman and skulk around ComiCon for kicks?"

I grinned. "Hey, nobody's perfect."

"Exactly." Grayson's cheek dimpled. "So use some of that logic on yourself, Cadet."

I took in a deep breath. "Okay. I'll try."

"Tell me, Drex. Why did you drop your whole life and join me a year ago? What were you hoping to achieve?"

"Well, at the time, it wasn't much of a life to drop, as you may recall. And, if I'm being totally honest, it isn't that much better now."

Grayson pursed his lips. "I see. You've had three months off to think about what you want to do with your life. I thought you would come back invigorated. Enthusiastic to continue our investigations. I'm disappointed to say I'm not feeling that."

I winced. "I'm sorry. I guess this hasn't turned out quite like I hoped it would. I want ... *more*."

"Diving into the unknown isn't enough for you?"

"No." I stared longingly into his eyes.

I want you, too.

Grayson sighed. "Well, if that's how you feel, Drex, I won't hold you to the next year of the internship."

I nearly gasped. "What? You won't?"

"No." He shook his head. "As long as you give this last investigation your *all*, that is. In return, I'll write you an outstanding recommendation. I'll even pass it along to a fellow investigator I know in Miami."

"You'd *do* that?"

"Of course. I want to see you happy."

I scowled. "I meant, you'd just *ditch me* like that? Without another thought? After all we've been through?"

Grayson's face puckered with confusion. "I don't get it, Drex. I thought that's what you wanted."

"Nick Grayson, for someone who's supposed to be a trained observer, you can't even see what's staring you right in the face! Fine. I'll help you catch your stupid dinosaur alligator. Then I'm leaving. For good."

Grayson reached for my hand. "I don't—"

Suddenly, a huge blast sounded outside. The RV rattled like a death trap.

The side door flew open. Earl scrambled inside like a cockroach after somebody turned on the lights.

"Y'all ain't gonna believe this!" he gasped, his eyes big as golf balls. "That ol' lady Tarminger's boat sank!"

I glared at my cousin. "Of course it did. It's a garbage scow. Now if you don't mind, we're in the middle of something import—"

"You don't get it," Earl said. "Denny's out there hollerin' her head off! Looks like Chomp went and got him the rest of Tommy Tarminger!"

Chapter Twenty-Eight

An evil smirk curled my lips at the thought of how the man who stole my father's business out from under me had met his untimely end.

Chomp finished off Tommy Tarminger. Couldn't have happened to a nicer guy.

As I followed Earl and Grayson out of the RV, we stumbled into a scene straight out of *Lord of the Flies*. Everywhere I looked, men in camo ran to and fro around the grounds, their faces streaked with brown, black and green war paint.

They banded together in circles, hooting, hollering, and thrusting their bang-sticks in the air like the spears of savage warriors.

"Geez," I said. "Are they shooting a remake of *Apocalypse Now* nobody told me about?"

The biggest crowd of men was gathered around a picnic table near the bait store. I stood on tiptoe, straining to see between two smelly men. One sported an unwashed mullet, the other a greasy rattail.

As I parted their body odor like a curtain, I got a glimpse of the main attraction. Lo and behold, standing atop the table was Denny Tarminger herself. She was wet as a drowned rat and pontificating like a preacher on the last day of a Southern Baptist tent revival.

"It was Chomp, I tell ya!" she hollered, her beady eyes shining like two black olives. "And I ought to know. I seen him afore!"

"What happened to Tommy?" somebody yelled.

"I'll tell you what happened!" Denny shouted back. "That monster gator leapt right into our boat, that's what! Before I could even holler,

'Watch out!' he snatched Tommy in his jaws and pulled him under that black water. I barely escaped with my life!"

"How big was Ol Chomp?" someone shouted from the crowd.

"I don't rightly know," Denny hollered back. "But I can tell you this. His head was the size of a ridin' lawnmower! And every one of his teeth as big as a slice of peach pie!"

I felt an elbow nudge my gut. "Tole you!" Earl said. "Teeth that big? It's gotta be Grayson's dookeysaurus!"

I glanced around. "Where *is* Grayson?"

"Right here."

I turned around and found my nose pressed into the black fabric covering his rock-hard chest. I looked up. "What are we gonna do now, fearless leader?"

He looked down at me, surprised. "You actually want to participate?"

"I told you I would. One last time." I poked a finger in his chest. "For a good recommendation, right?"

"Hey Denny!" someone yelled. "Where'd you spot that godawful beasticle?"

"Just past the bridge," the old woman said. "I believe that murderous monster's headed for Lake George. We gotta stop it afore it gets there. If we don't, we'll never find it!"

Somebody shouted, "Let's get that gator!"

A war cry rang out from the crowd. It was swiftly followed by a cacophony of whoops and howls. Then, like a herd of charging wildebeests, the whole dirty horde of men took off for their boats. Before I could even make a snide comment, I heard the first boat motor crank to life.

"Let's go with 'em!" Earl said.

I grabbed his arm. "This is a redneck feeding frenzy. It's not safe to get out in that free-for-all!"

"I concur," Grayson said. "Let the first wave of hunters head out, then we'll go. It's only three o'clock. Legal hunting hours don't start until five. Let's go back to the RV, gather our weapons, and make a rational plan before we partake in the search for Chomp."

"So, what's the plan?" I asked.

"Clean out your ears," Earl said. "Grayson just said. The plan's to not end up as rations partaken by Ol' Chomp."

Chapter Twenty-Nine

We were back inside the motorhome discussing various tactics to capture Ol' Chomp without ending up chomped ourselves. Between the murderous mescal moth larva, the strangling size-XS T-shirt, and now Earl captaining our gator-hunting boat, the odds of me surviving my last mission with Grayson weren't looking good.

Not good at all.

I was savoring what could very well have been the last blueberry Pop Tart of my life when a knock sounded at the RV door. I opened it to find a law officer standing there. I recognized his teeth. He, however, didn't recognize me. Not without my Aunt Vera old-lady wig on.

Aww, crap!

"Hello," he said. "I'm Officer McVitty. River Patrol. I'm looking for the man who gave me the ... uh ... *bait container* earlier today. Who are you?"

"I ... uh ..."

"Howdy, officer," Earl said, wrapping a heavy arm around my shoulders. "This here's my cousin Bobbie. She *ain't* my Aunt Vera. Nope. Not at all. That poor ol' gal just hightailed it outta here a minute ago. Poor ol' Tommy getting' swallered up by Chomp really spooked her good."

"I see," Officer McVitty said. "Strange. I didn't notice any vehicles leaving the campsite."

"Naw," Earl said. "Aunt Vera usually rides a broom." He glanced over at me. "She was pretty sore we used the handle to make gator plugs, wasn't she, Bobbie?"

I grimaced out a smile. "Yeah. You looking for Grayson? He's indisposed at the moment."

"No he ain't," Earl said. "He's on the john. Come on in. You want a cup a coffee, Officer McVittles?"

I TRIED TO DISCOURAGE Earl from telling Officer McVitty all the reasons I wasn't Aunt Vera, but my cousin had apparently developed callouses on his shins and was immune to my boot-toe suggestions. When Grayson finally emerged from the restroom, I jumped up from the booth to try and warn him. But he didn't give me the chance.

"Officer," Grayson said, looking past me toward the kitchen. "What brings you here? Don't tell me you've already gotten a DNA analysis on the container of mystery gravy we gave you this morning."

"No," McVitty said. "That could take a few days. I just wanted to let you know what we found during a search of the area. And I wondered if you had any more information for me."

"Nothing." Grayson made himself a coffee. "So, what did you find out?"

McVitty sat back in the booth. "There were signs of gator activity along that general area of the riverbank by the bridge."

"What kind of signs?" I asked.

"The usual. Mashed down reeds. Wallowed-out places. And a pile of rotting vegetation that could be an alligator nest."

"Could be?" I asked. "You can't tell?"

"Too dangerous to get close enough." McVitty angled an eyebrow. "Gators are masters of the ambush attack. And they don't take kindly to anyone messing with their nests. They'd attack a tank if it got too near." He glanced around at the three of us. "I'd appreciate you all keeping that information on the down-low."

"Sure," I said. "Would a gator really attack a tank to protect its eggs?"

"Absolutely," Grayson said. "For the primitive reptilian brain, there's nothing stronger than the survival instinct."

"I'd agree, with one modification," McVitty said.

Grayson did his Spock impression. "What's that?"

McVitty smiled. "There's nothing stronger than *maternal* instinct. A mother's love. But then again, what would any of us guys know about that?"

I sighed. "So, you think it was a gator that got him?"

"Can't say for sure." McVitty stretched his shoulders. "You might not know this, Bobbie, just joining us other guys here and all. But two men went missing four days ago. Buddy Barlowe and Fatback Taylor."

"Earl filled me in," I said. "He told me Denny Tarminger said you were the one who found their boat."

McVitty cleared his throat. "That's right."

"What do you think happened to them?" I asked.

McVitty sighed. "Knowing those two, they could've gotten in a fight and done each other in. Then fallen out of the boat and the gators got their leftovers. But there wasn't enough evidence in the boat to draw any conclusions. No blood. No sign of a struggle. Nothing."

"I thought the boat was bit half in two," Earl said.

"Just a rumor," McVitty said.

"Dang," Earl said. "Not even a tooth mark?"

"Well, when we searched the area, we did find *this*." McVitty reached into his shirt pocket and pulled out what appeared to be an oversized arrowhead. "Found this lying on the riverbank."

"*Otodus megalodon*," Grayson said, taking the object from McVitty.

"Otis who?" Earl asked. "Did he get kilt too?"

I frowned. "Grayson, what are you talking about?"

"A big tooth." He held the triangular object up to the ceiling light.

My face soured. "No kidding."

Grayson stopped staring at the tooth and shot me a look. "Otodus megalodon literally means 'big tooth.'"

"Did it come from that giant dookey-saurus?" Earl asked.

"No," Grayson and Officer McVitty said simultaneously.

Grayson handed the black, triangular object back to McVitty. "That's a fossilized shark tooth."

"You're exactly right," McVitty said. "We find them pretty often around the river banks and shorelines around here. I brought it by because I didn't want you greenhorns thinking this was some kind of monster alligator tooth, like some of the locals believe. But I see you all seem to know your stuff."

Grayson nodded. "Rest assured, Officer McVitty, we're not ones to go off on wild goose chases."

I nearly snorted.

Just wild monster *chases.*

"Glad to hear that." McVitty set down his empty coffee cup and began scooting out of the booth. "I best be going. As you saw for yourselves, there are a lot of yahoos out there who need supervising. You all be careful and try to stay out of trouble, okay?"

"We will," Grayson said. "And thank you for the warning."

"You're welcome. Thanks for turning in Buddy's eyeball. I appreciate the professional courtesy." He handed Grayson back the tooth. "Here, you keep this one. I got a pile of 'em at home."

Grayson smiled. "Thank you."

As the door closed behind McVitty, Earl turned to Grayson, crestfallen. "So there ain't no giant croc after all?"

I laughed. "Oh, there's a giant crock, all right."

"Perhaps not," Grayson said. "I could've been mistaken. We could be looking at the return not of Deinosuchas, but of Megalodon."

Good grief!

"Ol' big tooth is back?" Earl asked, his eyes wide. "Is it any kin to Bigfoot?"

"Yeah," I said. "Just like you're kin to Bigmouth."

"Big mouth, indeed." Grayson turned the tooth over in his palm. "Extrapolating from the size of teeth like this one, it's believed Megalodon could've reached up to 67 feet in length, with massive jaws that could exert a bite force of over 180,000 newtons."

"Boy howdy," Earl said. "That's a lot a figgy fruitcakes."

I shook my head. "It most certainly is."

Chapter Thirty

I snatched the big, black tooth from Grayson's hand. "Geez. From what you say, this Megalodon makes Deinosuchas look like a wimpy gecko. Do you really think whatever's killing people is a giant shark instead of a giant alligator?"

"That would explain the lack of sightings," Grayson said. "And why all the attacks apparently occurred in the water."

"But Denny said it was a gator what took Tommy," Earl said.

"That mercenary old hag's as legendary a liar as her lousy cousin Tommy," I said. "But Earl's got a point, Grayson. Alligators hang out in the water, too."

Grayson rubbed his chin. "True, but alligators prefer to stalk their prey on land, or along the water's surface."

I looked up at him from studying the fossilized tooth in my hand. "Why's that?"

"Simple anatomy. They're air breathers. They also typically employ their complete bodies during an attack."

"Complete bodies?" Earl asked.

Grayson nodded. "Yes. Instead of just using its bite as a weapon, an alligator's mouth and tail act together. Their tails sweep things toward their waiting jaws, like a broom to a dustpan." Grayson shot me a smirk. "But perhaps that particular analogy is lost on you."

I shot him a death glare. "Excuse me? I do my fair share of cleaning around here. And what's with all the stupid broom jokes, anyway?"

"What's wrong with adding a little levity to the situation?" Grayson asked. "Chasing potentially lethal cryptids can be a stressful occupation."

"So can avoiding potentially lethal gas attacks," I said. "But I don't make it my business to joke about it. By the way, on that note, no more franks and beans for dinner again. *Ever*. Got it?"

"Got it." Grayson smiled. "Listen, let's all lay down our arms and lighten up. Deal?"

I sighed. "Deal."

"Good." Grayson glanced at the clock on the wall. "And on *that* note, it's five o'clock. Time to head out."

"With our arms laid down?" Earl asked. "How we gonna catch a gator without no arms?"

I smirked. "The same way you manage to stay alive with no brain."

Grayson shot me a stern look.

I backtracked and tapped a finger to my temple. "By using your noodle instead, Earl."

My cousin beamed. "All right! I'll go get the pool noodles outta Bessie right now!"

AS WE MOTORED DOWNRIVER, I got to thinking. "Grayson, who's to say that whatever's killing people around here is the work of just one animal? What if it's both Deinosuchas *and* Megalodon?"

"The thought had occurred to me, but I dismissed it."

"Why?"

"The odds of two creatures undergoing reiterative evolution simultaneously seemed preposterous."

I blanched. "Seriously? *That's* your problem with it?"

Grayson put a finger to his lips. "Shhh! The bridge is coming up. I believe this could be the alligatoroid's lair."

"Alligatoroid?" I asked. "I thought we were looking for Deinosuchas, not a gator with hemorrhoids."

"I'm beginning to have my doubts about Deinosuchas. I'll defer to the scientific term alligatoroid from here on out."

My nose crinkled "Why not just *alligator*?"

"I feel it pertinent to distinguish the creature we seek from normal alligators," Grayson said. "An alligatoroid is an animal with alligator-like attributes. Just like something with human-like attributes is labeled humanoid."

"I get it." I glanced over at Earl. I was chomping at the bit to rip him a new one, but I thought better of it and changed my target. "I guess that makes Tommy Tarminger a *human* hemorrhoid, huh?"

"Shh!" Grayson shushed me as we passed under the small bridge's arch. His warning echoed off the span like the hiss of a tire going flat.

"Hey! Who's out there?" a voice called out from overhead. As we motored through to the other side of the bridge, we could see a man standing on the road in the middle of the span, a pair of binoculars in his hand.

"Howdy!" Earl called out. "We're looking for us a humongous gatoroid. What're you up to?"

"I'm the bridge tender," he called back.

"Excellent," Grayson said. "Have you seen anything unusual in the river lately?"

"Well, now that you mention it, yeah," the man said. "I'm usually gone by dusk, but with all the hullabaloo about Tommy getting eaten by Chomp, I stayed around today. About an hour ago, I saw something large go by underwater heading downstream. I was hoping to get another look at it."

"What do you think it was?" I asked.

"It looked like an overturned boat, at first" he said. "But then I realized it wasn't."

"How did you draw that conclusion?" Grayson asked.

The man glanced to his left, then right, then back down at us. "Because boats don't have tails."

I gasped. "The thing had a tail?"

The guy nodded. "Yeah. And arms and legs."

"Sounds like you got a fairly good look at it," Grayson said. "Do you think it could've been an alligator?"

"Maybe," he said. "If it was, it was the biggest one I've ever seen."

"Chomp?" I asked.

The bridge tender shrugged. "I dunno."

"Why didn't you call the police or something?" I asked.

He cringed. "Well, to be honest, I'd just smoked a number when the thing went swimming by. It gets pretty boring around here, you know?"

I can only imagine.

"That could prove to be a costly move," Grayson said. "You know there's a five-thousand dollar reward on Chomp's head, right?"

"Yeah." The guy shook his head. "But that's just it. The thing I saw didn't look like it had a head. It looked like something had bitten it clean off."

Chapter Thirty-One

"Don't tell me you actually believe that pothead?" I said as we motored out of earshot of the guy standing on the bridge.

"Why would he lie?" Grayson asked. "He admitted to being under the influence. To me, that adds credibility to his statement. And he also renewed my belief in Deinosuchas."

"But he said the creature he saw was as big as a boat," I argued. "That's not *that* off the scale for a regular alligator, is it?"

Grayson nodded. "I thought the same thing, until he said it was missing its head. If something truly did bite it off, that confirms there's a creature in this river that's well beyond the growth parameters of Alligator *mississippiensis*."

Earl grimaced. "If you're right, Mr. G., we're gonna need us a bigger boat."

I shook my head. "Gimme a break. The guy was *stoned*. He was just seeing things!"

Suddenly, our boat hit something on the starboard bow, sending me lunging forward. "What was that?" I asked, trying not to sound panicked.

Earl glanced over at the river, then back to me. "Looks like we hit a tree branch. But it's gettin' too dark to see. Bobbie, look over the side and see if that dad-burned limb damaged the hull."

I flipped on my flashlight and examined the side of the hull. "Just a scratch. Nothing to worry about."

Suddenly, a deep, rattling, cough-like sound echoed across the water. I jerked back upright into the boat. "Was that a gator talking?"

"Couldn't be," Grayson said.

"Why not?" I asked.

Grayson frowned. "Alligators don't have vocal cords. Instead, they suck in air and expel it from their lungs, like a bellows."

"Sure sounded like somebody bellowin' to me," Earl said.

"That term does more accurately describe the reptile's vocalizations," Grayson said, shining his flashlight around in the water. "I'm surprised we haven't heard more of them before now."

"Seriously?" I groaned. "So you're saying alligators are the *chatty*?"

"Actually, alligators are among the most vocal reptiles on the planet. They can make a variety of sounds, depending on whether they seek to find mates, warn off competitors, defend their territories, or whatnot."

I scowled. "Thanks for the science lesson, Mr. Wizard. So, what kind of call was *that*?"

Grayson rubbed his chin. "I'd say it was a chumpf."

"A what?" Earl and I asked in unison.

"A chumpf," Grayson repeated. "It wasn't a growl or a hiss or a roar. So it must be what's called a chumpf."

"Okay," I said. "I'll bite. So why do gators chumpf?"

Grayson's eyebrow shot up like Spock's. "I don't know."

The cough-like rattle sounded again. Closer this time. It was coming from somewhere upriver—between us and the route we had to traverse to get back to the docks of the Rangler Resort.

"Let's head over and check it out," Grayson said. "Earl, make it so."

"You got it, Chief." Earl turned the boat around, then gunned the throttle. "Hey Bobbie, what's that shinin' up there in the water ahead of us?"

I leaned over the side. My flashlight caught the amber glint of what appeared to be a bicycle reflector. I laughed. "McVitty's right. People throw all kinds of garbage into this poor river."

I reached a hand into the water to try and grab it. Then I yanked back my fingers as if the water were boiling hot.

The amber glint I'd spotted wasn't coming from a bike reflector.

It was an eyeball.

An eyeball attached to the head of a gigantic, open-jawed, prehistoric beast.

Chapter Thirty-Two

"Mwwaaaack!" I screeched. "Dalimater!"

"What?" Earl said.

"Dangosaurus!" I gasped.

"What?" Grayson asked.

I sucked in a lungful of air and screamed, "Get us the hell out of here!"

Chapter Thirty-Three

"Lawd a Mercy!" Earl hollered. "Denny weren't lyin'! That gator's head's as big as a John Deere!"

"Shut up, Earl!" I screamed. "And get us the hell out of here!"

Earl gunned the skiff's outboard. We took off with a mind-jolting jerk, whipping up a foamy wake as we sped upriver away from the monstrous, orange-eyed beast lurking in the black water below us.

The sun was gone. A spooky mist was coming off the water. It was the perfect horror-movie scene for a massive beast to spring from the murky depths and swallow us whole.

"Faster, Earl!" I screeched, aiming my headlamp to illuminate the river ahead.

The white arch of the bridge appeared in the gloom, shimmering like a portal to another dimension. I hoped it was. Better to end up on another planet than as a dinosaur's dinner.

"I didn't get to see it," Grayson said, sounding disappointed as we blew beneath the bridge. "Was it Deinosuchas?"

"How the hell should I know?" My knuckles clamped a white death grip on the side of the boat hull. "But it sure as shit was no shark!" I tightened my grasp then turned my head and yelled, "For crying out loud, Earl! Can't you make this thing go any faster?"

"I'm givin' it all she's got," Earl hollered. The skiff bounced on the surface of the river as if propelled by a jet engine. "Hold on, Cuz. The bend's comin' up ahead. We ain't got that much farther."

Thank God. We're in the clear!

But we weren't. As our skiff rounded the bend in the river, I spotted another boat making its *own* waves—and it was on a collision course right for us!

"Watch out!" I screamed.

Earl swerved just in time.

"Lawdy, we must a missed each other by two inches," he hollered, throttling down the engine.

"I'd estimate ten millimeters," Grayson said, adjusting his headlamp.

"Thanks for that observation," I said to Grayson. "You can't see a forty-foot gator, but you can see a two-inch near miss."

Behind us, the boat we almost collided with circled back around and pulled up beside us. "You all okay?" the driver asked, giving me the once over. "Geez. You look white as a ghost!"

"Willie!" I gasped. "You guys watch out. There's a giant alligator out there! Just past the bridge!"

Willie shot a glance at the other man with him. Then he looked back at me and grinned. "Did it have big, orange eyes?"

I blanched. "Yes! Did you seen it, too?"

Willie laughed. "Yeah. Lots of times. That's McGatortail's mascot. It blew off their roof when that tornado came through here last July."

"Oh," I said.

Behind me, Earl snickered.

A wave of relief and embarrassment coursed through me, leaving me uncertain whether to laugh or cry. I shook my head. "But it looked so *real*."

"Hey, guys!" Willie called out to the other boats angling around nearby. "Looks like old McGatortail got him some more tourists!"

A chorus of hoots and guffaws echoed off the riverbank. Whether we were being heckled or honored, I couldn't tell.

"Drex, you should've known better," Grayson said, leaning over and putting a hand on my shoulder. "I told you that alligators' eyes reflect *red*, not orange. Because of the "tapetum lucidum."

"Right," I said, my own eyes seeing red. "What could I *possibly* have been thinking?"

Earl winked at me and tapped a finger to his noggin. "Should a used your ol' pool *noodle*, Cuz."

I glared at him.

I'll use a noodle, all right. A metal *noodle—right upside your big, fat head!*

I reached for the bang stick fastened to the inner side of the hull. As my fingers wrapped around the pipe, a man's voice blasted across the water.

"Listen up, y'all!"

I let go of the bang stick and my plan to murderize Earl. There were too many witnesses around, anyway. I turned back to face the small armada of flats boats gathered in the dark at the river bend.

"Everybody give a listen!"

I stood on tiptoe and squinted into the fading light, trying to see who'd called out for everyone to listen. I spotted him in a battered old jon boat. A beer-bellied old hillbilly standing atop a Coleman cooler.

He held his hands to his lips like a megaphone, then hollered, "Everybody to the Rangler Resort! Somebody just dragged in a big'un!"

For a moment, dead silence fell across the river as everyone's reptilian brains seized up, trying to process the information.

Then someone let out an audacious, "Whoooeeee!" and all hell broke loose.

The river exploded, whipped into a frenzy of white foam by a stampede of rednecks, each stoking their big Johnsons for all they were worth.

Chapter Thirty-Four

As we pulled up to the rickety docks of the Rangler RV Resort, we got our first glimpse of the huge gator that had caused a flotilla stampede back to the campgrounds.

"That feller weren't kiddin'," Earl said. "That's a big'un, all right!"

Though night had fallen like a thick, wet blanket, the campground along the docks was lit up like the noon-day sun. Someone had set up spotlights—and they all appeared to be aimed at one particular section of shoreline.

And rightly so. Because lying on the riverbank was the biggest damned alligator I'd ever laid eyes on.

The lower half of the beast was still in the water. A milk jug bobbed lazily in the water beside it, attached with a yellow nylon stringer to a harpoon in the gator's back. Even though the reptile was only partially in view, I could tell it had to be one for the record books.

Whoever had trapped the gator had also finagled a noose around its neck and right front leg. At the other end of the rope, a conga line of sweaty men were fully engaged in a tug-of-war with the carcass of the beast. The grunts and groans were audible from fifty feet away, as they labored to haul the reptile's huge, limp carcass to shore.

"There's an eyeball drawn on that milk jug," I said to Grayson. "That must be the same gator we saw when we were out with Denny. You think it also rammed our boat?"

"Indeterminable," Grayson said.

"Terminator or not, I'm tellin' ya, that's one monster-ass gator," Earl said, tying off the boat. "Let's go check it out!" He tossed the end of the rope, then turned and sprinted down the dock toward the crowd gathered around the spectacle.

"Is the creature still alive?" Grayson asked, as we worked our way to a ringside view.

"Geez. I sure hope not," I said as we broke through to the front of the crowd.

Our timing was impeccable.

With a final grunt, the sweaty gator hunters pulled the rest of the beast out of the water. When the bulk of its torso hit the slick grass beyond the riverbank, the friction must've lessened. The gator's body suddenly shot forward, sending half the tug-of-war champs tumbling backward onto the ground.

As they gathered themselves up and onto their feet again, a guy with a long gray beard and a cowboy hat stepped forward and yelled, "Make way, y'all!"

The crowd parted like the Redneck Sea.

"Who's that?" I asked, elbowing Willie, who'd ended up beside me.

"The guy in the cowboy hat? That's Moses. He's the one who caught the gator."

"No," I said. "The *other* guy."

The "other guy" I was referring to was buff, handsome, and a foot taller than most of the other men on the scene. He strutted along beside Moses through the gap parted in the crowd. Clad in nothing but a pair of well-fitting, low-rider jeans and a devilish grin, he strode confidently over to the dead gator.

"That's Johnny Rango," Willie said. "He's a genu-wine Seminole Indian. And a professional alligator wrestler, to boot."

Saliva pooled around my tongue as I stared at Johnny's smooth, hairless chest. "What a man!"

"I know," Willie said. "Every guy here wishes he was Johnny Rango."

Johnny turned and waved to the crowd, sending the long, black braid running down his rippled back swaying like a pendulum. Wielding a roll of silver duct tape, he stepped over the gator with one leg, straddling the animal where its thick neck met its front legs. As the crowd cheered, he slowly lowered his fabulous buttocks onto the gator's back.

Damn. Never thought I'd wish to be a dead gator.

But just as Johnny's fabulous butt hit the infamous gator's hide, the beast suddenly sprang to life. The humongous reptile let out a hiss worthy of a steam engine. Then, as quick as lightning, its massive tail whipped around, knocking poor old Moses clean out of his cowboy boots.

"Watch out, Johnny!" I gasped as the gator's eyes and jaws snapped open simultaneously.

But it was Moses who had to worry. The gator stood up on its short legs and roared. Writhing under the weight of Johnny Rango, it tried to swing its head around to take a chunk out of Moses, who was laid out cold on the ground. But like a superhero from an action movie, Johnny yanked hard on the noose around the beast's neck, distracting it from the old man sprawled in the grass.

"Did you see that?" Grayson said, elbowing me. "The gator employed the 'broom and dustpan' move, just like in the article I read."

"Uh-huh, whatever," I said absently, feeling a bit swept off my feet myself.

"Stay back!" Johnny called out to the crowd.

Everyone responded with a gasp and a step backward.

While Johnny got busy wrangling the gator, two men crept forward and grabbed old Moses, who'd woken up and was crawling away like a drunk toddler. As they helped the poor guy to safety, I watched in awe as Johnny gripped the gator with his muscular legs and held onto the noose like a rodeo star atop a bucking bronco.

"Get 'em, Johnny!" someone in the crowd yelled out. I think it was me ...

Johnny smiled, then put a finger to his lips to hush the crowd. "Time for this one to go to sleep," he said.

The men all went silent. Then, to my surprise, the gator actually settled down for a moment.

That's when Johnny made his move—so swiftly I almost missed it.

Johnny leaned over and pressed his bodyweight onto the gator's head, forcing its top jaw to the ground. The massive maw of the gator clapped shut with a *click* that reminded me of the sound Grandma Selma's Sunday pocketbook used to make when she'd snap it closed.

Afraid for Johnny and what may come next, I wanted to close my eyes. But I couldn't. Morbid fascination overtook me.

I found myself cheering with the others as Johnny held the gator's jaws closed with one hand, and wrapped silver duct tape around its snout with the other. Then (I suspect just for show) Johnny tore off the end of the duct tape with his perfect teeth, tied it into a bow, and stuck it atop the beast's head.

The crowd exploded into hoots and hollers—me included. After a minute or so, Moses stepped forward and raised his hands. The noise of the crowd died down.

"Your kill," Moses said to Johnny.

"You sure?" Johnny asked. "You caught it."

Moses nodded. "And you saved my life. Do me the honor, would you?"

Johnny grinned. "Gladly."

Without another word, Johnny pulled a ten-inch dagger from a leather sheath on his waistband. He looked up at the heavens for a moment. Then he took aim and plunged the knife into the base of the gator's huge skull.

The knife went in so deep the blade disappeared all the way to the handle. A lungful of air escaped from between the gator's taped-up jaws. The life deflated out of it like a punctured tire.

Johnny patted the beast's head. Then he stood, raised his dagger in the air, and let out a warrior yell.

The crowd returned his cry with their own whoops and catcalls. Then they rushed toward Johnny like he was giving away beef jerky and ball caps.

Chapter Thirty-Five

A few brave souls dared to poke the giant gator to be sure it had been thoroughly dispatched by Johnny and his dagger of death. Then fifteen or twenty men grabbed ahold of the beast and hauled it up to the concrete slab of the parking lot for further inspection.

"That guy's a walkin' legend," Earl said, nodding toward the dashing gator wrestler in tight-fitting jeans.

I admired Johnny's butt. "You can say that again."

Earl shook his head. "I ain't seen nobody that brave since that orderly at the old folks' home tried to take away Aunt Vera's puddin' cup afore she was done with it."

"Johnny might've been hard on that gator," I said, "but he sure isn't hard on the eyes. I'm gonna go talk to him."

"What for?" Grayson asked.

"To see if he knows the way to San Jose," I quipped. "Or maybe Funky Town."

I took off, making a beeline for Johnny. The stunning Chippendales doppelganger had escaped the gawking crowd and was walking alone toward an old, black pickup truck parked behind the camp store.

"Hi, Johnny!" I called out.

In the glow of the parking lot lamppost, I saw Johnny turn and glance around, searching for whoever had called his name.

"That was quite a show," I said. "Can I buy you a beer or something?"

His dark-brown eyes landed on me. "Oh. Thanks, but I don't drink."

I blanched. "Never?"

He laughed in the way I envisioned Apollo did.

"Not if I don't want to get scalped by my wife when I get home," he said,

"Oh," I sighed, feeling the air go out of me like Johnny'd just put a dagger through *my* brain.

He turned back to his pickup and tossed a rope into the open bed. I noticed the back was loaded with five coffin-shaped wooden boxes. Empty ice bags littered the truck bed around them.

I suddenly shivered despite the hot, humid night air. "Uh, you don't have any dead bodies back there, to you?"

"What?" Johnny did a double-take at the truck bed, then shot me his killer smile. "No. I use those crates to haul around live gators."

"Oh. For your show?"

He shrugged one broad, muscular, naked shoulder. "Yes, sometimes. But at the moment, I'm hoping to pick up a few gators during the annual hunting season. I'm nobody special. I can only trap the permitted limit myself. So I have to buy the rest."

"What do you do with all of them?"

He shot me a sly grin. "I take the good-looking ones back and mount their hides. I also sell their meat to the highest bidder."

"Oh."

"Hey Johnny!" I heard Earl bellow from behind me. "You got you one a them wrestling shows in the Everglades?"

I turned and shot my cousin a *get lost* look. But it was no use. Grayson was coming up right behind him.

"Not in the 'Glades," Johnny said. "Outside of Orlando, near Gatorland."

"Aw, yeah!" Earl said. "I used to go there when I was a kid. I ain't been in ages!"

"What are the boxes and ice for?" Grayson asked.

"Like I was telling these guys," Johnny said, "they're for transporting gators. The crates keep them calm. The ice keeps them from overheating in this summer weather."

"I see." Grayson studied Johnny. "Those are some pretty nasty scars on your arms."

I admired the thin, pinkish-white ribbons crisscrossing Johnny's forearms. "I think they look cool."

"How did you acquire them?" Grayson asked. "Knife fights with your quarry?"

"Carelessness, mostly," Johnny said. "Gators don't always give up as easy as that one did. I figure that harpoon and buoy already took most of the fight out of it."

"You think that gator could be Chomp?" I asked. "The one that's been killing people?"

"Killing people?" Johnny's face registering surprise. "I don't know about that. But I seriously doubt it."

"Why?" I asked.

He laughed. "That gator's so old, it's barely got any teeth left."

I blanched. "It sure looked like it had teeth to me!"

"What I meant was—"

"Hold up!" Earl hollered. "Looks like they're fixin' to cut that critter wide open!"

We turned to see the gator lying upside down on a wooden table made for cleaning fish. In the glare of the overhead lights, the table looked to be about twelve feet long, with legs made of fence posts. Even so, it squeaked precariously under the load. The end of gator's tail hung off so far it touched ground.

"Here we go," the old cowboy named Moses said as we scurried over to see the show.

He stood over the beast, wielding a large knife with a hooked end. In one quick movement, he sliced open the gator's belly. A pool of clear liquid poured out. Moses reached inside the gator's body and pulled out the gut sack. It looked like a big, saggy tote bag made of white leather.

My nose crinkled as Moses sliced open the stomach and dumped the contents into a metal washtub on the ground. To everyone's surprise, out tumbled half a blue crab, a pink plastic flip-flop, and a wooden spoon.

"If that don't beat all," Earl said.

"*Omnivorous maximus*," Grayson whispered absently to himself, a fascinated expression on his face.

"There's no accounting for taste," a man standing beside me said. I glanced over to see it was Cheech.

"I guess not," I said, then turned back to the macabre show.

"There's something stuck inside its craw," Moses said. We all stared in silence as he shook the leathery gut sack to empty whatever was hung up in there. Unsuccessful, Moses adjusted his cowboy hat, then reared back and swung the gut balloon against the side of the wooden table. It hit with a sickening, wet *smack*, dislodging whatever was inside.

The unknown object came flying out. It landed inside the metal washtub with loud *clang*. We all waited with bated breath to see what it was. Moses bent over and plucked the object from the washtub. As he stood and held it up, I recognized it immediately. It was the metal pincer prosthesis that used to be attached to Tommy Tarminger's left arm.

"Well, that solves *one* mystery," I said.

"Sheesh," Cheech said, shaking his head. "Can you believe that?"

"Believe what?" I asked. "That the gator ate Tommy?"

"No." He nodded toward the gator. "If that thing really *is* Chomp, then Tommy's story about it biting his arm off is true. At least, it is *now*, anyway."

"What's so hard to believe about that?" I asked.

Cheech shook his head. "It's just that ... well, I never thought I'd live to see the day somebody managed to make an honest man out of Tommy Tarminger."

Chapter Thirty-Six

Officer McVitty turned Tommy Tarminger's pincer prosthesis over in his rubber-gloved hands. "Well, that's something you don't see every day, thank goodness."

After taking pictures of the huge gator, its busted gut sack, and the washtub full of innards, the officer placed the metallic arm into an evidence bag. Then he loaded it—along with the rest of the gruesome items—into his patrol vehicle.

"That's just his arm," I said. "Where's the rest of Tommy?"

McVitty let out a long breath. "The gator probably stuck him up under a submerged log somewhere, to wait for him to soften up."

My gut churned at the thought. That was a fate even someone as repellent as Tommy Tarminger didn't deserve.

"Tommy was one tough old bird," Moses said. "I'm sure he didn't go down without a fight. McVitty, you got what you need here?"

"I suppose so." The game officer washed his hands in the fish-cleaning sink. "Moses, where'd you catch that gator?"

"That's confidential information," he said, adjusting his cowboy hat. "You wouldn't tell nobody your favorite fishing hole, would you?"

McVitty shot him a look. "Gators guard their larders. I'm going to need to call in some divers as soon as day breaks."

Moses' shoulders slumped. "Right out yonder." He pointed out at the river. "Just the other side of the camp store."

McVitty's brow creased in alarm. "And the bait?"

"A chunk of my wife's pot-roast."

"Must've been pretty enticing," McVitty said.

Moses smirked. "You ain't never tried my wife's pot-roast. It was either that gator or *me*."

McVitty laughed. "Tough as a Tarminger, was it?"

"You got that right." Moses shifted in his boots. "So, can we go ahead and process the gator meat?"

"Sure. I don't see why not. But let me know if you find anything else of value to the investigation."

Moses smiled. "Will do." He turned to two guys standing by the gator carcass, knives at the ready. "Go ahead, boys. Skin it up!"

"You heard him, boys," one of the guys holding a knife said. "Let's get to cutting those scutes."

"Scutes?" I asked, turning to Grayson.

"The hemispherical osteoderms," Grayson said.

I frowned at him. "Why can't you ever just use a normal human word for things?"

Grayson's eyebrow shot up like Spock's. "Are you implying I'm not a normal human?"

I smirked. "Absolutely."

We watched as two men took positions on either side of the gator. With knives as big as their forearms, they began slicing along the boney ridges running down the center of the alligator's back.

"Y'all ain't saving the hide?" Earl asked, his eyes transfixed on the men as they peeled off a foot-wide strip of dinosaur hide running down the middle of the gator's back.

"Nope. See here?" One of the men held up what looked like a long strip of tractor-tire tread. He pointed to the boney ridges reminiscent of a stegosaurus' spikey lumps. "These here scutes are all busted up from bein' harpooned and buoyed. This old gal's too tore up to taxidermy."

I gulped. "Chomp's a *girl*?"

The man grinned. "Well, if I got my anatomy lessons right in high school, yep."

"What about her head?" McVitty asked. "Size alone would make it a prize mount."

The guy sucked his teeth. "Would 'cept for her choppers ain't too purty, either."

He was right. Chomp's teeth were smooth and rounded, no sharper than my own human canines.

"I thought they got new teeth throughout their lives," I said. "What would wear them out like that?"

"Crunching bones," McVitty said. "And chewing metal arms all to hell."

Chapter Thirty-Seven

Against my protests, Grayson purchased the massive gator's head from Moses for fifty bucks. He and Earl were busy hauling it back to the RV in a wheelbarrow.

"Come on, Grayson," I argued, trailing behind them. "What are you going to do with that nasty thing?"

"I want to examine its braincase."

I nearly swallowed my tonsils. "Not in my new kitchen, you're not! Keep that thing outside." I ran past them to block the door to the RV. "And if you ask me, *you're* the one who needs to have your braincase examined."

Grayson studied me as I sprinted past him. "Why? As you may recall, Deinosuchas had a similar, but distinct braincase. A comparison of this skull with fossil records could provide a definitive answer as to its geneology. If so, this would be the best fifty dollars ever spent in the history of humanity."

I stifled an eye roll. "Fine. Keep it. But you bring even one ounce of gator flesh into my new RV, and they'll be searching for *your* fossil records. Comprende?"

Grayson's eyebrow rose an inch. "Comprende."

I TRIED TO TAKE A NAP, but thanks to the odd hours we'd been keeping with the hunt, my internal timeclock was all messed up. It also wasn't helping that every time I was just about to nod off, I'd be startled awake by Earl shouting something idiotic. Usually, "Good golly!"

"Good golly!" Earl yelled again.

"Arrgh!" I flipped onto my side and mashed the button to turn my bed back into a chair. Then I got up and stomped outside, determined to get to the bottom of their idiocy.

My efforts did not go unrewarded.

Like something out of a comedy skit about white-trash cannibals, Earl and Grayson were standing around a giant stew pot fashioned from the bottom half of a fifty-gallon drum. My cousin held a big stick, and was using it to poke at whatever was boiling in their makeshift kettle. Meanwhile, a shirtless Grayson stood watch over the scene, wielding that metal bang stick like a warrior's spear.

I guess I should be grateful I was spared seeing Earl in a loincloth ...

Even so, the scene was surreal. I blinked, thinking I must be dreaming. "What are you two doing?" I asked, keeping a few feet of distance between me and the stewpot. "Reenacting *Lord of the Flies*?"

"Not me," Earl said. "It's Grayson's job to keep the flies off."

"What?" I edged closer for a peek inside the drum.

"We got that big ol' croc in our big ol' crock pot!" Earl quipped.

My nose crinkled. "What for?"

"We're boiling the specimen to remove soft tissues," Grayson said. "That will facilitate comparison of this creature's skull with Deinosuchas. I thought I'd already explained all of this."

"Right." I bit my tongue. "I'd tried to forget. Anyway, to change the subject, you think the rest of Tommy Tarminger's body is out there in the river?"

"Perhaps." Grayson shot me a look. "Or it *could* be on ice in the back of a certain pickup truck."

I nearly gasped. "You don't think *Johnny* had anything to do with killing Tommy!"

Grayson shot me a dubious glance. "You can't rule out someone on the basis of how attractive they are, Drex."

I frowned. "I know that." I studied Grayson for a moment.

Wait a minute. Is Grayson shirtless because he's trying to compete with Johnny?

I laughed. "Don't tell me you're *jealous*!"

"Not at all," Grayson said primly. "I'm a detective. Avoiding suspects' deadly charms is rule number one."

I frowned. "Are you saying I don't have the basic skills required to be a P.I.?"

"Well ..."

Earl grunted behind me. I turned to see him using the stick to haul the gator skull to the surface of the pot liquor by its eye socket.

"It appears she may be done," Grayson said.

I scowled and headed back toward the RV.

Oh, she's done all right. Completely done.

Chapter Thirty-Eight

After swearing off Grayson, Earl, and men in general last night, I awoke the next morning to the aroma of coffee brewing.

I took a deep sniff.

Ahh! Maybe the world doesn't suck so much after all.

I swiveled around in my chair-bed and peered into the main cabin. Grayson was at the banquette, sipping coffee and pecking away at his laptop. I was about to declare a truce when I spotted it. Perched atop the sofa nearby was an alligator skull the size of an industrial Hoover vacuum cleaner.

What the hell!

I bolted out of my chair-bed like it was an ejector seat and scrambled into the kitchen. "I thought I told you not to bring that inside!"

Grayson glanced up at me, nonplussed. "You said not to bring *an ounce of flesh* inside. The skull, as you can see, is completely devoid of soft tissues."

Well, he had me there. With the gator's flesh removed, its teeth were a lot easier to see. They were ground nearly to nubs.

"I see it's devoid of sharp teeth, too," I quipped, mashing the *cappuccino* button on the automatic coffee dispenser.

"Uh ... Drex," Grayson said.

"Hold on," I said. "I was thinking about something you said yesterday."

His eyebrow rose. "About Johnny Rango?"

"No." I frowned. "Why would you bring *him* up?"

Grayson shrugged. "Association."

Dear lord! The man won't even let me get a cup of coffee before he starts in already.

My upper lip snarled. "Association?"

"Well, yes." Grayson eyed me up and down. "You think Johnny is *hot*. Coffee is also *hot*. And you forgot to put a cup in the coffee machine."

"Wha—? Oh, crap!"

I scrambled over to the cupboard, snatched a mug from a shelf, and stuck it into the coffee machine just as black brew began to dribble from the spout. As my cup filled, I turned to Grayson. "Geez. Why didn't you just tell me that in the first place?"

"I tried to. But you interrupted me. Something about what I said yesterday?"

"Oh. Right." I grabbed my cappuccino and took a step toward the booth, then changed my mind. The gator skull on the sofa was creeping me out. I decided to lean against the wall instead, in case I needed to make a quick getaway.

"I was thinking about Buddy," I said. "And the gravy stuff with his bobber eyeball in it."

"Drex, please. I'm trying to drink my coffee."

I snorted. "Since when did *you* develop a sensitive stomach? And excuse me. But isn't that a *dead alligator* staring at you from the sofa?"

Grayson's cheek dimpled. "Excellent, Cadet."

"What's so excellent about a dead gator?"

"No. I mean that you noticed me acting out of character. That skill is key to good detective work."

My nose crinkled. "Grayson, you're *always* acting out of character. And anyway, it doesn't matter now. This is our last case, remember?"

"I remember. So what was your question? About Buddy's dead-eye gravy, I mean."

"Oh. You explained that the goo was probably created by the partial digestion of his remains. And that at some point after ingestion, the gator became agitated and disgorged Buddy's remains before they were completely digested."

"Correct."

I nodded toward the skull. "It would take something pretty big to agitate a gator that size, don't you think?"

"Absolutely."

"So, like what could do it?"

"My theory?" Grayson said. "An even bigger alligator. Like Deinosuchas."

The side door opened. Earl came in carrying a hacksaw. "Found it," he said. "Doctor Earl reporting for surgery."

I frowned. "Surgery?"

"Yes." Grayson scooted out of the booth. "We're going to cut open the skull to examine the braincase."

"Then we're goin' out to eat," Earl said. "You hungry?"

I EMERGED FROM A LONG, hot shower to find Grayson and his hillbilly hacksaw henchman both studying the sawed-in-half skull with a pair of magnifying lenses.

"So, what's the verdict?" I asked. "Has Earl got a brain or not?"

Grayson looked over at his computer screen displaying images of Deinosuchas' fossilized skull. "Well, disappointingly, this specimen is *not* Deinosuchas." He snapped his laptop shut. "But she could still be the *mother* of reiteration."

"Is that like the mother of invention?" Earl asked.

Grayson's eyebrow shot up, then went down just as quickly. "Surprisingly, in a way, *yes*. This creature could be the alligator that *reinvents* Deinosuchas. After all, all it takes is one egg to express the required latent genes as dominant."

"One *bad* egg," I said.

Earl grinned. "You mean one bad-*ass* egg."

"Indeed." A smile curled Grayson's lips, giving him the appearance of a mustachioed *Grinch* about to steal Christmas.

I'd seen that look many times before.

I recognized it instantly as a tarminger of doom.

Chapter Thirty-Nine

Grayson pushed aside the dissected gator skull and got up from the banquette table. "I've got an idea," he said.

I grimaced. "I was afraid of that."

Ignoring me, Grayson plowed on. "This whole campground will soon be swarming with law-enforcement officials and search-and-rescue divers combing the river for Tommy Tarminger's body. I say we get out of here and head back to the scene where we found the bait bucket with Buddy's artificial eyeball in it."

My nose crinkled. "Won't the search team be *there*, as well?"

"No. That area's already been searched, remember?"

I frowned. "But ...."

"But what, Drex?"

"But we'll miss Cheech's food truck!"

Grayson's brow furrowed. "Sometimes, detective work requires sacrifice."

I snorted. "Says the guy who brakes for every taco stand we come across."

The toilet flushed. Grayson and I instinctively glanced toward the hallway. Earl emerged from the restroom looking proud of himself.

"Earl, my good man," Grayson said. "How soon can you get the boat ready for a morning troll?"

Earl glanced at me and grinned. "Aww, Bobbie don't look *that* bad."

"Ha ha." I wasn't sore about my cousin's comment, but the fact that I hadn't come up with it myself.

"How long?" Grayson asked again, glancing at the clock on the wall. "I want to set off before things get too hectic around the Rangler Resort."

"I'm ready," I said. "I have absolutely zero desire to see that rat bastard Tommy Tarminger ever again—dead *or* alive."

Earl stretched his arms over his head. "With my mornin' constitutional outta the way, I guess I could get her going just as soon as the Pop Tarts is done."

Grayson nodded. "Good. Make it so."

"EXCUSE ME, GRAYSON," I said as we putted along the river in the early morning mist. "I don't mean to question your judgment, but do you really think messing around with that huge alligator nest over by McGatorTail's is such a good idea?"

Grayson sat up straighter. "I don't see the problem with it."

"Yeah," Earl said. "What could possibly go wrong?"

I winced. "What about all that motherly instinct stuff you and McVitty talked about yesterday? If we go poking around with the nest, we could set the brooding female off on a rampage. You said it yourself—there's nothing stronger than a mother's love."

Earl laughed. "What would you know about any of *that*, Bobbie?"

"I *am* a woman," I said. "In case you two forgot."

Grayson shushed us. "Shh! We're almost there. But I'll concede, Drex. You make a good point. We'll need to employ stealth not to disturb the mother. She may be lurking nearby guarding her nest."

"Should I call him on my cellphone?" Earl asked.

I shot my cousin a look. "Call who?"

"That Stealth guy," Earl said. "You know, to employ him."

As I stared at my cousin, something deep inside me came loose and unwound. I gave in to it, and no longer wished for anything further from this life than a swift, painless end.

Chapter Forty

With Officer McVitty suspending gator hunting for the day, we'd motored in solitude downstream to the bridge. Once there, Earl maneuvered the skiff up alongside the riverbank, just in front of the abandoned McGatorTail's restaurant.

Grayson surveyed the shoreline, then lowered his binoculars. "It appears we may be too late."

"What do you mean?" I asked.

"The nest has already been tampered with."

I squinted through the thin, morning fog coming off the water. The mound of dirt we'd seen earlier beside a stand of cattails was still there. But amid the brown layer of fallen reeds and dead leaves that covered the nest, I could see patches of white jutting out. It was unmistakable—they were the torn remains of leathery alligator eggs.

"Did they hatch, or were they eaten by predators?" I asked.

"Indeterminable from here," Grayson said. "We'll need to examine the nest closer to find out. Earl, pull us up to shore."

"You got it, Mr. G."

As the nose of the boat touched the sandy shore, Grayson stood, making the boat wobble.

"Careful!" I said. "It might be dangerous!"

But it was too late. In a flash, Grayson stepped past me, then leapt onto the soggy shoreline.

"Great," I said to Earl. "I guess I better go with him. You stay here in the boat."

Earl pouted. "Why?"

"In case that guy Stealth shows up."

"Oh." Earl nodded. "Right. Okay."

I jumped out of the skiff, pulled out my Glock, and trailed behind Grayson. He was picking his way closer toward the nest like an egret stalking prey. I only hoped he didn't become another birdbrain victim of whatever was making people disappear around here.

To my relief, nothing sprang out of the reeds or charged Grayson from the riverbank. In fact, the whole area seemed devoid of wildlife altogether. I tucked my Glock into my back pocket and walked up to Grayson.

"It's affirmative," he said. "Predators got the eggs."

I peered at the mangled eggshells in the nest. "Raccoons?"

Grayson shook his head. "Not unless they've learned how to ride bicycles."

I blanched. "What?"

Grayson pointed a long, thin finger to a line in the soft ground. "See these tread marks? They're too small to have been made by a car. I think the nest was harvested by someone on a bicycle or small motor-bike."

I chewed my lip. "Before or after the eggs hatched?"

"Both, probably." Grayson picked up an empty egg shell. "I'll collect samples. We may be able to retrieve Deinosuchas DNA from the ovum and albumen."

"The ova album?"

Grayson turned and shot me a pained look. "Excuse me. In *normal human language*, that would be the shells and egg whites."

"Thank you," I said sourly. I watched him drop the remnants of a deflated, leathery egg into a baggie and seal it. "But seriously, Grayson. Why would you be looking for Deinosuchas DNA in *this* nest?"

He shrugged. "This could belong to the same alligator that rammed our boat when we were out with Denny. Or the one caught by Moses last night. If so, she's huge for a female of the species. Therefore, she would possess superior genetic lineage for the reiteration of Deinosuchas."

I chewed my lip. "And if this nest *doesn't* belong to that gator?"

"Statistically, it's still as good as any. Do the math, Drex. With 1.25 million alligators in Florida, that's easily half a million breeding females. At fifty eggs per clutch per year, that's 250,000 possibilities per annum for iterative evolution to take its course."

My nose crinkled. "I suppose. But—"

"Finding Deinosuchas is the whole point of our investigation, Drex. Otherwise, we're just three random people on an ordinary alligator hunt. What would be the point of that?"

"Meat and hides," Earl said, tromping up to us. He leaned over and took a good look at the strewn clutch of empty eggshells. "If that don't beat all. Why would somebody take an alligator's young'uns? They ain't got enough hide on 'em to make a durned wallet. And the tail meat don't add up to a measly chicken finger's worth."

"Lots of reasons," Grayson said. "But the main two would be for personal pets, or to sell to the illegal pet trade. Man has a long history of antagonizing this species. It's no wonder they're now seeking to avenge themselves."

"Come on," I said. "Isn't that nature's way? The apex predator gets to make the rules?"

"Yes." Grayson rubbed his chin. "And that may be *exactly* why the rules are now changing."

Chapter Forty-One

With his plastic baggie full of sticky, deflated alligator eggshells tucked into his backpack, Grayson took off. He followed the trail of the narrow tire tread from the gator nest up the steep slope of the riverbank.

The tire mark's trajectory took a straight shot up the muddy bank. Then it crossed a patch of weedy ground and disappeared into the parking lot of McGatorTail's.

As I followed behind Grayson, the morning sun finally made its appearance. As it breached the horizon, it shot laser beams of golden light through the trees and onto the asphalt parking lot and the roof of the abandoned restaurant.

But the bright promise of a new day couldn't staunch the cold shiver worming its way down my spine. It was back. The same creepy feeling I'd had the last time I was here. The feeling of being watched by someone ... or some*thing*.

I squinted and slowly surveyed the premises. To the left of the lot, the bridge tender's parking spot stood empty. To the far right, the dumpsters still stood where they'd been the day before. But Cheech's food truck was gone.

I frowned.

He's no doubt serving up red-eye gravy at the Rangler Resort right now. And I'm missing out on it!

My stomach gurgled. I glanced over at Grayson. "So the bike tracks disappeared into the parking lot. What do we do now?"

"Let's spread out and look around for anything odd," he said. "Especially eggs the nest poacher may have dropped or left behind."

"I'll take the road front and restaurant," I said.

Grayson nodded. "Good. Earl, you check the grass along the riverbank. I'll search the parking lot perimeter."

We split up and went our separate ways. As I walked toward the restaurant, a car came creeping up the road. It looked like a dark-blue sedan. The same kind of car Grayson thought was following us. My heart began beating a drum solo in my chest. I dove behind a bush and pulled out my Glock.

I was about to sound the alarm when the sedan pulled into the spot reserved for the bridge tender. A man with bushy black hair got out carrying a brown paper bag. It either contained a sawed-off shotgun or a sub sandwich. I squinted for a closer look. His T-shirt read, *Prisms don't die. They just cross over the rainbow bridge.*

I blew out a sigh of relief.

Sub sandwich. Definitely.

"Hey," I said, coming out of the bushes. "Do you have a white Buick, too?"

He turned to face me, looking startled. "What?"

"I was here the other day. A white Buick was parked in a tender spot."

He smiled. "How tender?"

My nose crinkled. "What?"

"Never mind. Old bridge tender joke." He laughed. "No. I don't drive a white Buick. This is the only car I have."

"Okay, thanks." I turned to go, then asked, "Hey. Have you had anymore sightings of the huge, headless gator from the day before?"

"Uh ... no. You must be confusing me with Charlie. He works weekends." The guy glanced over at Earl and Grayson milling about on the other side of the lot. "What are you guys doing out here?"

"Looking for egg poachers," I said. "Have you seen any around here?"

He smiled. "No. But you'd probably have better luck in the kitchen department at Walmart."

My brow furrowed, then went slack.

Ha ha. Everyone in this stupid town's a freakin' comedian.

AFTER WALKING AROUND the restaurant grounds, I went in search of Grayson. I spotted him standing in front of one of the dumpsters Cheech had hidden his food truck behind to avoid the greedy palms of Tommy Tarminger.

As I approached, I noticed Grayson was staring at a sign stenciled onto the side of the middle dumpster. It read, *Empty When Full.*

I smirked. "Contemplating Schrodinger's Garbage?"

Grayson turned and locked his serious green eyes on me. Then he actually broke out in laughter. "Ah. Not bad for a layman."

"Lay*woman*," I corrected.

"Fair enough. So, did you find anything, lay*woman*?"

"No. But I did notice someone has started painting the restaurant blue. I'll give you one guess who."

"Tommy Tarminger," Grayson said. "That man was definitely on a roll."

"Yeah," I laughed. "Can't say I'm sorry his last one ended up being a gator's death roll."

"*What* kind a roll?" a voice called out from inside the dumpster. Earl's shaggy head popped up, startling me.

"Geez, Earl! What the hell are you doing in there?"

"Special assignment from Grayson," he said, a smug grin on his face. "And looky what I found." He disappeared, then popped up again holding up a bucket of paint. "You can see from that there dot of sample paint that it's Tarminger's signature color."

"Interesting," Grayson said. "What else is in there?"

Earl disappeared again. I heard him grunting as he kicked stuff around. He reemerged. "Just a bunch a egg cartons. Got some empty grits sacks, too. Maybe four jugs a old grease."

"Probably stuff from when McGatorTail's used to be open," I said.

Grayson shrugged. "Or Cheech is using it for his own personal garbage can."

"They's a pile a these here frozen biscuit bags, too," Earl said, holding up an industrial-sized plastic bag.

My mouth fell open. "Cheech said he made those biscuits from scratch!"

Earl shook his head. "Dang Yankee used instant grits, too."

"Ungh," I grunted indignantly.

"Not everything is as it first appears, Drex," Grayson said. "You should know that by now."

As I tried to think of a comeback, Grayson's phone beeped with a weird tone I'd never heard before.

"I need to get this," he said. "I programmed my phone to alert me to any internet news about people going missing in Lake County."

Before I could say anything, he turned his back on me to read his phone screen. Meanwhile, Earl climbed out of the dumpster like a bear wearing overalls.

"How'd you like your special assignment?" I asked as he brushed a glob of old grits off the knee of his pants.

"It was cool," he said. "Not as good as huntin' gators, but I did find me a souvenir." He held up a bottle opener. It was shaped like an alligator. Half its tail was missing.

"Gee. I'm almost jealous," I said.

Grayson glanced up from his cellphone. "Looks like they found the missing woman, Shirleene Parker."

"The town floozy?" Earl asked. "How many pieces was she in?"

"Just one. According to the news feed, Ms. Parker was found alive and well, still clinging to her flamingo float in the St Johns River. She'd made it all the way to Jacksonville."

"Geez, that's a long haul," I said.

Grayson nodded. "Over a hundred miles. But the St Johns flows north, so she was traveling downstream. She made it all that way in under two days."

"Did that there article say how Shireleene ended up in the river in the first place?" Earl asked. "Somebody push her in?"

Grayson shook his head. "No. The reporter who interviewed her said Ms. Parker's trip was intentional. Her goal was to use the flamingo float as transportation all the way out into the Atlantic Ocean."

"What for?" I asked. "Suicide?"

Grayson cleared his throat. "According to the article, Ms. Parker stated, and I quote. "I didn't have enough money for a water taxi to take me all the way to the Lost City of Atlantis, so I planned to float there."

I closed my eyes and shook my head. "Only in Florida."

"Don't be so quick to dismiss Ms. Parker," Grayson said. "We know more about the surface of the moon and Mars than we do about the depths of our own oceans."

My nose crinkled. "What's that supposed to mean?"

Grayson shrugged. "Only that if someone wanted to keep something hidden, the ocean would be the best place on this planet to conduct covert operations."

I blew out a breath. "Gimme a break, Grayson!"

"I'm serious. The darkness of the ocean depths offers a kind of cover one could only dream of here on land."

My mouth fell open. "So you're saying you actually believe that crap about Atlantis?"

"I believe in the possibility of it." Grayson studied me for a moment. "Have you ever heard of the Lost City of Cuba?"

My chin lowered. "No. But I have a feeling I'm about to."

"It's a real place," Grayson said. "Just off the coast of the island nation of Cuba. It's been sitting there underwater for over six thousand years. Yet no one noticed it until the year 2000."

"Uh-huh," I said. "That's because it's probably just a rusted out old taco truck."

"Not in the least," Grayson said. "It's a full-scale city covering well over a square mile. It's got buildings, roads, and even an impressive pyramid."

My right eyebrow rose an inch. "Really?"

"Really. It exists, Drex. So who's to say there's no possibility that Atlantis is out there, too?"

"Yeah, Bobbie," Earl said. "Who's to say?"

"Fine," I said. "But for now, could we keep the conspiracy theories down to just one at a time?"

Chapter Forty-Two

"Okay, let's get out of here," I said, trying to herd Earl and Grayson out of the McGatorTail's parking lot and back to the RV for a badly needed Pop Tart. "And Grayson? Could you put a lid on your squirrelly theories about the Lost City of Atlantis and that giant shark of yours, Megamouth?"

"Megalodon," Grayson said.

"Whatever. Like I said, let's stick with one weirdo legend at a time. Grayson, you've got your gator egg samples for testing. I say we get the heck out of here before that mother gator comes back from lunch and has *us* for dessert."

"Fine by me," Earl said. "I could use me some vittles myself."

We turned and headed for the riverbank. "Y'all keep a sharp eye out for that mama gator," Earl warned as we got closer to the bank. "I'm surprised she ain't already snapped at us. I wonder why she ain't guardin' her nest."

"Good question," Grayson said, scooting down the ridge toward the riverbank. "I'd speculate she's either been caught and killed herself—quite possibly by Moses—or she knows her nestlings have been murdered, and now she's somewhere else, plotting her revenge."

"Revenge?" I said, surprised at Grayson. "Animals aren't capable of plotting *revenge*."

Earl shot me a look. "You ain't never met my friend Skeeter's bulldog. If'n you did, you'd think different, Bobbie."

"Come on," I said, following Grayson toward the skiff on the riverbank. "Giving human characteristics to animals is anthropomorphism. Even *I* know that. It's pure crap. Pseudoscience!"

Grayson shrugged. "Perhaps. But keep in mind, *every* theory is pseudoscience until proven otherwise. And from the stories I've read, alligators have plenty of reasons to be on the warpath with humans."

My nose crinkled. "You keep saying that, but what exactly have we done to deserve for alligators to declare war on us?"

Grayson took a tentative step inside the boat. "Well, take for instance that man in Palm Beach. He threw a three-and-a-half foot gator through a Wendy's drive-thru window."

"What in tarnation did he do that for?" Earl asked.

Grayson shrugged. "Apparently, he wanted to use it for payment for a burger and fries. The man was charged with illegal possession of an alligator and petty theft."

"Why?" Earl giggled, winking at me. "Was that gator somebody's 'petty'?"

Grayson ignored Earl's attempt at humor. Instead, he settled onto a boat bench and offered up another example of man's inhumanity to gators. "Not too long ago, a Florida man was charged with picking magic mushrooms while carrying an alligator."

I snorted. "Nothing beats tripping with a friend."

Earl hooted. "Good 'un, Cuz."

Grayson frowned as Earl climbed past him to the seat beside the trolling motor. "Okay, you two," he said. "How about this one? A few weeks ago, a man in Daytona tried to throw a live alligator he'd stolen from a miniature golf course onto the roof of a beachside cocktail lounge. He said he wanted to 'teach it a lesson.'"

"What lesson?" Earl asked.

I smirked. "That drinks *aren't* on the house?"

Earl and I exchanged glances, then cracked up into a giggling fit.

"Laugh all you want," Grayson said, folding his arms across his chest. "But it may very well be the *alligator* that gets the last laugh. And as we all know, he who laughs last, laughs best."

AS WE PUTTED ALONG the St. John's River on our way back to the Rangler RV Resort, something Grayson said was plaguing me worse than the mosquitoes buzzing around my face. I looked back to find him scanning the riverbank with his binoculars.

"Grayson, were you serious? Is the reptilian brain really capable of revenge?"

"Perhaps not in its primitive state." Grayson lowered the binoculars. "But as we discussed, the brain is capable of evolving. It's theoretically possible that the old reptilian brain model is adapting to the challenges presented by Homo sapiens."

"Over the past hundred years?" I argued. "That's virtually overnight. Evolution takes a lot longer than that."

"That depends on which theory of evolution you believe. Darwin's natural selection model only allows for slow, gradual changes. But there is a longstanding debate about whether a species evolves gradually, or in rapid, punctuational bursts."

"Punctuational bursts?" I stared into the black water of the river.

"Yes. The theory of punctuated equilibrium says that evolutionary change is characterized *not* by long, slow development, but by short bursts of rapid evolution, followed by longer periods of stasis in which no change occurs. Perhaps the reptilian brain is, as we speak, sprouting extra nodes and capabilities, just as the mammalian brain once did."

I chewed my lip. "I don't know about that, Grayson."

Earl laughed. "Hey Bobbie, if *you* can grow you an extra brain part, why can't a poor ol' gator?"

"He's right," Grayson said.

I frowned and locked eyes with Grayson. "Gimme a break."

Grayson shrugged. "The supernumerary section removed from your brain demonstrates that when it comes to genetic expression, literally *anything* is possible."

"The super hootenanny what?" Earl asked.

"Supernumerary," Grayson said. "It means a number beyond what's normally expected."

Earl hooted. "You mean Bobbie growed her a fourth brain?"

Grayson cocked his head and studied me. "In a manner of speaking, yes."

Earl giggled. "Too bad it didn't make you no smarter, Cuz."

I glared at my cousin. "That's rich coming from a guy who doesn't have two brain cells to rub together!"

"Uh-oh." Earl grinned from ear to ear. "Better watch out, Grayson. I think the chains done broke on Bobbie's mood swing again."

Chapter Forty-Three

When we arrived back to the Rangler RV Resort, it was nearly lunchtime. Officer McVitty was there, announcing over a megaphone that the search for bodies had been called off for the rest of the day.

"I've got to make an urgent pit stop," Grayson said, climbing out of the boat. "Drex, grab McVitty and find out what the divers discovered during their search."

As Grayson ran for the RV and Earl tied the boat to its moorings, I jumped out and edged my way into the sweaty knot of men gathered around McVitty. The tension in the air—as well as the body odor—were palpable.

"You boys can resume your gator hunting after 5 p.m," McVitty said over the megaphone. "But mind you, be careful. The gator Moses caught yesterday might not be the beast that got Tommy. And if that's true, that means the monster is still out there. You could be next!"

The men grunted and mumbled among themselves like a den of confused cavemen. As they began wandering away, McVitty turned and headed for his patrol boat. I ran after him.

"Officer McVitty!" I called out. "I just got here. Did you find Tommy's body?"

McVitty stopped and turned around. "No, we didn't."

"So he's still missing?"

McVitty sighed tiredly. "Yes, I'm afraid so. Along with Buddy and Fatback Taylor."

"Golly," Earl said, joining us. "It's like they all vanished out of nowhere."

"No. They're *somewhere*," McVitty said. "My bet is in a gator's belly, or softening up in its underground lair somewhere out there on the river."

Earl shook his shaggy head. "Whew! That gator they cut open yesterday what had Tommy's metal arm in it? Was she big enough to swallow him whole?"

McVitty shook his head. "No. And even if she was, we'd have found his body inside her."

"Then how'd his prosthesis end up in her stomach?" I asked.

"Gators can't chew," McVitty said. "They tear their prey into pieces small enough to swallow whole. The gator that got Tommy could've torn his arm off, then the old sow gator Moses caught helped herself to the scraps. With that milk-jug buoy slowing her down, she could've been forced to scavenge."

"So she couldn't have caught Tommy, like Denny said?" I asked.

McVitty's face looked grim. "Unlikely. I think it would have to be a much larger gator. If such an animal is out there, it's not impossible that it could've swallowed Tommy whole. Or torn him up and devoured him completely, part by part. Tommy wasn't that large a man. And gators are capable of eating up to a quarter of their body weight in one sitting."

"I weigh 250 pounds, give or take a snack cake," Earl said. "How big would a gator have to be to get me?"

I shook my head. "Do the math, Earl. Four times 250 is 1,000." I turned to McVitty. "There's no such thing as a half-ton gator, is there officer?"

"Sure there is," he said. "Just a couple of years ago, a guy up in Alachua County caught a gator weighing in at 1,008 pounds. When he pulled him out of the Apalachicola River, the beast was just an inch and a half shy of thirteen feet."

"Geez," I said. "That guy must've had a big rig to take down *that* monster."

"Nope. He did it in a twelve-foot jon boat, just like yours."

I cringed. "That's crazy! That gator was bigger than his boat!"

"Yeah." McVitty pursed his lips. "But that gator's not the state record. That goes to a 1,043 pound male fished out of Orange Lake. It was just shy of fourteen feet long."

"If that don't beat all." Earl scratched his head. "Do gators grow bigger in lakes?"

"I couldn't say," McVitty said. "But if there's gonna be a monster gator around there, my money is on it living in Lake George."

I crinkled my nose. "Why?"

"Because that lake is *huge*," McVitty said. "Six miles across and eleven miles around. That's plenty of habitat for the Loch Ness Monster, much less a giant gator. You all might not know this, but the St Johns River dumps into Lake George just a few miles north of here."

I grimaced. "You don't say."

McVitty eyed us both. "So, where were y'all this morning?"

I shifted on one foot. "Grayson wanted to check out an alligator nest up by McGatorTail's."

"Some jerk done plundered it," Earl said.

"You can bet that was Tommy Tarminger." McVitty shook his head. "He owns half the county, and *thinks* he owns the rest."

"You think that gator got Tommy as payback for killin' her young'uns?" Earl asked.

I elbowed my cousin. "Earl, we've already been over this. Gators don't have the brain capacity for revenge!"

"History would argue that point," McVitty said.

"What do you mean?" I asked.

"I'm guessing you two have never heard of Gator Joe or Two-Toed Tom before."

Earl and I glanced at each other, then turned and shook our heads. "No, sir."

A faraway look filled McVitty's eyes. He smiled grimly and said, "Okay. Buy me a Yoo-hoo and I'll fill you in."

Chapter Forty-Four

"Twenty bucks for a six-pack of Yoo-hoos?" I asked, holding up the carton in disbelief.

"You want 'em or not?" Denny asked, taking a puff from her Marlboro and blowing it in my face. "They're cheaper at Walmart, if you don't mind the half-hour drive."

I slapped a twenty on the counter. "Sorry to hear about Tommy. You look really broken up about it."

"People mourn in different ways," she said. "And this store ain't exactly gonna run itself."

"Yeah, right." I turned and stomped out of the bait store. As I flung open the exit door, I spotted Earl sitting down at a picnic table with Officer McVitty. I joined them and handed out the Yoo-hoos.

"Crap," I said. "I need a bottle opener."

"I got me one." Earl fished in his pocket and pulled out the broken gator bottle opener.

"You get that at the bait shop?" McVitty asked.

"Dumpster," Earl said.

McVitty laughed. "That's where they belong." He picked it up. "Cheap crap. But Denny still sees fit to charge eight dollars a pop for 'em."

"Her mercenary charms know no bounds," I quipped.

McVitty laughed, opened his Yoo-hoo, then raised a toast. "To Tommy Tarminger, wherever that rotten bastard may be."

I was popping the top on my Yoo-hoo when Grayson walked up. He raised an eyebrow. "Drinking your curds and whey, I see."

I frowned. "What are you talking about?"

"Yoo-hoos," Grayson said. "They're made primarily of water, high-fructose corn syrup, and whey."

"No whey," Earl said, then chortled at his own joke.

"I can understand their appeal for you, Drex," Grayson said. "They're made by the same company that manufactures Dr Pepper."

I shook my head. "Thanks for yet again making us victims of your random, drive-by facting. Sit down, Grayson. Officer McVitty was about to tell us a story about some vengeful alligators."

"Really? Excellent. But ..." Grayson glanced around.

"Don't worry." I pulled a Yoo-hoo from a bag at my feet. "I got you one, too."

"Thanks." Grayson smiled and sat down at the table with us. "Officer McVitty, you have the floor."

"Right." McVitty set down his Yoo-hoo and placed both hands on the picnic table. "Y'all may not know this, but it was a spiteful gator that took down the infamous Ma Barker Clan."

Chapter Forty-Five

"What?" I gasped, nearly spewing my Yoo-hoo.

"The Ma Barker Clan," McVitty said. "You heard of them?"

"Who hasn't?" I said.

McVitty nodded. "Well, Ma Barker and her four sons started out their life of crime stealing from the church collection plate. Then, in the 1930s, her killer brood set out terrorizing half the country, committing a string of kidnappings, robberies, and murders. Then, of course, they ended up here in Florida."

"Of course," I said sourly.

"Anyway, with the FBI on their tails, the Barker Clan hid out in Ocklawaha in a two-story cracker house on Lake Weir. Little did they know, that was also the home of Gator Joe, a humongous alligator with a reputation almost as notorious as the Barkers themselves."

"How'd Gator Joe bring down the Barker Clan?" I asked.

McVitty smiled. "Hand me another Yoo-hoo and I'll tell you."

I grinned and handed him a bottle. "Geez. Mercenary talents run deep in these parts."

McVitty laughed and popped the top off the bottle. "You see, Gator Joe was a local legend in Ocklawaha long before the Barkers arrived. In fact, it was people curious to get a look at Gator Joe that eventually led the FBI to find the crooks' hideout."

"Is that so," Earl said, his pondering face busy pondering away.

"Sure was," McVitty said. "Though the Barkers tried to shoot and kill Gator Joe on many occasions, they never could. Ironically, all that ruckus helped lead the FBI to them. And that instigated what became the longest FBI shoot-out in history."

"Seriously?" I asked.

"It's all documented," McVitty said. "On January 16th, 1935, Federal agents shot the shit out of that house on Weir Lake for four solid hours. At the end of it, what was left of the Barker Clan was dead."

"What happened to Gator Joe?" I asked.

"He lived on for a couple more decades, until he crossed paths with a local gator hunter named Vic Skidmore. Vic shot Gator Joe dead. They say when they went to skin him, that gator measured fifteen feet, seven inches."

"That's incredible," Grayson said.

"You can check out his foot, if you don't believe me," McVitty said. "Far as I know, it's still on display at Gator Joe's Beach Bar and Grill in Ocklawaha."

"Have you seen it?" Earl asked, his eyes big as boiled eggs. "Gator Joe's big ol' foot, I mean?"

"Yes I have," McVitty said. "Biggest animal claw I ever laid eyes on."

"Huh," I grunted. "That's interesting, for sure. But you said you had proof that alligators can plot revenge. This Gator Joe story seems like a simple case of being in the right place at the wrong time."

"True enough," McVitty said. "Perhaps you're right. But I think you'll find the tale of Two-Toed Tom can't be so easily dismissed."

"Why not?" I asked.

"Because Two-Toed Tom actually stalked the man who took his toes off—all the way from Alabama down to Florida."

Grayson smiled sinisterly. "Intriguing. That's hundreds of miles. What more do you know about this creature?"

"Well, as you can guess, back in the 1920s, alligators were everywhere," McVitty said. "But Two-Toed Tom stood out from them all."

I frowned. "How?"

McVitty waggled his eyebrows. "Accounts of Tom say he was massive. With red, glowing eyes. He didn't act like normal gators, either."

"What do you mean?" Grayson asked.

"Two-Toed had a penchant for eating the local farmers' livestock. Some accounts of him say he was so large and powerful, he could tear a horse to shreds with one swift thrash of his teeth."

"That's hard to believe," I said.

McVitty shrugged. "Believe it or don't. But there are recorded tales of Two-Toed Tom not only devouring livestock, but people as well."

"Geez!" Earl said. "Couldn't somebody just shoot him?"

"Reports say a bunch of boys tried to do him in with their .22 rifles, but Two-Toed just shrugged them off like it was nothing."

"His hemispherical osteoderms must've been massive," Grayson said.

McVitty shot Grayson a funny look. "I don't know about that. But after losing cows and mules to the beast, a farmer named Pap Haines made it his mission to kill off old Two-Toed."

"Did he get him?" Earl asked.

"Maybe. Maybe not. You see, one day Pap thought he had Two-Toed Tom trapped in a pond. He threw 15 syrup buckets full dynamite into the water trying to kill him."

"That ought to do it," I said.

"You'd think so, wouldn't you?" McVitty said. "But after the sounds of the explosions died down, Pap heard the shrieks of his granddaughter. He and his kin ran over and found the poor girl's mangled body on the shoreline of another pond nearby. Old Two-Toed Tom had outsmarted them, yet again. They say it was as if the creature somehow knew what they were planning."

Grayson rubbed his chin. "Fascinating. This Two-Toed Tom could've been exhibiting characteristics of an evolving reptilian brain."

"I can't speak to that," McVitty said. "But back then, folks who encountered him came to think Two-Toed Tom was too wily to be a normal gator. They said he must've been a demon sent from hell."

"Or Deinosuchas returned from the graveyard of extinction," Grayson said.

"How'd Tommy lose his toes?" Earl asked.

McVitty sighed. "Some accounts say his toes were shot off. Some say they were cut off in a bear trap. Either way, it riled the gator enough to seek revenge. Accounts say Two-Toed Tom followed the farmer who cost him his toes all the way from Alabama to his new homestead in Esto, Florida."

"How do they know that?" I asked.

"Within a week or two of arriving, the farmer's livestock started to go missing. And he spotted Two-Toed's unmistakable tracks all around his farm. Despite his best efforts, though, he never could bring old Two-Toed down."

Earl gasped. "So he's still out there?"

"Could be," McVitty said. "Or his offspring. That's why I think it's possible that a gator could grow big enough to swallow Tommy whole and then disappear for a while. In a couple of months, there'd be nothing left of Tommy but his metal parts."

"But why single out Tommy?" I asked. "And what's this got to do with revenge?"

McVitty locked eyes with me. "My guess is old thieving Tommy Tarminger finally went and messed with the wrong nest eggs."

"Intriguing," Grayson said, rubbing his chin.

"But you haven't recovered any bodies," I argued. "So how can you be so sure a gator got Tommy? And what about the other folks who've gone missing?"

McVitty glanced around. The campground was empty except for the four of us. All the other gator trappers were inside their campers and tents, resting up for the coming night's hunt. All around us, their snoring droned and hummed like a Dixieland band made up of lawn mowers and leaf blowers.

Seeing the coast was clear, McVitty leaned in over the picnic table closer to us. "I wasn't going to say anything. But remember that bucket of gravy you all gave me with Buddy's bobber eyeball in it?"

I grimaced. "Yeah. That's kind of a hard thing to forget."

McVitty nodded, then whispered, "Preliminary results say that goop contains partially digested human remains, just like we thought."

"Buddy's?" Grayson asked.

McVitty shook his head. "Too soon to tell." The game warden stood up. "Well, I better get going. I could use a nap myself."

"Thanks for sharing the info on Buddy," Grayson said. "We should rest up for tonight, too."

McVitty took a step to leave, then turned back around. "You folks want some friendly advice?"

"Uh, sure," I said.

"Don't go out on the river again. Leave the gator hunting to the professionals." He glanced over at Earl. "No offense, son."

Earl beamed, then saluted him. "None taken, Mr. McVittles."

McVitty smiled. "You all have a nice day, now." He tipped his hat, then ambled back toward the docks.

I turned to Grayson. "Did you test *your* sample of that goop yet?"

"Not yet. But that reminds me. Don't eat the baggie in the freezer marked 'BG.'"

Earl gulped. "You mean that didn't stand for burger gravy?"

Chapter Forty-Six

We were walking over to Earl's truck to head out for lunch when I spotted gorgeous Johnny Rango leaning over the tailgate of his pickup. He was tying bungee cords over the wooden crate-coffins stacked up in the bed of his truck.

"You heading out?" I asked the handsome gator wrangler.

"Yes." His smooth, black hair glinted in the sun. "I've got my quota of gators, so it's time to go."

"Oh," I said, a little disappointed.

"Well, have a good trip," Earl said. "Come on, Bobbie. I'm starvin'!"

As I stared at Johnny for the last time, I felt a hand grab my bicep and try to tug me away. I glanced over and was surprised to see it wasn't Earl, but Grayson.

"What?" I asked.

Grayson leaned in and whispered in my ear, "How did Johnny manage to bag gators when no one was hunting today?"

I shrugged. "How should I know?"

Grayson glanced back at Johnny's truck. "I think we need to check those coffins for human bodies."

I nearly fell over. "What?"

"We need to take a look before he gets away," Grayson said. "Drex, go distract Johnny so Earl and I can check out those crates in the back of his truck."

My nose crinkled. "Are you serious?"

"Yes." Grayson gave me a gentle shove. "Go!"

I cringed. "What am I supposed to say to him?"

"Chat him up," Earl said. "You're good at that."

"Hurry," Grayson said, pushing me toward Johnny. "He's heading for the cab of his truck."

"Ugh! Fine!" I sprinted toward Johnny's black pickup truck, trying to think of a way to stall him. To my surprise, instead of getting in his cab, Johnny turned and walked back toward the bait store.

"Where you going?" I asked, jogging up to him.

"What?" Johnny turned toward me. His expression didn't exactly convey that he was happy to see me. "Oh. You again. I just need to get a few more bags of ice before I hit the road."

"Uh ... what for?" My eyes darted back for a look at Grayson and Earl. They were descending on Johnny's vehicle like a pair of hungry raccoons.

"It's a long trip, and it's hot out," Johnny said, stepping up to the ice vending box outside the door of Denny's bait shop.

"So you need ice for a cooler?" I asked, scrambling like a lamebrain for something to say.

"For the gators in the boxes," he said, pulling bags from the freezer.

"Oh, right." I smiled wanly. "So, where'd you get them?"

Lines crossed Johnny's handsome brow. "From the icebox. You just saw me pull them out."

I winced. "I meant the *alligators*."

"Huh?" Johnny asked, his voice tinged with annoyance. "Why?"

"It's just that ... McVitty cancelled last night's hunt. You know. After they found Tommy's arm in that gator."

"Yeah. So?"

"So if nobody was hunting, where'd the gators come from?"

"Oh." Johnny's brow smoothed. "A couple of hunters had bagged a few smaller gators early last night. I bought them all. We already had them loaded in the truck before Moses came in with the big one."

"Oh." I smiled. "I see."

Johnny laid the bags of ice on the concrete beside the shop door. "Look, I gotta go pay for these."

"Oh. Sure. Okay."

Johnny went inside. I took off like a bullet around the corner of the building. Earl and Grayson were still messing around at Johnny's truck, trying to pry open a box with a crowbar. I saw Earl jump back and wring his hand, as if something had nearly snapped his finger off.

"Well?" I shouted. "What gives?"

Grayson shook his head. "Nothing but gators. I guess the whole thing with Johnny's a bust."

I sighed.

You can say that again.

"I TOLD YOU JOHNNY RANGO had nothing to do with the missing people," I said as we cruised around the tiny town of Astor in search of a lunch spot that appeared both appetizing and survivable.

"Yes," Grayson said. "But we couldn't rule him out simply because you think he's good looking."

"Well, at least Johnny's an actual *human being*," I said. "And not made of silicone boobs and hot air!"

Grayson blanched. "Are you implying that the blow-up doll was my girlfriend?"

I shot him some side eye. "Why else would you have her?"

Grayson stared down at his hands. "Because I missed you, Drex."

I was touched, until I pictured Grayson caressing Ms. Floozy and pretending it was me. "Gross!"

Grayson's eyes widened as he caught my drift. "I didn't have ... *relations* with her. Why would I, when you and I have never had sex?"

Earl nearly drove Bessie off into a ditch. "What? Hold up! You're sayin' y'all ain't never done the deed?"

I folded my arms and scowled. "No. We haven't."

"Why in tarnation not?" Earl asked. "Don't tell me you're one a them Frigidaire women, Bobbie!"

"Arrgh!" I yelled. "It's *frigid*—ugh! No, I'm not! But I tell you what, Earl Schankles. If I had a Frigidaire, I'd lock you inside it and throw away the key!"

Suddenly, a thought hit me like a ton of gator meat. I turned to my cousin. "Earl?"

He grinned at me. "Whut?"

I opened my mouth to speak, but vomited all over Earl's lap instead.

Chapter Forty-Seven

"Are you okay?" Grayson asked, pulling me back to sitting after heaving a puddle of vomit onto Earl's lap.

"Yeah." I wiped my mouth with a tissue I found in the ashtray. "I want to go to McGatorTail's."

"You're *hungry*?" Earl asked, pulling the truck over. "Lawd, after smelling that batch a puke, I don't think I'll eat for a week." He rolled down the window. "Sheesh! What'd you eat for breakfast, Bobbie? Collard greens and vomit?"

"Sorry," I said.

He looked down and cringed. "Good thing I got me some spare britches in the back of the truck."

"Are you delirious?" Grayson asked, placing a hand across my forehead. "McGatorTail's doesn't serve tacos. Besides, they're closed."

"I *know* that," I said, slapping his hand away. "Just do it. *Please*?"

"All right," Earl said. "But I gotta do something else first." He reached into the glove box and pulled out an aerosol can. Then he spritzed the cab's interior down with pine-scented air freshener.

"Seriously?" I grumbled. "That can wait. This is an emergency!"

"You better *believe* it is," Earl said. "If I don't get this smell under control, we're all gonna have to be hospitalized."

"Gimme that!" I snatched the can from his hand. "Now crank the truck and let's get going!"

WE PULLED INTO THE abandoned parking lot of McGatorTail's restaurant reeking of pinesap and vomit.

"I want to check the dumpsters," I said, pushing Earl toward the driver's door of the cab. "Get out!"

"Are you crazy?" Earl asked. He looked pleadingly over at Grayson. "Mr. G. You think she's turnin' into some kind a dumpster divin' zombie or somethin'?"

Grayson snorted, but still managed to say, "Indeterminable."

"Ha ha," I said. "Now get out! Both of you!"

"Yes ma'am." Earl climbed out of the cab. I hopped out onto the asphalt beside him. "Earl, when you were in that dumpster, you found evidence to substantiate that Cheech uses instant grits and frozen biscuits."

"Uh ... yeah. So? It ain't exactly against the law, no matter what my mama says."

"He's right," Grayson said. "What's your point, Drex?"

I chewed my lip. "I guess it just makes me wonder what *else* Cheech has been lying about."

"What do you mean?" Earl asked.

I took my cousin by the shoulders. "When you were in the dumpster, what else did you see in there?"

"Just the usual garbola," he said. "But it still smelled better'n your nasty ol' puke, Bobbie. What you been eatin' girl?"

"Listen to me carefully," I said, shaking Earl. "While you were dumpster diving, did you happen to find any empty packages labeled *alligator meat*?"

Earl's face puckered with thought. "Huh. Nope. Not as I can recall."

I let go of him. "So tell me. Where is Cheech getting his supply from?"

"Fresh," Earl said. "From the gator hunters, like Johnny does."

"But no one had caught a gator until last night," I said.

"None that were *reported*," Grayson said. "Are you thinking Cheech might have killed the alligator that made the nest on the riverbank here?"

I nodded. "Yes. I think he fattened her up on scraps. He probably took the hatchlings, too."

"I don't think so," Grayson said. "Whoever did left a single tire tread. Cheech doesn't appear to have a bike or a motorbike."

"Not out in the open," I said. "But maybe stowed away inside his trailer?"

Grayson rubbed his chin. "It's possible. Let's check it out."

We walked over to the pull-behind trailer. The door on the back of it was secured by a padlock. A dark green extension cord poked out from the bottom of the trailer's sliding door and snaked along the ground to an outlet on the exterior wall of the restaurant.

"Cheech is stealing electricity," Grayson said.

"I'd say Tommy owed him at least that," Earl said. "After cheating him outta his house and home an' all."

"You still have that crowbar?" Grayson asked.

Earl nodded. "You betcha, Mr. G."

"Go get it."

Earl saluted, then sprinted over to Bessie and fished the crowbar from the toolbox in the truck bed. With the brute strength of a bear, he broke open the lock on Cheech's trailer and pulled up the sliding door.

A wheelbarrow came tumbling out.

"Ha!" I said. "There's your single-tire tread-mark."

"Hmmm. That explains one mystery," Grayson said. "But what about this one?" He picked up the electric cord. It lead to a chest freezer in the back corner of the trailer. "What's he got stored in there?"

I grimaced. "That's what turned my stomach earlier, guys."

"Why?" Earl asked. "I thought you liked frozen food."

"Ugh!" I grunted. "What I mean is, what if the 'scraps' Cheech has been feeding the gator are actually Buddy, Fatback, and Tommy?"

Grayson blew out a breath. "I see. Well, there's only one way to find out. Earl, climb in there and open that freezer."

"Why me?" Earl asked.

"Another special assignment," Grayson said.

Chapter Forty-Eight

"Woooeeee!" Earl exclaimed after throwing open the freezer lid. "You was right, Bobbie. We done hit the jackpot!"

"Jackpot?" I asked, bile rising in my throat.

"Yeppers! This thing's plum full of Hot Pockets!"

"What?" I gasped. "Are you sure?"

Earl held up a box and tapped a finger to his temple. "Bobbie, I might not know much, but I know me a Hot Pocket when I see one."

AFTER DIGGING DOWN through ten layers of frost-covered Hot Pocket cartons in Cheech's freezer, Grayson and I decided it was probably time to recalibrate our thinking. Cheech might've committed the sin of using instant grits and frozen biscuits, but apparently he was no murderer.

As we walked back over to the truck to head out, I heard a strange half-grunt, half-chirp sound.

"Did you guys hear that?" I asked.

It sounded again.

"Yeah," Earl said. "It's coming from over by the river."

Cautiously, we walked over to the edge of the riverbank. There on the shore, we spotted a couple of small hatchling gators feasting on a mound of raw hamburger inside a Styrofoam container.

"Well, at least *that* part's true," I said. "Somebody's feeding the hatchlings all right."

"How do you know that the mama gator didn't regurginate that for her young'uns?" Earl asked.

"Impossible," Grayson said.

"Why not?" Earl asked. "I thought dinosaurs came from birds."

Grayson sighed tiredly. "Two reasons. One. Alligators don't use dishware. And two. They can't chew."

"Huh," Earl grunted. "I guess they can't use wheelbarrows, neither."

"Wait a minute," I said. "Cheech plugged his freezer into an outlet."

Earl laughed. "Yeah, genius. Where *else* is he gonna plug it in?"

I glared at him.

I can think of one other place.

"Listen," I said. "That means the electricity is still on in McGator-Tail's."

"Sure," Grayson said. "They would need to keep it on to run the commercial freezers. Otherwise, they'd mildew and become unusable."

I nodded. "Right. So I wonder what *else* is going bad inside there." I glanced over at my cousin. "Earl, there were some keys hanging on the wall inside Cheech's trailer. Maybe one of them opens the back door to the restaurant."

"Are you thinking what *I'm* thinking?" Grayson asked me.

"Well, I'm definitely not thinking what *Earl's* thinking."

We both stared at Earl for a second, watching him twirl the broken gator-shaped keyring he found in the dumpster around his index finger, grinning like a toddler.

I shook my head, then took off in a race back to Cheech's trailer. Grayson followed suit. His long legs got him there a few seconds before me.

"There are several keyrings here," he said, gawking into the trailer as Earl and I came running up behind him.

"That one there's got a gator bottle opener thingy on it, just like this one a mine," Earl said.

"They sell those at the bait store," I said. "Let's try that one."

Chapter Forty-Nine

"This is highly illegal, isn't it?" I asked Grayson while Earl fumbled with the keys trying to see if one would open the back door to McGatorTail's restaurant.

"Only partially," Grayson said. "It's not breaking. Only entering."

Earl snickered. "Somethin' *you two* cain't be accused of. Not *yet*, anyway."

My molars pressed together. "Could you can it with the stupid jokes already? This is serious business!"

"Ah!" Earl said as the third key turned the lock. "What we lookin' for, anyway? More a them Hot Pockets?"

"Yeah," I said. "Especially if they still have a body attached to them."

Earl's face puckered. "Huh?"

Going inside the shut-down restaurant was an eerie experience. All around, abandoned equipment and empty chairs gave me the feeling I was getting a glimpse into a future, post-apocalyptic world. I took a step. A squeak worthy of a horror movie slammed my focus back to current-day reality.

"What was that?" I squealed.

"There's a meat grinder in the dishwasher," Grayson said. He lowered the door of it, causing another identical eerie squeak to echo in the abandoned space.

"So what?" I said.

"The machine's recently been through the wash cycle," Grayson said. "It's still warm."

"Oh, good!" Earl said, wiping his hands on his jeans. "They got a washing machine here, too? I could use doing me a load while we're here!"

"Forget it," I said. "Go check out those big refrigerators over there."

Earl ambled over to the commercial upright coolers and flung open a glass door. "Nothing in here but eggs and butter and milk," he said. "And a bunch a baggies full a chicken meat."

"Chicken meat?" I grimaced and walked over for a closer inspection. The baggies actually *did* look like raw chicken breast.

"Could be alligator meat," Grayson said from behind me.

I nodded. "Okay. What about the freezers?"

Grayson opened one up. "Looks like we've got a gator in this one."

"Cool!" Earl said, scurrying over for a look.

I followed him to the freezer and stood on tiptoe to get a peek over his shoulder. Sure enough, wrapped in clear plastic was a long, tapered hunk of flesh about four feet in length. It had the same pale, pinkish-white color of chicken or pork, but the shape of a gator's tail was unmistakable.

"Huh. I guess that's it," I said, blowing out a breath. "Cheech is legit."

"Hold up a second," Grayson said.

He leaned over the freezer and picked up the gator tail. Lying underneath it was another kind of white meat.

And it wasn't pork.

Not unless pigs had begun wearing cowboy boots.

"Oh my lord!" I screamed. "Is that a human leg?"

"It would appear so," Grayson said. "And I think we can all guess who the half-stump arm lying beside it belongs to."

"Tommy Tarminger!" Earl gasped, his eyes as big as boiled eggs.

"Bingo." Grayson tossed the gator tail back into the freezer and slammed the lid shut. "Let's get out of here before we leave biological evidence of our own."

But it was too late.

Grayson and Earl locked eyes with each other. Then they both bent over and spewed their guts all over the kitchen floor.

"And now," I said, feeling the bile rising again in my own throat, "you're both finally caught up to me."

Chapter Fifty

"We've got to ... tell McVitty that ... Cheech is a murderer," I said, fighting the urge to throw up.

"Of course," Grayson said, his face the color of Swiss cheese. "But to be fair, any number of people could possess keys to this place."

"And any number of people can be stuck in these freezers," I said.

"Fair enough," Grayson conceded.

I glanced around McGatortail's semi-abandoned kitchen. Besides feeling nauseated, I had the worst case of heebie-jeebies I'd ever experienced. And having once dated a guy named Newly Ledbetter, that was saying a lot.

"Look, Grayson," I said. "Can't we leave this horrible freak show for someone *else* to figure out? After all, what have these murders got to do with Deinosuchas? Right? Unless, of course, you think its brain has evolved enough by now to use meat grinders and freezers."

"And wheelbarrows," Earl gasped between heaves.

Grayson wiped his mouth with a tissue and nodded. "Okay. Point conceded. Let's get out of here."

The three of us crept out of the restaurant, queasy and stunned to silence by the macabre collection of body parts we'd just discovered in the freezer. As Earl locked the door behind us, I told him to keep the keys to McGatorTail's.

"We'll hand them over to Officer McVitty," I said. "Now come on!" A shiver ran up my spine. "Let's get the hell out of here and report this to the authorities."

"I second that," Grayson said, trailing after me.

"I third it," Earl said, then bent over in a dry heave.

Fighting the urge to upchuck myself, I lead the way past Cheech's pull-behind trailer. As we rounded the corner of the dumpsters, I heard the sound of an engine approaching.

"Hold up!" I motioned for the guys to stop. Cautiously, I peeked around the dumpster. A white panel truck was driving slowly into the parking lot.

"Shit. It's Cheech!" I whispered. "What are we gonna do now?"

"Okay, be calm," Grayson said. "Act naturally, and he won't suspect that we know."

"Know what?" Earl asked. "That he's servin' up Dahmer dinners out a that food truck a his?"

"Exactly," I said. "Now, *be cool*, Earl."

"As a cucumber," Earl said. "You can count on me."

We walked around the corner of the restaurant and out into the open parking lot.

Cheech spotted Earl's monster truck first. Then his dark eyes darted over to us standing by the dumpsters, standing stiffly and smiling woodenly like *The Three Stooges* caught doing meth.

Cheech smiled and started to wave. But the looks on our faces must've told him all he needed to know.

His calm, casual smile vanished.

Then Cheech tried to make *us* disappear, as well.

Chapter Fifty-One

Ping! Ping!

For a brief nanosecond, the noise didn't register.

Ping! Ping!

"Look out!" Grayson shouted. Then he body-slammed me. "Cheech has a gun!" he said as we fell to the ground behind the dumpster.

Another shot pinged off the dumpster, just as Earl dove for cover, too, landing with a grunt beside us.

"I've got my Glock," I said, pulling it from my pocket. "Should I return fire?"

Ping! Ping!

A glass bottle lying three feet away exploded into a million pieces.

"That's six rounds fired," Grayson said. "He must be out of ammo by now." He poked his head around the side of the dumpster, then waved his arm, wildly motioning us to follow him.

"Let's go!" he shouted. "He's getting away!"

Earl and I scrambled to our feet. While my cousin barreled full steam ahead, I cautiously peeked out from behind the dumpster. Cheech's food truck was busy burning up the asphalt. Tires squealed and rubber smoked as he frantically tried to turn the clunky vehicle around in the parking lot.

"What do we do now?" Earl asked.

"I've got him!" I shouted. "Earl, get out of the way!"

Earl dove to the ground again. I fired at the food truck's back tire. It hit the rim with a *clang*.

"Try again!" Grayson yelled.

I did. This time I hit rubber. The tire blew.

But Cheech had already managed to do a 360. He hit the gas. The food truck made a wobbly beeline for the road leading out of McGatorTail's parking lot.

"We've got to go after him!" I shouted.

"Roger that," Earl said. "But you gotta drive Bessie."

"Why?" I asked, then glanced over to see he was dry heaving again. His grunting set off Grayson's gag reflex. He started heaving, too. The two guy's faces were as green as a pair of Granny Smith apples.

"Fine. Let's go," I said. "Earl, gimme your keys. Now the two of you get in the truck. And try not to ... you know what!"

Chapter Fifty-Two

Chasing Cheech in his food truck was pretty anticlimactic. After all, the guy was driving on three rims in an old panel truck not exactly designed for maximum aerodynamics. We, on the other hand, were cruising along in Bessie, a monster truck equipped with a chrome periscope, a hemi engine, and tractor tires with enough traction to make it through the middle of the Mohave in a rainstorm.

But Cheech had a gun. So I kept my distance.

While we slowly tailed him down Highway 40 through the heart of Astor, Grayson called McVitty and alerted him to our recent discoveries.

"Drex," Grayson said, putting a hand over the phone receiver. "McVitty wants to know where Cheech is headed."

"How should I know?" I said. "I'm no criminal mastermind!"

Suddenly, to my surprise, Cheech pulled into the last place I expected.

"Wait!" I said. "Tell McVitty he's turning into the Rangler RV Resort." I glanced at Earl. "Why would Cheech go back there?"

"Maybe he misses his mama," Earl said.

I shook my head. "Don't be an idiot."

Earl shrugged. "All I'm sayin' is, I know that if I was in as big a heap a trouble as Cheech, I'd want my mama."

I sighed. "Well, that makes *one* of us."

We followed Cheech into the Rangler RV Resort. When he got to the bait store, he hit the brakes and sounded the dinner horn on his truck.

Suddenly, I realized why he'd come here.

In an instant, dozens of RV doors and tent flaps flew open. Before I could even unlock the driver's door, Cheech's food truck was swarmed by a sea of starving rednecks, all waving twenty-dollar bills in the air like they didn't care.

"Great," I said. "How are we gonna find him in *that* hoard?"

"I have an idea," Grayson said, clicking off the phone with McVitty.

I glanced over at him, and was glad to see Grayson's skin tone had returned to a shade within normal human parameters. "So what's the plan?" I asked.

"To use his secret weapon against him," Grayson said. Then, without further explanation, he opened the passenger door and jumped out.

"But—"

"Wait here," Grayson said, then he took off.

Earl and I watched from the elevated seats of the monster truck's cab as Grayson ran over to the food truck and climbed in the side door.

"What on earth's he doing?" Earl asked.

"I have no idea."

A moment later, I heard Grayson's voice blast over Cheech's megaphone.

"Attention everyone! Cheech's gator gravy is made of people!"

"Wha—?" the crowd grumbled, their twenty-dollar bills wilting in the humidity.

"Cheech is killing people and serving them up as gator meat!" Grayson announced. "We need your help to catch him!"

A communal gasp echoed from the bumbling crowd.

Then dead silence.

Then everyone bent over and began to hurl.

Chapter Fifty-Three

"So much for garnering assistance," I said to Earl as we picked our way through the crowd of rough-and-ready gator hunters spewing their guts on the ground. Grayson had escaped the food truck and was standing atop a picnic table, scanning the boat dock using his hand as a visor.

"Did either of you see where Cheech went?" he asked as we got to the table.

"He's holed up in the bait store," Earl said. "I seen him go in the back door."

I shot my cousin a look. "And you're just telling me this *now*?"

Earl flinched. "I thought you knew!"

The three of us stared at each other for a moment. Then, in one fluid motion our primitive reptilian brains engaged. We hightailed it toward the bait store.

I got there first. I ran up to the glass front door and tried it. "It's locked!" I yelled, peering inside. "I can't see squat. The lights are out!"

"Are they closed?" Earl asked as he stumbled up beside me, huffing like a wildebeest.

"This time of day?" I said. "When there's money to be made? Not unless Denny's in the freezer next to Tommy. Have you still got the keys?"

Earl's head cocked to one side. "Why would I have the keys to the bait store?"

"*Cheech's* keys! Do you still have them? One might fit the store."

"Oh. Yeah." Earl fiddled the gator keyring out of his shirt pocket. "Move over. I'll give it a try."

"Be careful," Grayson said. "He could be—"

Blam!

A gunshot blast rang out from inside the bait store. The clear entry door exploded into a heap of glass cubes at Earl's feet.

"What the?" was all Earl managed to utter before Cheech himself came barreling through the giant hole in the glass door. He jumped over the pile of shattered remains and skittered past us. He hooked a left at the gas pumps and scrambled toward the docks, running for all he was worth.

"Get him!" I yelled.

"You think?" Earl said.

Then we all took off after him.

Chapter Fifty-Four

Caught between us and the river, Cheech didn't get far. After a brief chase, we cornered him down by the riverbank.

"Give it up," Grayson shouted.

"No way!" Cheech yelled. "You'll never take me alive!"

"Let's form a human net," Grayson said.

"Huh?" Earl asked.

"Like Red Rover," I said. "Just don't let Cheech come right over."

"Oh." Earl grinned. "Got it!"

Earl, Grayson and I formed a line and stepped slowly toward Cheech, who'd sought refuge by crouching inside the stone walls of a fire pit.

"Has he still got a gun?" I asked.

"I don't think so," Grayson said.

"Cheech!" I yelled. "You don't have anywhere to go. Come out with your hands up!"

"No way!" A cloud of ashes swirled up from the fire pit. Then Cheech sprang up as ashy as a ghost himself. He shot a glance our way, then bounded like a deer across the lawn and onto the boat docks.

"Don't let him get to the river!" Grayson yelled as we ran toward Cheech.

But it was too late.

Cheech jumped into Denny's battered old boat and cranked the feeble engine. Before we could reach him, he'd putted out into the river beyond our grasp.

I laughed. "You're not gonna get very far in that old scow!"

"The hell he ain't," a raspy voice hollered from behind us.

I turned around to see scrawny old Denny Tarminger aiming a shotgun at us with one hand. Her other hand was busy pumping gas into an old milk jug—one with a crude eyeball drawn on it.

I took a step toward the old woman.

"Move another muscle and you're toast," she said.

"I'd advise you to—" Grayson said.

"Shut your pie hole!" Denny yelled, then stuck a wadded strip of T-shirt into the top of the milk jug. She lit it with her cigarette, then reared back and hurled it like a Molotov cocktail.

I followed the jug's trajectory as it sailed through the air over our heads, then landed on the boat dock. It skittered across the rickety planks, then fell into the water with a plunk and a hiss.

I turned back and grinned victoriously at Denny. The cigarette dropped from her mouth.

"Aww, the hell with it!" she yelled. Denny cocked the shotgun, aimed it at the gas pump beside her, and pulled the trigger.

A red mushroom cloud raced toward us.

Followed by a sonic boom.

Then everything went black.

Chapter Fifty-Five

I woke up in the hospital.

Again.

This is one bad habit I definitely *need to break ...*

I glanced around. Earl was sitting in a chair to the left of my bedside. At least, I think it was Earl. Whoever it was looked like Mr. Clean—after a failed attempt at sealing a core breach in a nuclear reactor.

"Geez!" I said. "Are you okay?"

"Bobbie!" Earl jumped up from the chair "Yeah, I'm fine. Just got me one heck of a sunburn from that blast Denny set off."

"Your hair is gone," I said.

He grinned. "I ain't the only one."

I closed my eyes and let out a breath. "Don't tell me. Mine is, too."

He winked. "You always was the smart one, Cuz."

"What about Grayson," I asked. "Is he okay?"

"Well, he survived, but his moustache didn't."

I couldn't help but smirk. "So it wasn't a total loss, after all."

WITH MINOR BURNS AND major hair loss, the three of us were treated and released from the hospital. We walked out looking like a trio of balding, slightly roasted mummies.

Waiting to greet us in the parking lot was Officer McVitty.

"Glad to see you three are okay," he said.

"Yeah," I said. "Just a mild concussion and a few singed body parts."

He nodded grimly. "Well, I can't thank you enough for figuring out who was killing our town folk. At least now we know it wasn't a gator, but a whole different kind of beast altogether."

"Right." I cringed. "I'm curious. What happened to Denny?"

McVitty's face turned grim. "She didn't fare as well as you all. Ended up burned beyond recognition."

My nose crinkled. "And Cheech?"

"We caught up with him just a few miles down the river. Ironically, he'd run out of gas."

I shook my bald head. "I don't get it. Why did Denny help out a murderer like Cheech?"

"You didn't know?" McVitty appeared genuinely surprised.

"Know what?" Grayson asked.

"Cheech is Denny's son. And like I told you all before, ain't nothing stronger than a mother's love."

Earl grinned and looked down his red nose at me. "Told ya, Cuz!"

McVitty frowned. "Now as for his daddy, Tommy Tarminger, that's a different story."

Earl gasped. "Tommy was Cheech's own daddy?"

McVitty shrugged. "Well, they never did an official DNA test or anything, but that's what we all were told."

"Why would Cheech kill his own father?" Grayson asked.

"Cheech always carried a chip on his shoulder about Tommy. He wouldn't marry his momma and make an honest woman out of her."

"So he *killed* him?" I asked.

McVitty locked eyes with me. "Freezers don't lie."

I swallowed hard. "I guess not."

McVitty shook his head. "Turns out, Tommy Tarminger was worth a lot more to Cheech and Denny dead than alive. A *whole lot* more. They were set to get all his real estate holdings."

"That makes sense," I said. "But why'd they kill Buddy and Fatback?"

"Good question," McVitty said. "According to Cheech, he and Denny didn't kill them. *Tommy* did. Cheech confessed to killing Tommy. But he said he found Buddy and Fatback in the freezer at McGatorTail's when he went to scab electricity off his daddy's newly acquired restaurant."

"That must've been a shock," Grayson said.

"You should know," McVitty said. "Anyway, Cheech told his momma about finding them. They got to thinking about it, and worried that if they let Tommy keep breathing, they might end up in the freezer, too."

"But why didn't they just call the po-lice?" Earl asked.

McVitty shrugged. "I asked Cheech the same thing. He said Denny was worried that if Buddy and Fatback's families found out Tommy had killed them, they might sue to try and get some of their inheritance."

"Huh," I grunted. "So I guess the last question is, did Cheech really serve up human flesh as gator tail?"

McVitty sucked his teeth, then spat on the ground. "Now that, I can't say for sure. We found a few assorted arms and legs in the freezers. Cheech could've just been trying to get rid of the evidence a bit at a time, fattening up the local gators with the body parts. But either way, anybody who ate food from his truck got a taste of human flesh, either firsthand or secondhand."

Chapter Fifty-Six

After our stint in the hospital, all three of us were ready to get out of the Florida sun and back to the shade of the RV. As we waved goodbye to Officer McVitty, I suddenly realized I didn't see Bessie and her shiny chrome periscope anywhere in the parking lot.

"How'd we get to the hospital?" I asked.

"By ambulance," Grayson said.

He and Earl glanced at each other. Then Earl reared back and hollered, "Officer McVitty! Hold up!"

"I GOTTA SAY," MCVITTY said, driving us along Highway 40 in his patrol car. "You all make a pretty good team."

"Thanky," Earl said. He was sitting up front with McVitty. My cousin had called shotgun, fair and square. He tapped a finger to his temple and said, "You know, I'm kind a the brains behind the operation."

From the backseat, I saw McVitty smirk at Grayson and me in the rearview mirror. "That so?"

"Yep," Earl said. "Anyhoo, I got a question."

"What's that?" McVitty asked.

"You think ol' Tommy's fake pincer hand ended up in that gator's craw from the critter biting it clean off a him? Or you think Cheech throwed it in the river to get rid of it?"

"I don't know," McVitty said. "But I'll tell you what. This whole crazy mess is one for the record books."

"You can say that again," Earl said. "Hey. I got one more question."

"What's that?" McVitty asked.

"That big old gator Moses caught. Was it Chomp?"

"We don't know yet, son. But if it turns out to be the biggest one caught by the end of the season, we'll say it is. And after all we've been through this year, I think I'll call an end to the whole Chomp contest business for good."

I sighed. "Officer McVitty? What's the biggest gator ever caught out there on the St. John's?"

"Hard to say. But the biggest one caught around here without a gun or a bang stick was a thirteen-footer named Lumpy."

"Another man-eater?" I asked.

"I don't know about that," McVitty said. "But any gator interacting with humans only has to be four feet long before it's deemed a nuisance."

I smirked. "How tall are you again, Earl?"

MCVITTY PULLED HIS patrol car into the scorched remains of the Rangler RV Resort. The blast had leveled the bait store, the docks, and the fish-cleaning station. Thankfully, the campers and the tire wall surrounding the place were left unharmed.

As we piled out of the car, McVitty got out too. He shook each of our hands.

"Well, I guess this is where we part ways." He rested a hand on Grayson's shoulder. "Sorry you didn't find your big gator, Grayson."

"Not *yet*," Grayson said. "But he could still be out there."

McVitty eyed him with skepticism. "Uh-huh. Anyway, the good news is, your boat's one of the few that survived Denny's bait-store inferno. Y'all can probably get a good price for it, seeing as how many went down in the blast. And we've still got five full weeks of gator season left."

"Right," I said. "We'll think about it."

McVitty walked over and opened the trunk of his car. For some reason, it made me flinch. I half expected him to grab an Uzi from inside it and mow us down. But he handed us each a ball cap instead.

"These are genuine River Patrol hats," he said, eyeing our bald, sunburned heads. "Put 'em on and try to keep out of the sun, you hear?"

"Yes, sir," Grayson said.

Earl saluted. "Thanky, Mr. McVittles."

I smiled, slipping the cap over my bald head. "Thank you."

"Y'all take care, now," McVitty said. He climbed into his car and drove away.

I watched him go, then turned to the guys. "I think McVitty's right. Let's sell the boat to the highest bidder and get the H-E double toothpicks out of here. This place gives me the creeps."

Grayson frowned. "Okay. Under one condition."

I frowned. "What's that?"

"Since this is our last investigation together, let's take the skiff out for a final pleasure cruise before we go our separate ways."

I gulped. Grayson's somber words slammed home the reality that this might very well be the last time I ever saw him. When I'd offered to quit a few days ago, I hadn't thought Grayson would so readily agree.

I let out a sigh.

I guess my time as Experiment #5 is up. He'll soon be on the lookout for Experiment #6.

"Okay," I said. "One last cruise it is."

"Woohoo!" Earl hollered. Then he ran for the RV like a scalded gorilla, yelling, "I'll get the RCs and the Moon Pies!"

I watched my cousin disappear behind a huge RV, then I turned to Grayson. "What happens after the boat cruise?"

He shrugged. "We'll go back to Plant City. I'll figure out a way to pay you for the RV. We'll get you set up with a car and finalize that internship with my friend in Miami."

I chewed my lip. "And you?"

"Me? I'll go on looking for Deinosuchas."

Chapter Fifty-Seven

Earl toted two giant coolers to the dock and loaded them into the skiff. Their combined weight, along with his, lowered the boat's waterline six inches.

"That oughta do us," he said.

I smiled. "Geez. I would certainly hope so. We're only gonna be gone an hour."

Earl angled his way to the back of the boat and sat by the engine. He patted a five-gallon gas can at his feet. "Good thing I filled up the tank afore Denny blew the pumps to smithereens. I got us this here backup, too."

"Thanks," I said. "Good thinking."

"You ready to go?" Grayson asked, joining me on the dock.

I nodded. "Ready as I'll ever be, I guess."

"Y'all quit your jibber-jabberin' and hop in," Earl said, cranking the engine.

"Hold your horses a minute," I said to Earl. Then I turned to Grayson. I wanted to say something smart and meaningful. But one look in his green eyes and my brain turned to mush.

"Grayson, I—"

Then I spotted it out of the corner of my eye. A blue sedan. It was racing toward us and the burned-down docks.

"Who's that?" I asked.

Earl squinted at the car. "Is that the bridge tender fella?"

"I don't think so," Grayson said. "I've never seen the guy before. Is that blood on his shirt?"

I squinted to get a better look at the guy climbing out of the car. My blood turned cold.

"It's Ariel," I said. "The bartender from the Budget Motor Inn."

Grayson's eyebrow shot up like Spock's. "*He's* the one who's been following us? What for?"

I shook my head. "I don't know. But I have a feeling he's not after college tuition money."

Grayson's head cocked. "What?"

I watched as Ariel reached into the side pocket of the car door. Something metallic glinted in the sun. Whether it was a cellphone or a pistol, I wasn't waiting around to find out.

"Come on!" I said, grabbing Grayson's arm. "Get in the boat. *Now!*"

Chapter Fifty-Eight

"Get us out of here, Earl!" I yelled as Grayson and I tumbled aboard.

For once, Earl did as he was told. He throttled up the engine. The skiff took off like a ballistic missile, heading downstream in the direction of the bridge. By the time Ariel reached the riverbank, we'd cruised too far away to tell whether he was waving goodbye to us or brandishing a firearm.

"Don't tell me you skipped out on the bill," Grayson said.

"No. They had my credit card on file."

I thought about the three months I'd spent at the Budget Motor Court. What had Ariel *really* been doing there? Had he been spying on me the whole time? If so, why?

I glanced over at Grayson. He was holding the binoculars with both hands, peering at Ariel. Was it just my imagination, or was one of his long thumbs pointing skyward in a covert thumbs-up?

A horrible thought crossed my mind. "Grayson! Did you hire Ariel to spy on me?"

Grayson lowered the binoculars and stared at me, puzzled. "If I had hired him to spy on you, why would I tell you to keep a lookout for a blue sedan?"

I frowned. "How should I know?"

"Hey," Earl said. "Don't the feller that tends the bridge drive a blue sedan?"

I ground my teeth. "Apparently *everybody* does."

Grayson rubbed his chin. "Perhaps no one was following us at all."

"Excuse me," I said. "Then how do you explain Ariel?"

"You *sure* you didn't skip out on the motel bill?" Earl asked.

I frowned. "Yes!"

Earl shot me a sideways look. "What about the mini bar?"

My upper lip snarled, then my face went slack.

Could that really be it?

"Ha!" Earl laughed. "Thought so." He tapped a finger to his noggin. "I know you think I ain't nothin' but a dumb redneck. But you ain't no better, Bobbie. You're just a bubba yourself."

"A bubba?" Grayson asked.

"Yep," Earl said. "That's somebody who thinks they done rose above their redneck heritage."

"I see." Grayson turned to me and opened his mouth to say something.

"Not one word," I said. "Or we turn this boat around right this instant."

Chapter Fifty-Nine

For the past ten minutes, we'd been motoring along the scenic St Johns River in silence. Neither Grayson nor Earl had dared to risk ending our outing by uttering a single syllable. I knew it was up to me to break the ban I'd laid down.

"Like I said before, the Budget Motor Court had my credit card info," I said. "Ariel couldn't have been following me for that." I turned to Grayson. "What other reason could there be?"

"Indeterminable," Grayson said. "It may be possible Ariel is connected in some way to whatever Warren Engles was working on before he disappeared."

I chewed my lip. "So you think Ariel might be Engles' replacement? Or one of his cronies, tracking us in the hope we'll lead them to aliens or some kind of cryptid creatures?"

"Correct." Grayson's eyes stared into the dark river water. "That scenario fits the experiences we've had with them so far. They follow us without making contact. And whenever we get close to finding out the truth, they swoop in and confiscate whatever physical evidence we've gathered."

"As part of their mutual alien-FBI cover-up operation, I suppose?" I asked sourly.

"Exactly. Either that, or they're tracking us because we're ... *us*."

I frowned. "What do you mean by *that*?"

"The theft of our vestigial organs," Grayson said.

"You mean the stuff in the pickle jar?" Earl asked.

Grayson nodded.

"Whew!" Earl shook his head. "I sure am glad I didn't eat *them*!"

Grayson's brow furrowed. "Perhaps we would all be better off if you *had*."

"What?" Earl gasped.

"Whoever took the jar now has our DNA," Grayson said.

I shrugged. "So?"

"It might have fallen into the wrong hands."

My nose crinkled. "Wrong hands? Geez, Grayson. You're not saying Ariel is working for that Intergalactic Freak Show collector business you talked about on the drive over here, are you? Please tell me you just made all that crap up!"

Grayson shook his head. "I can only speculate at this point, Drex. But if that *is* the case, whether the collector is from Earth or some other planet, they successfully obtained biological samples from us. Now they may be after complete specimens."

"You mean *you and me*?" I gulped. "Geez. You're more of a conspiracy theorist than I ever dreamed!"

"Maybe, maybe not," Grayson said. "Hear me out. Before our body parts were stolen, I had them tested. They both came back with unusual DNA markers."

My lip snarled. "What do you mean?"

"It turns out we're both one third English, one third Irish, and one third uncategorized."

I nearly swallowed my tonsils. "Are you saying we're like *brother and sister* or something?"

"No," Grayson said. "I'm saying we both possess uncategorized DNA."

I cringed. "You mean like *alien* DNA?"

"Not necessarily. Some indigenous tribes don't allow their DNA lineage to be shared, as a matter of privacy. After what the rest of mankind has put them through, you can't blame them."

"I guess not," I said. "But that must mean that my biological father, Mr. Applewhite, has some Native American blood in him."

Grayson shrugged. "Either that, or he's an extraterrestrial."

I blanched. "What?"

Grayson locked eyes with me. "I'm just saying it's another possibility."

"Woohoo, Bobbie!" Earl hooted. "If your daddy's a Martian, that'd be outta this world!"

I shot Earl some major side-eye, then leaned over and whispered, "Did you send in his DNA, too?"

Grayson nodded.

I cringed. "Are he and I related?"

"Why?" Grayson asked. "Would that be so bad?"

"It would be a freaking disaster."

"Aww, come on, Bobbie," Earl said. "Admit it. You're a bubba, just like me."

Grayson grinned. "I don't know about that Earl. She looks more like a hubba bubba to me."

"Ha! Good 'un, Mr. G!" Earl grinned, then took a slug from a bottle of RC Cola.

"Gimme one of those," I said to Earl.

"Your wish is my command, Hubba Bubba." Earl lifted the cooler top and pulled out a cold one.

I stood up and reached over to grab the bottle. Suddenly, the boat jerked to a dead stop. The force sent me skittering headfirst across the boat seat, over the edge, and into the river with all the grace of a one-legged harbor seal.

"Dang it, Earl!" I yelled as I came up for air. "This is *not* funny!"

"I didn't do nothin' on purpose, Bobbie," he said. "I think we must a snagged something."

"Yeah, sure!" I growled.

"I don't see anything," Grayson said. "Drex, do you?"

I scanned the surface of the river. "No. He just did that on purpose!"

"I did not!" Earl said.

"Check underwater," Grayson said.

Angry as a wet hen, I dipped my head in the water for a quick look. The tannic water was dark as tea. I bobbed back to the surface.

"Nothing," I hissed.

Then something rough brushed by my thigh.

It felt humongous.

Chapter Sixty

"Get me out of here!" I screeched, swallowing a cup of river water in the process. "There's something down there!"

"I'm comin'!" Earl yelled, ripping off his shirt. He cannon-balled into the river beside me like an albino manatee.

"I think it's a gator," I whimpered as Earl wrapped me in his big arms.

"Try not to splash," he said, swimming toward the boat. "That only gets 'em riled up."

"Give me your hand," Grayson said, leaning over the side of the boat.

I grabbed ahold of his long, tapered fingers. With one mighty tug, Grayson yanked me over the side and into the boat. "Help me get Earl in," he said.

Floundering like a wet seal, I righted myself and joined Grayson at the side of the boat. I held my arm out alongside his. Each of us grabbed ahold of one of Earl's beefy arms.

"Ready?" Grayson asked.

I nodded. "Ready."

"Go!"

Both of us pulled with all our might. But trying to lift Earl was like trying to hoist up a fully-laden refrigerator. He slipped out of our grasp and fell back into the water with a giant splash.

"Forget it," Earl said. "I'm gonna swim over to the shoreline. Y'all can pick me up over there."

"Good plan," Grayson said. "We'll follow right behind you."

I chewed my fingernails to the quick as Earl dog-paddled toward shore. When we got within ten feet of the bank, Earl stood up and waved.

"Touched bottom!" he said, grinning.

Then the smile disappeared from his face.

"That wasn't the bottom," he said.

Suddenly, the water around him exploded.

Then a gator with jaws as big as a truck bed opened its mouth wide and lunged for Earl.

Chapter Sixty-One

"Earl!" I screamed. "Earl! Earl!"

I lunged forward. Grayson grabbed me from behind and held me tight.

Together, we watched in horror as the monster gator flipped Earl into its cavernous mouth. As its jaws closed around my cousin, swallowing him whole, the beast watched us with a pair of glowing red eyes the size of saucers.

"Let him go!" I screamed.

But the gator didn't. Instead, it calmly turned and headed downstream, keeping its head and snout above water as if to taunt us.

The beast's head alone was as big as half of our boat.

Grayson was right.

Deinosuchas was back.

Chapter Sixty-Two

"We have to save him," I screeched. "What can we do?"

"You still have your Glock?"

"Yes." I fumbled it from my pocket. I wanted to shoot at the gator, but my hands were shaking so badly I was afraid I'd shoot a hole in the boat hull.

"Put that away for now," Grayson said. "Come here and man the trolling motor. We're going to follow it."

"And then what?" I asked, sitting down beside the motor.

Grayson, pulled out his Ruger. "I'm going to shoot it once I get a clear shot at the base of its skull. Try and keep the boat steady."

"I'll try." My hand was shaking on the throttle. I was a trembling mess. But Grayson was cool as a cucumber. He stood steady on the bow, aimed his Ruger, and shot the gator.

Bang! Bang! Bang!

"Incredible," he said. "The bullets are just ricocheting off its hide."

I began to cry. "Oh, Grayson! What else can we do?"

"I don't know. Let me think." He put his gun back in its holster. "Let's keep following it. Hopefully we'll think of something along the way."

"Okay," I whimpered, and blew my nose on my sleeve.

"Don't give up, Drex. As long as we can keep the gator in sight, Earl might still have a chance."

"Right."

But I didn't believe it.

Then, as if it had understood our words, the monstrous beast dived under the dark water and disappeared.

Chapter Sixty-Three

As the gator submerged out of sight, I burst into an uncontrollable crying jag.

"He's gone!" I wailed. "Earl's gone!"

Grayson pursed his lips. "No. Don't say that. We'll get him when he comes back up."

I shook my head. "Earl told me gators can stay underwater for over *two hours*, Grayson. What chance does he have?"

"Bubbles," Grayson muttered. He grabbed his binoculars and stood back up. "Bubbles!"

I blinked back tears. "What?"

"The alligator's leaving a trail of bubbles, just like a scuba diver." He turned and shot me a grim but earnest smile. "We can follow them, Drex!"

I sniffed. "Okay. Just tell me where to go."

"He's still heading north. Downstream, toward the ocean."

My heart lurched. "But he'll stop, right? Alligators need fresh water."

Grayson chewed his lip. "They can live in brackish water, too. And this may be a whole new species adapted to saltwater, like the crocodiles in the Keys."

"Oh, Grayson!" I cried. "If that thing makes it out into the Atlantic, we'll never find it! How long do we have before it gets there?"

"According to the maps I've looked at, the Atlantic is about a hundred miles from Astor. At the creature's current speed, it should take it three to five hours, depending on wake zones."

I shook my head. "I don't think that monster cares about wake zones."

"You're right. What was I thinking?"

I stood up. "Grayson, come and take the throttle. I better call Beth-Ann."

"Okay." Grayson hugged me, then took the helm.

I was about to punch my best friend's speed-dial number when a call popped up on my screen. When I saw who it was, I nearly dropped my phone into the river.

"Aaack!" I gasped.

"Who is it?" Grayson asked.

I looked up at him. "It's Earl!"

"Well? Answer it!"

"Oh! Yes!" I clicked answer and put the call on speaker. "Earl is that you?"

Grayson and I stared at each other as we listened to a bunch of muffled grunts and groans. I thought it might just be the beast itself, digesting Earl. Then I heard my cousin's voice say, "Let go a me, you dad-blasted gatoroid!"

"The waterproof cellphone case," Grayson said. "Earl must've butt dialed you!"

"Earl!" I screamed into the phone.

A string of muffled noises echoed from the phone's speaker.

"What's he saying?" Grayson asked.

"I don't know." I held the phone to my ear. "The line went dead."

"Right." Grayson rubbed his chin. "But by some miracle, *Earl* is still alive."

Chapter Sixty-Four

Grayson and I chased the monster gator for hours, past Lake George and beyond, following the eerie trail of bubbles it left in its wake. All the while, I didn't dare make a call for fear I might miss another butt dial from Earl.

But he never made another one.

I had to face the fact that it wasn't looking good.

The gator remained submerged. But even if it ever came up to the surface, it hardly mattered. Grayson and I hadn't been able to come up with any kind of plan to rescue Earl from its clutches.

Grayson tried contacting the River Patrol, but they took his call as a prank by drunken gator hunters. Desperate, Grayson even tried Warren Engles, but his number was still disconnected.

"It's hopeless, isn't it?" I asked.

"No, not yet." Grayson came and sat beside me. He wrapped his arm around my shoulder. "Earl hasn't called, but he may not be able to access his phone if it's in his back pocket. His current quarters may be too uh ... tight."

I sniffed. "Right."

"Don't give up, Drex. Even if we lose the bubble trail, we can still track him by the GPS in his phone."

I nodded. But to be honest, I didn't hold out much hope of ever seeing my annoying—but beloved—cousin again.

Chapter Sixty-Five

The sun was low in the sky when Grayson and I reached the Atlantic Ocean. Helpless, hopeless, and out of ideas, we kept following the gator because it was all we could do.

When the beast exited the river, it turned right and skirted the shoreline briefly, then headed out into the open ocean. I turned the boat east and followed it, my hope waning faster than the setting sun.

"I wonder if he's suffering right now," I said, tears welling in my eyes.

Grayson squeezed my shoulder. "Drex, you may not know this, but there exists a half-second, unbridgeable gap between what's happening to us and the time it takes the brain to process it. So, in a way, we're always living in the past—for half a second, anyway. Every 'right now' moment is already gone."

My shoulders slumped even further. "Is that supposed to make me feel better?"

"Yes. I mean, I hope so." Grayson took my hand. "Does it?"

I shook my head softly. "Not really."

"Sorry."

I glanced into Grayson's eyes. "Tell me something."

"What?"

"Why didn't you fight for me?"

Grayson's brow furrowed. "What do you mean?"

"When I said I wanted to quit working with you. Why didn't you try to talk me out of it?"

"Oh." Grayson's face grew serious. He locked his green eyes on mine. "I didn't because forcing you to do something against your will would be breaking my own personal prime directive."

"Oh."

"Does that make sense to you, Drex?"

I shrugged. "As much as any of this craziness has." I looked him in the eye again. "Grayson, you and I got Earl killed."

Grayson grimaced. "Don't look at it that way."

"What other way *is* there to look at it?"

"Remember when Earl told us he wanted to spend his life hunting and fishing?"

I nodded. "Sure."

"And hunting cryptids with us?"

"Yeah."

"He was doing exactly what he loved doing. I guess that's another reason why I didn't try to talk you into staying, Drex. You don't seem to have the passion for it the way he and I do. *Did.*"

"That's because I wasn't in it for the cryptids, Grayson."

"You weren't?"

I shook my head. "You're always so busy trying to discover what's out there that you don't notice what's right under your nose."

"You mean my moustache?"

"No. *Me!* I mean me. *Me!*"

"But—"

"Grayson, I wasn't in it for the cryptids. I was in it for *you.*"

His eyebrow shot up like Spock's. "Seriously?"

I smiled sadly. "To quote a certain person I've come to admire, 'The heart wants what it wants, or else it does not care.'"

Grayson looked down. "I see. Why are you just telling me this now?"

I shrugged. "Because it's now or never, I guess. I really don't have anything left to lose."

"Not even me?" Grayson pulled me to him and kissed me hard on the mouth.

I felt the earth move under my feet.

Then I remembered we weren't on solid ground.

We were on a boat.

A boat that was about to be rammed by a giant alligator.

"Look out!" I screamed, as the monstrous gator's jaws crunched down on the front of the boat. It sliced the bow in half. We tumbled to the floor.

"Don't look," Grayson said softly as he held me tightly in his arms.

The boat pitched. Slowly, we slid closer and closer toward the waiting maw of the beast.

As its jaws closed around us, sealing our doom, I held tight to Grayson, my face pressed into his chest, and listened to his heartbeat for as long as it would last.

Chapter Sixty-Six

I could hold my final breath no longer. As I gave up and let the air escape my lungs for the last time, I felt Grayson's hand squeeze mine. I opened my eyes for one more gaze into his, before we both drowned.

I breathed in, anticipating the sting of salt water as it filled my starving lungs. I could scarcely believe it when air coursed through them instead.

"What?" I gasped. "I'm breathing. How is that possible?"

"I'm not sure," Grayson said. "Perhaps Deinosuchas gulped a massive amount of air before submerging. But who cares? I don't want to waste what precious minutes we have left talking about a stupid cryptid."

My eyebrows rose an inch. "You *don't*?"

"No." Grayson squeezed me tight. "Drex, if you're game, I thought we might as well go out with a bang."

"We can't," I said. "I lost my Glock when the boat went down."

"I didn't mean that kind of bang."

"What?"

Grayson's green eyes twinkled. "I'm no Johnny Rango, but I do come with my own personal bang stick."

I grinned, my fear melting as I gazed into his eyes. "You pick *now* to develop a sense of humor?"

His cheeks dimpled. "Shut up and kiss me."

As he pressed his lips against mine, he whispered, "Close your eyes, Bobbie. Let me make love to you with my final breath."

I did as Grayson requested.

In my mind's eye, the gator's tongue became a silken mattress. Grayson's body became my whole reason for being.

As we wriggled out of our clothes, Grayson said, "I think I've longed for you since the day I was born."

I whispered back, "Every moment's been worth it, Grayson. I would do it all over again, no matter the cost."

SOMEWHERE ON THE OUTSKIRTS of St. Petersburg, Florida, a blue sedan sat parked in front of a single-wide trailer. On a desk inside the mobile home, a green anole clung to a plant in a terrarium. Beside it, a ham radio crackled with static.

A man took a slug from a Dr Pepper can, then turned a knob on the radio. It crackled to life. He reached for the microphone. "Agent A here. Come in Agent E. Come in. Over."

In a smoke-filled room, a man's spidery finger tapped lightly on a pickle jar containing two intertwined globs of flesh. "Engles here, over," he said into a microphone.

"According to Agent Ariel, project *Adam & Eve* is a go. I repeat. A go. Both subjects underway. Over."

"Excellent work, Applewhite," Engles said. "The other five pairings have failed. This one took a year to develop. Do we have reason to hope this one will succeed? It had better, if we're to avoid the appearance of nepotism. Over."

"Engles, even though your son's supernumerary stimulator was cut off, and my daughter's supernumerary brain capacitator was removed, this shouldn't affect their ability to bear offspring with both enhanced characteristics. And as I've come to learn, this species fares exponentially better alongside mates of their own choosing. Over."

"Affirmative," Engles said, his eyebrow angling sharply. "But do you have reason to believe this *is* such a pairing? Over."

"If you're in doubt, I can plug you into the live camera feed. Over."

"No need," Engles said. "I'll take your word for it. Over."

"Once they reach the underwater city of Vlak, it shouldn't take them long to adjust. After all, what choice do they have? Over."

"As they say, once you go Vlak, you never go back. What about redirects? We'll need to bury their disappearance. Over."

"Already on it," Applewhite said. "I've got three stories ready for release to media outlets now. Over."

"Good. Give me the highlights. Over."

"Story one: *Florida man serves up human Buddy to human buddies via food truck*. Over"

Engles nodded. "Intriguing. Go on. Over."

"Story two: *Florida man washes up on Jacksonville Beach, claims to have been abducted by both aliens and a giant 'dookey-saurus.'* Over."

Engles smiled. "Excellent. It's unfortunate that particular subject's samples proved to be 100% human. He's quite the character. Over."

"Indeed," Applewhite said. "An inexplicable combination of opposing characteristics. Typical human, through and through. In a few weeks, I'll doubt even *he'll* believe his own story about being spit from the mouth of a giant alligator. Over."

"Right." Engles sat up in his chair. "But how will we explain the disappearance of our two love progeny? Over."

"Boringly," Applewhite said. "*Another pair of ill-equipped boaters go missing in the Atlantic*. Over."

Engles nodded. "Well done. Not a conspiratorial note in that well-orchestrated headline. Over."

"Exactly." Applewhite smiled. "But as we both know, love is, quite often, the greatest conspiracy of all. Over."

DEEP INSIDE THE BERMUDA Triangle, the gigantic mechanical alligator swam due east for 3.3 miles, then adjusted its trajectory 16.7 degrees to the south.

Hidden from detection by the ocean depths, the gator-shaped submarine followed the preset coordinates further and further from Florida's shoreline. Inside its airtight holding compartment, its precious cargo lay safe and warm, basking in an unusual afterglow.

The End

I hope you enjoyed ***Half Crocked****. If you did, it would be freaking fantastic if you would post a review on Amazon, Goodreads and/or BookBub. Thanks in advance for being so awesome!*

https://www.amazon.com/dp/B09JCKDPCR#customerReviews

Already jonesing for more Freaky Florida Investigations? Well, you never know which of your favorite characters might drop by in my brand new "Val Fremden Strikes Again" series! Click the link below to check out *That Time I Kinda Killed a Guy*, the first book!

https://www.amazon.com/dp/B0C2VZT3LM

Get a Free Story!

INTERESTED IN MORE Florida-based mysteries? Sign up for my newsletter and be the first to learn about sales, sneak previews, and new releases! I'll send you a free copy of the *Welcome to Florida, Now Go Home* as a welcome gift!

https://dl.bookfunnel.com/ikfes8er75

For more laughs and discussions with fellow fans, follow me on Facebook, Amazon and BookBub:

Facebook:

https://www.facebook.com/valandpalspage/

Amazon:

https://www.amazon.com/-/e/B06XKJ3YD8

BookBub:
https://www.bookbub.com/search/authors?search=mar-
garet%20lashley
Thank you!

More Mystery Series by Margaret Lashley

FREAKY FLORIDA INVESTIGATIONS

https://www.amazon.com/gp/product/B07RL4G8GZ

Val Fremden Midlife Mysteries

https://www.amazon.com/gp/product/B07FK88WQ3

Val Fremden Strikes Again

https://www.amazon.com/dp/B0C2VZT3LM

Doreen Diller Humorous Mystery Trilogy:

https://kdp.amazon.com/en_US/series/W34F3Z8FNY5

Mind's Eye Investigators

https://www.amazon.com/gp/product/B07ZR6NW2N

About the Author

Why do I love underdogs? Well, it takes one to know one. Like the main characters in my novels, I haven't lead a life of wealth or luxury. In fact, as it stands now, I'm set to inherit a half-eaten jar of Cheez Whiz...if my siblings don't beat me to it.

During my illustrious career, I've been a roller-skating waitress, an actuarial assistant, an advertising copywriter, a real estate agent, a house flipper, an organic farmer, and a traveling vagabond/truth seeker. But no matter where I've gone or what I've done, I've always felt like a weirdo.

I've learned a heck of a lot in my life. But getting to know myself has been my greatest journey. Today, I know I'm smart. I'm direct. I'm jaded. I'm hopeful. I'm funny. I'm fierce. I'm a pushover. And I have a laugh that lures strangers over, wanting to join in the fun.

In other words, I'm a jumble of opposing talents and flaws and emotions. And it's all good.

I enjoy underdogs because we've got spunk. And hope. And secrets that drive us to be different from the rest.

So dare to be different. It's the only way to be!

Happy reading!

Made in the USA
Coppell, TX
27 February 2025

46437163R00152